"For My flesh is true food, and My blood is true drink."

John 6:55

Madness Heart Press
2006 Idlewilde Run Dr.
Austin, Texas 78744


Cover by Luke Spooner



Second Edition
ISBN: 978-1-955745-88-8
www.madnessheart.press

# LOW BLASPHEMY

JUDITH SONNET

A Madness Heart Press Publication

# PROLOGUE

Reece Brampton had precious few memories of her mother. She could recall, with ease, an occasion when she was five and the family had gone on a picnic together. Her mother, Becca, had held her hand tightly and refused to let go. Even when Reece had expressed interest in climbing on the jungle gym with the other children at the park, Becca was unyielding. She remembered her father, Stewart, confronting her mother on the car ride home.

"She would've been fine."

"I don't trust that group." Becca moaned. "They looked rough."

"She's going to be in kindergarten soon, sweetheart. You're going to have to let her hang out with other kids at some point."

In the back seat, Reece flexed the fingers of her right hand, where her mother had gripped her tightly. The skin had grown red and purple. She hadn't complained or cried. She was used to her mother's hold. It was hard and firm, as if Becca feared that letting go of young Reece would send her flying up into the heavens and beyond like a balloon. As if Becca was the only thing anchoring her five-year-old child to the ground.

Reece couldn't remember if she loved her mother or not. Becca Brampton was an odd woman. Even to an imaginative child like Reece, Becca seemed *peculiar*.

She had been young. She had given birth to Reece in her twenty-second year … only to die on her twenty-seventh birthday. But despite her age, she seemed old and weary. Her hair was a shallow brown that reminded Reece of mud, and her eyes were equally drab. Her lips looked gray in Reece's memory, and she spoke in a thin voice that lacked the self-assurance Reece observed in other parents.

Her mother looked weak, but her hands were so strong. Reece wondered if that was out of urgency. Whenever Becca Brampton was around, Reece was prepared to be handled. Her shoulders were pinched, her hair was ceaselessly plucked at, and her hands were held so tightly they buzzed as if they were filled with static.

Stewart often chided Becca, sometimes in good humor and other times with an uncomfortable snort. "She'll be fine, hun. You let her be."

"No!" Becca had once spat. "She's not fine. Look at her cheeks." Becca pinched Reece's baby fat. "She's so thin. She's going to wilt away. We really shouldn't be here."

Where had they been? Reece dug around her

head for the memory. Ah, yes ... they had been at church. Stewart was a religious man and had insisted on raising a religious family. And so, every Sunday, Reece wore itchy church clothing and prepared for her mother to pick at her body with her curved fingers as if she was a primate pulling lice from Reece's fur.

Reece was not a fan of church. She didn't understand any of it. A white-haired man stood in front of a crowd of somber-faced adults and spoke about some flowery text that got all scrambled in her head. It wasn't special; it was boring.

She didn't mind the reception afterwards, when everyone lumbered downstairs and sat at circular tables, eating chili and discussing the sermon. She liked the food, she liked the presence of other squirming children, and she liked preoccupying herself with her sketchbook, which she was not allowed to use during the service.

Another memory she had of her mother was during one of these soft discussions. Becca put her chin on Reece's head and whispered: "What is that?" She pointed a hooked finger at the drawing Reece was working on.

"Just a turtle."

"It's beautiful." Becca seemed in genuine awe.

Feeling proud of herself, Reece began to overcrowd the drawing with details. She put jewels on the turtle's shell, tried to give him big black eyes, and added candy-cane shaped claws at the ends of his rounded feet. She drew a background as well, a wide African safari with a multi-fingered tree right behind the large turtle.

"I love it." Becca cooed like a pigeon.

"Thanks, Mommy." Reece looked at the drawing with a self-satisfied smile.

It was that night when Becca Brampton killed herself. And so, Reece liked to pretend this was her last memory with her mother. A gentle moment wherein her mother complimented a cute drawing of a turtle that Reece had conjured. But it wasn't. In fact, her last memory with her mother tainted this sweet one. It had curdled it so egregiously that Reece had torn the turtle up and thrown the paper into the trashcan shortly after the funeral. She had sobbed into the black arms of her black jacket and tugged at the hem of her black skirt and wished that her mother had just died peacefully in her sleep. She cried on her bed, feeling bad for herself and bad for the all-too-innocent turtle that had done nothing to anyone.

She recalled sitting in her room long after her last tears had dried into a scratchy paste on her cheeks and trying to recall good memories with her mother. Even at five, it was an enormous task. Her memories were deformed by her mother's closeness. Her protective touch. The weird seal she had drawn over herself and her daughter.

All due to the terrible thing that Becca Brampton had done before she killed herself.

Reece almost wished she could have seen her mother die. This thought came to her on her more vindictive days when she blamed every trouble she had ever experienced on Becca.

People told her how important it was that she forgave and understood Becca.

There was nothing, Reece figured, *understandable* about what had happened.

After returning home from church, Reece had hung the drawing of the turtle up on the fridge with pride. Becca and Stewart had mooned over it for a few minutes before becoming detached and finding interest in their own adult things. Stewart turned the television on to catch a football game, and Becca sat down beside him with a set of knitting needles. She was working on a sweater—which she would never finish. She had already bragged that it would be perfect for Reece to wear to church. Reece never admitted it, but the thought was dreadful to her. Usually, handmade sweaters were scratchy and frayed easily, and her mother would be overly cautious with it. There would be no hope of running outside after service with the other children to play in the sandbox as long as Reece was trapped in one of her mother's sweaters.

The image of her father drinking a beer and her mother knitting was so stereotypically male and female, Reece would later wonder if this was what had killed Becca Brampton—the dim awareness that she had been fit into a neat little box. She had slid in easily without any hesitation or revolt. She had just naturally become a woman who knitted while her husband asked for a beer midway through the game.

"Sure, honey." Becca set her needles aside, stood, and went to the fridge without argument.

Reece grew tired of playing with her dolls and asked if she could watch a movie.

"Not now, darling," Stewart whispered, his eyes

affixed to the television and his beer hanging below his pink lips. His hair was already thinning, giving him a crafty widow's peak. Stewart Brampton also wore thick coke-bottle glasses that—as Reece often said—"made him look like a bug." Like a bug surprised to be caught under the looming shadow of a rolled-up magazine.

Reece grumpily stamped upstairs and played in her room for the next hour. She rolled underneath her bed and imagined she was exploring a cave, but this fantasy was short-lived since the bed could only get so dark and she could only crawl around so much before her knees began to ache. Still, to a five-year-old, the underside of the bed held a plethora of potential. There were secret scratches she had made in the soft wood, just for her eyes alone. Symbols that made no sense but were so intrinsically *hers* that they didn't have to. The cave fantasy was fun while it lasted.

Reece was considering a future as a "cave explorer." She had brought it up to Becca once before and had been met with a polite: "That's interesting, dear." She hadn't talked to her father yet because Stewart would ask far too many questions that hurt her brain.

"How much money do cave explorers make? What college will you need to go to? Would you live in a cave?" Sometimes, listening to her dad talk was mind-numbing. It was just as bad as church.

And so, like the secret scratches in the wood beneath her bed, she kept her ambitions to herself.

She didn't recall hearing her mother enter her bedroom. She had been crawling underneath the bed, imagining herself trying to silently bypass a patch of hanging bats. If she made a single noise, then the bats would flutter around her and become entangled in her hair. She almost shrieked when her mother sat on the mattress and the wooden frame creaked beneath her. Reece crawled out, afraid that she was somehow in trouble.

"I was just playing!" Reece began to explain, but she quieted when she caught her mother's eyes.

Becca Brampton looked scared. She was sitting solidly on Reece's bed. Her hands were clenched together, and her eyes were wet with tears. Her gray lips rolled against her teeth as she tried to figure out what she was going to say.

Reece was dressed in her pink PJs, and she was holding an oversized flashlight. The beam fell directly on Becca's left foot, which was bare. Reece noticed that Becca hadn't trimmed her nails in a while. Her toenails were curled and yellow. Some sock gunk clung in the pits between her toes like black moss.

"Momma?" Reece asked. "What's wrong?"

Becca shook her head. "Hey, baby. What were you doing under the bed?" Her voice was wavering. She sounded both mad and indefinably scared. "Were you hiding from me?"

"No, Momma. I was just playing. Just playing." Reece didn't know how many details she should give. After a second of silence, she divulged some precious information. "I was exploring a cave."

"A cave?" Becca gasped. "Under your bed?"

"It was just a game."

"Reece, it's never just a game. If you say that

there's a cave under your bed … I believe you."

Another awkward beat passed between them.

Downstairs, Reece could hear her father shouting at the television. The game had turned, and not in his favor.

"Can I see it?" Becca tilted her head like an owl in the rafters of a barn. "Can I go under your bed and see it?"

Reece didn't want Becca under her bed. Her mother didn't look … okay. Her eyes were big, and her cheeks were fluttering. Her tears were running in streaks beside her runny nose, and her fists had grown tighter. Something was wrong with her mother, and she didn't know what it was.

Reece was only five. As far as she knew, the world was an innocent and playful place … and the only thing she really needed to worry about was beings known as "strangers." She pictured strangers like shaggy haired brutes with dog-like teeth and uncleaned hands. They smelled and barked and ran on all fours. They were cold, cruel, and they did *terrible* things. She had received several talks about strangers from her mother. But at this moment, Becca Brampton looked like a stranger. Her voice was shaky; her eyes were furtively taking in the room, as if she was preparing her escape. She looked like a snake ready to strike.

"Sure." Reece swallowed the lump in her throat.

With rapidity she did not expect, her mother lurched down on her hands and knees and scuttled under the bed. Reece stood in confused silence.

"Oh wow! You were right, Reece! There *is a* cave down here! I'm glad I believed you!"

Reece didn't know what to say or do. She clicked her flashlight on and off and looked out the window over her bed. Sometimes, on stormy nights, she imagined a monster outside that window. She had never worried about anything sinister living underneath her bed. The real horrors were outside her room.

*Strangers.*

Becca's skeletal arm slithered out from beneath the bed, and she whispered: "Come down here and guide me through the cave, Reece. I don't want to get lost."

*Don't.* A godly voice bellowed in Reece's ear. *Don't go under there with her. She'll hurt you.*

Reece didn't understand. She felt an intuitive pull toward the door. She wanted to run down the stairs, leap into Stewart's arms, and demand that he take her outside. She wanted to be as far away from Becca as she could be.

But it was raining outside. Lightning skittered across the roiling clouds. Droplets hit the window, blurring her view. Reece felt her little knees knock together. This felt like a scene out of a very grown-up movie. The type of film her parents told her she wasn't even allowed to look at when they visited the video-rental store. The types of films that promised monsters, and blood, and crying people being tortured.

"Come on, Reece." Becca's voice aimed to sooth, but it reminded Reece more of a robotic hiss. "Come on." It was as if she was trying to coax an animal down from a tree. As if repeating the same phrase would goad Reece into her arms.

"I have to go to the bathroom," Reece said.

Becca was silent.

"I have to go." Reece was unsure if she should be asking for permission or not.

Becca's hand slunk back beneath the bed. The grown woman was completely hidden now. Reece didn't want to admit it, but her innards were spinning with fear. She had been lying about needing the restroom, but her stomach felt nonetheless squirmy.

"Come back soon, okay?" Becca croaked.

Reece turned and left the room. When her back was turned, she expected Becca to scuttle out like an agitated spider and chase her down. Reece expected her mother to hook her claws into her back and drag her under the bed—*into the cave*. But nothing happened.

Reece left the room, walked down the hall, went into the bathroom, closed the door, and locked it. One step at a time and with the fluid ease of a machine. She was safe there, she decided. Safe behind her locked bathroom door.

She had neglected the light. The darkness of the bathroom did not alarm her. She was comforted by it. Still, she clicked her flashlight on and scanned the room. There were white towels hanging from a glinting rack. There was a bar of soap, dipped through its middle by ferocious scrubbing. There was the faded glass surrounding the shower. The flashlight pointed out tidbits of familiarity, one at a time.

She hugged her flashlight close to her chest, allowing its beam to glow hotly beneath her chin.

She took comfort in its presence.

*You'll be okay,* she thought to herself. *It will all be over soon.*

She heard footsteps. They were clicking up the hall at a steady pace. They were coming to the bathroom door.

Reece slunk back until she was pressed against the towel rack. She braced herself against her bulky flashlight and bit down on her lower lip. Her sharp little baby teeth drew blood, but she dared not yelp.

The footsteps stopped just outside the door.

Rough fingers rapped against the door.

"Becca? You in here?" It was Stewart.

An exhale gusted through her teeth.

The knob rattled desperately. "Hey, Becca? You okay in there?"

"It's me, Daddy!" Reece shouted.

"Oh." A beat of silence passed between them. "Hey, do you have the lights off in there?"

"Yeah."

"Have you seen your mom?"

Reece didn't respond.

"She's not in our room. Not in either of the bathrooms ... I think ... She didn't say she was going out, did she?"

"No." Reece's voice was slow.

"Sorry. It's just strange. I'll leave you—"

There was a sound like scissors ripping through paper. What followed was the noise of a foot battering a puddle. Wet, sloppy gulps that scared Reece so much that she dropped her flashlight. Its beam fluttered against the ground and landed on the bottom portion of the bathroom door ... where a red tide was flowing.

Outside, she heard Stewart gasp deeply.

Then there was a damp thud.

The stillness that followed was unbearable. Reece hadn't realized it, but her bladder had released itself. She gripped the nearest towel and stuffed her face into it. She didn't want to look at the crimson flood pouring beneath the bathroom door and inching toward her bare toes.

Even worse, she didn't want to listen to mother's soft laughter. It was a horse whinny that creeped through the door and filled the dark bathroom.

Becca's laugh broke into a cackle and then a braying cry.

Reece wanted to scream. She wanted to weep. She wanted, most of all, to be comforted by her parents. Not the dead or evil things outside the bathroom door—she wanted to be held by her mother and father. She wanted them to grip her hands so tightly that they bruised. She wanted them to take turns kissing her sweaty brow and telling her that it would be okay.

*It's just a nightmare, Reece. A horrible, awful dream. God sends us good dreams; the Devil sends us nightmares. Don't cry. You're awake. That's all that matters.*

The sound of her mother's laugh faded away.

"Praise be!" Becca Brampton shouted in a raspy moan. "Praise … be!"

Reece heard her loping down the stairs.

She heard the front door open and slam shut.

Then … she heard nothing.

Until the police came to get her.

# CHAPTER ONE

Paisley kissed August quickly. They were new to the whole "kissing thing"—as Paisley called it—and so when they did smooch, it was only for a few fleeting seconds before they pulled away. Still, those seconds were precious, and Paisley hadn't felt so electrified before in her seventeen years of life.

"Reece is gonna see you up here." Paisley laughed.

"She ain't a tattler," August drawled.

Paisley thought that he could turn the accent on and off whenever he pleased. Some days, he could be so well spoken. On other occasions, August Patch sounded as much of a hick as was expected from a farm boy that wore a pair of ratty overalls and a straw hat. She called him Sawyer whenever he wore that ridiculous hat, and she was fond of pulling it away from him and holding it just out of reach. She could do that too. Paisley Karkoff was a good two heads taller than her boyfriend of three weeks, and a year older.

Paisley felt the urge to kiss him again, and so she did. She pecked him on his chapped lips and watched as his eyes glittered with puppy-like glee.

They were sitting on a wooden board nailed between the boughs of the tree just beside Paisley's window. Some nights, she climbed out from the room she shared with her adopted sister and held flirtatious congress with August on this board. They would lie on their backs, let their legs drape over the board, and stare up into the night sky. Other nights, they would scamper down the tree and run through the woods. August would tell her spooky stories, and they would explore the creeks and furrows on Momma Karkoff's seventy-acre woods.

Unlike Reece, Paisley wasn't afraid of the dark.

Paisley never chided Reece for her worries. Paisley understood; after going through the type of shit Reece had gone through, the little one was deserving of her fears.

August once gently asked what had happened to Reece. The story made Paisley too sad, so she only shared sparse details.

"Her mother was crazy. Like dangerous-*scary*-crazy. She killed Reece's dad, then went outside and killed herself on the front lawn. Reece heard the whole thing, poor dear."

"Oh, wow." August gawped. "How old was she?"

"Five."

"So … that was half a lifetime ago, huh?" August said.

"Yup."

And then, like the sweetheart he was, August didn't push for more explicit details. He knew that if Paisley—or, for that matter, Reece—wanted to discuss it any more, they would do so of their own volition.

August had never been one to poke or prod his way into anyone's favor. In fact, he was a simple boy who communicated in simple terms. He said, "yes, ma'am" and "no, sir," and he minded both his Ps and his Qs. Paisley thought that he was just darling, a courteous farm boy with all the charm and suave of a nostalgic radio ad.

She also thought he was handsome. He sure didn't know how to dress to impress—unless it was Sunday—but he had a rugged look to him. His face was dotted with insubordinate hairs, his arms were muscular, and he had avoided the farmer's tan that plagued all the other boys at school. Instead, he had two slender strips of white where the shoulders of his overalls rested, while his arms, chest, and belly were a dark brown. His hair was wiry and untrimmed. It fell down his shoulders when he didn't have it pulled back. When he did put it in a tail, stray strands curled around his scalp like lichen.

August had only been Paisley's boyfriend for three weeks, but they had known each other their whole lives. He was too modest to say, but she was sure he had loved her since primary school.

When August had asked her out for ice cream,

Paisley had balked. "Why?"

"Cuz, I like you and I like ice cream." He shrugged. "Would you rather go to a movie?"

She wondered, on days her self-esteem was low, what there was to love. She was a hard strung young woman with all the grace of a falling scarecrow. She played rougher than August did and had been the cause and recipient of many bruises and busted lips. Where he minded his manners, Paisley spat and swore. He had never even seen the detention hall, much less been invited into it. Paisley, on the other hand, was on a first name basis with Mrs. Hoover, the crotchety old woman that was lenient on repeat offenders if they asked her how her day was and engaged in real conversations with her.

Sometimes, Paisley thought that punishment would be worse than listening to Mrs. Hoover ramble on about her bunions and her gardening woes. While she yammered, Paisley would repeat her offenses in her head as if she was putting it on the chalkboard.

*I will not get into fights in the lunchroom … I will not get into fights in the lunchroom …*

*I will not call my teachers hypocrites … I will not call my teachers hypocrites …*

*I will not hand in papers filled with profanity just to check if my teachers* really *read them. Because they do. And not only will they circle every word but they'll also call your mom and print her a copy … and you really don't want your mom reading about George Washington partaking in a gang bang while signing the Declaration of Independence, do you?*

On days when Paisley's self-esteem was higher,

she was a no-nonsense queen who could destroy any obstacle in her path. Her noncompliance was equal to the rebellions she read about from the '60s and '70s. She was an officer monitoring the authority figures while the sheep slept.

It felt foolish, but she really could think that highly of herself. She was beautiful too, with short brown hair, a sharp nose, and brown eyes. She often wore stylized "cowboy" outfits. She currently had on a pair of cowboy boots, a shaggy purple sweater, and a pair of rough jeans with holes torn through the knees. August had jokingly asked if the jeans came that way. They had, but she wouldn't let him know that.

Paisley felt August's calloused hand and brought up an ultimatum. "We either gotta go out for the night or I go back inside and fall asleep."

"I can't be out late." August frowned. "Mom's probably going to check on me after her shows are done."

"Pussy." Paisley smirked at him before planting another kiss on his lips. "You need some chap stick."

"Sorry." He rubbed his lips with the back of his hands. "I didn't really think about it."

"I didn't brush my teeth." She giggled. "And I had eggs for dinner."

"Yeah," he said coyly. "I could tell."

An awkward and bubbly beat passed between them before August spoke again.

"Okay, before I climb down, we need to make plans. That's why I came over here."

"I thought it was cuz you *waz* lonely." She

imitated his accent, feeling only slightly bad about the joke. They had been friends for far too long for a jest like that to matter.

"I wasn't." He stuck his tongue out. "Not that my mom isn't great company, but—"

"She don't kiss like I do."

"Gross." He nudged her. "Too far. Uhm, for real, though. What are you doing Saturday?"

"This Saturday or next Saturday or the Saturday after?"

"Every one. From here on out."

"Oh." She paused pensively. "Nothing."

"Good."

August began to crawl down the tree. The little wooden slats had been a great help when they were children, but now that they were almost adults, he had to wrap his legs around the tree and scuffle down like a bear.

"What's our plan?" Paisley asked.

"We're hanging out, dummy." He laughed.

"Yeah but, what are we *doing*?"

"Well, I don't know."

"I thought you came over to make plans!"

"No. I came over *cuz I waz lonely*!"

She tilted off the platform and kissed him again. And then he was down the tree and dashing through the yard. He would go into the woods and cut across the road to his house.

She watched him as he left, impressed by his swiftness and his silence. The only thing she could hear was the soft whoosh of his feet tearing through the grass and then the rickety clatter of sticks when he entered the tree line. Like a ghost, August Patch was gone. His tanned face disappeared into the woods as he took one last look over his shoulder. Of course he wanted to see her one last time before he was whisked away by the shadows. He always did.

Paisley Karkoff missed him already.

"August Patch and Paisley Karkoff sitting in a tree …"

She whispered to herself as she crawled off of the wooden platform and back into her open window.

"K.I.S.S.I.N.G."

She didn't feel like singing the rest. She didn't want to think about love, marriage, or a baby carriage. That was all a world away. But still, her lips thrummed where they had been kissed, and her fingers crackled where they had grazed his hand.

"That you?" Reece asked—a little too loudly—as Paisley jumped off of the windowsill and onto their floor.

"Who else would it be?" Paisley snickered.

Reece didn't respond.

"I thought you were asleep." Paisley began to hobble into her nightwear. "You okay? It's late. It's eleven-thirty. You should really have been asleep at nine. We've got school—"

"You woke me." Reece didn't present this as an accusation; it was merely a fact. "I wasn't sleeping great."

"Oh, hun." Paisley sat down on her bed, which sat on the opposite side of the room from Reece's. When Reece had moved in, they feared she would not fare well on her own. And so, despite the massive size of their house, Mom had plopped Reece right across from Paisley. At first, Paisley had been upset, but she grew accustomed to the company pretty fast.

Reece's side of the room was decorated with posters. She had several pop stars above her bed, everyone from BTS to Harry Styles. She had a small vanity mirror decorated with red smooches and a humble closet lined with neat outfits. Sometimes Reece would play *model*. She would strut back and forth as if she was at a high-end fashion show, treating the space between her and Paisley's bed as a runway.

Paisley's side of the room had a darker hue to it. She didn't hang up posters or decorate all that much. She did have a bookshelf filled with young adult and graphic novels and a few thick slabs of narrative poetry by Ellen Hopkins—she'd read *Identical* so many times the spine was almost broken in half. Atop the shelf stood a vigilant row of dinosaur toys she had outgrown but never had the heart to throw out. There was a stegosaurus with brown plates and a heavy tail. Its mouth hung stupidly open and was decorated with inaccurately sharp teeth. Then there was a gruesome Spinosaurus, which looked like a bipedal crocodile adorned with a considerable dorsal fin. Next to him was an average looking T-Rex, which had a crooked leg and a stubby tail.

Paisley drew her blankets to her chin and spoke in a whisper.

"You won't tell Mom, will you?"

"That you were out with Auggie? No." Reece

had adapted that nickname herself, and as far as Paisley knew, no one had even considered calling him that until Reece did. Now it was what everyone referred to him as. "I ain't a tattler."

"We were talking that loud, huh?"

"You forget yourself when you're with him." Reece yawned. "Don't you wanna hear about my dream?"

Paisley had, truthfully, been afraid to ask. Sometimes, Reece had bad dreams. Dreams about details she had learned after being rescued from the bathroom in her old house ... dreams of when she had been Reece Brampton and not Reece Karkoff.

Five years ago. *Has it only been five years?*

Paisley shivered. She had heard scant details from her mother about what had happened at the Brampton house, but her schoolmates had filled her in on the more troubling and sordid details ...

"Her mom went nuts. They say she had been acting weird all week before—you know—she did *it*." Jessica Cherry had said this as she leaned against Paisley's locker. "Said she had set up a secret shrine in the garden shed. Had a picture of Jesus and a couple wax candles ... and, like, Reece's hair. She had been cutting it off of her at night. While she was sleeping? I don't know if I'd believe that, but Keegan Peterson's dad's a cop, and she said she overheard him talking about it. A little Jesus shrine."

Paisley had confronted Keegan, asking for more details. The mousey kid—who later became Paisley's best friend and would come out as nonbinary to her before anyone else—had spilled the beans immediately.

"Dad said that shrine ain't a rumor. It's real, all right. It was in the back corner of the shed. They said they found grooves in the dirt where she had *knelt*. For hours, she'd go in there and worship it. Made a circle around it out of hair. They thought it was Reece's cuz it was all blonde, but ... I don't know."

"How'd she do it?" Paisley had asked impatiently. She wanted to know. All that the adults would say was that Becca had been "disturbed" and that what she had done had been "tragic." Paisley didn't know nor care what any of that meant. At the time, she had wanted the gory details.

Keegan had gone ashen-faced as they recounted the story they had overheard their daddy tell their mommy.

"Daddy was shaking when he told my momma about it. He said Mrs. Brampton cut Mr. Brampton's throat with a kitchen knife. Then she ... stabbed him right below the eye. Right here." Keegan touched the soft space just above their cheek and beside their nose. "Pinned him to the bathroom door. Reece was right behind it ... poor little girl. She must have heard it all."

"How'd Mrs. Brampton kill herself?" Paisley had asked.

"She went out on the front lawn. Daddy said she dug her eyes out with her hands before she cut her wrists. Her eyes were sitting on her palms when they found her. She was cross-legged and leaning up against the porch. They didn't know she was dead until they got close … I don't want to think about it anymore. I had nightmares all night." Keegan pulled their books closer. "You just give Reece a hug for me whenever you can, okay? Tell her it's from Keegan Peterson, and if she ever wants to come to one of our sleepovers, Paisley, then just bring her. We won't tell scary stories if she doesn't wanna hear them."

After Reece had become friendly with Paisley, Keegan, Jessica, and their other girlfriends, she told them what had happened herself. That was only a year ago, when Reece was nine. They were camping in the backyard and roasting marshmallows when Reece said:

"Do you wanna hear about the things I remember?"

No one had responded, and so Reece began to talk.

She told them about how Becca Brampton had crawled under her bed. She told them about the weird way her mother had acted. She even told them about the little voice that told her to hide.

"That's God!" Jessica, a stout and devout Christian, applauded. "God told you to get on out of there."

"Maybe." Reece shrugged. "But I was too scared to have been praying to him."

Paisley shook her head and resurfaced into the present. Reece was sitting up and staring across the room at her, expectantly awaiting a reply.

"What did you dream about?" Paisley asked.

"I dreamed about sharks."

Paisley was relieved. Sharks were manageable. Becca Brampton and the squishy sound of the blade searing through Stewart Brampton's throat were not.

"You were there." Reece's eyes turned pale, as if she'd drifted back to sleep. "We were floating on a piece of driftwood. They were circling us."

"Were they big?" Paisley asked.

"They were." Reece nodded. "And they had huge teeth." Reece curled her lips over her own teeth, and in the strips of moonlight sifting through their open bedroom window, her teeth looked luminescent.

Paisley felt a weird tingle crawl up her back. "You're spooking me." Paisley giggled.

Reece's teeth disappeared behind her lips. "Sorry."

"Nah, don't be." Paisley fell back into her bed with her arms splayed over the sides. "Do you think Mom is still up?"

"I heard her turn off the TV, like, fifteen minutes ago, but she hasn't come up the stairs yet." Reece's mouth fell. "She's been staying up real late."

Hollie Karkoff always had trouble sleeping, and yet Reece acted like every late night was a new and exciting development. Hollie had been the "weird" sister before Becca had committed her atrocious deed. Sometimes, Paisley wondered if her mother was jealous of her sister's notoriety. It was an odd thought to have, but Paisley wouldn't deny it. Still, Reece and Paisley were lucky to live under Hollie's roof.

Hollie was a kind woman who refused to raise

her voice. Even when Paisley was in her worst spats at school, Hollie's silence and composure never wavered. On better days, her laugh could be absolutely shrill and overpowering. Just that morning, they had heard her howling over the phone with a friend over some tasty gossip. It had been a pleasant alarm bell that had urged them out of bed.

It had taken Reece no time at all to start calling Hollie "Mom." In fact, her biological mother had been reduced to nothing more than "Becca." Paisley understood that resentment. She wouldn't want to be associated with a freakish murderer either.

Too many thoughts had been wasted on Becca Brampton that night. Paisley resolved to get the woman out of her head before she became nightmare fuel.

"What do you think?" Reece asked.

"About?"

"Anything."

Paisley bit her tongue. "I think it's about time we went to sleep."

Outside, a dirty rain began to fall over the Karkoff residence. Seventy acres worth of woods sat between them and the highway. The only other neighbors they had were the Patch family, who lived across from them, and a row of trailers just beside the highway and behind their property.

The Karkoff land had been handed to Hollie by her father, who raised Christmas trees beside the house. Hollie had no interest in Christmas trees. She allowed the land to become burdened with overgrowth.

The rain thickened steadily, nurturing the overpopulated forest.

In the woods, a deep creek began to fill as the rain increased. Water trickled over mud-encrusted stones and wove between tangled roots. Every divot became a pool, and every tilt became a rushing slope.

While the young Karkoff sisters found sleep, a shadowy figure slumped through the forest.

August Patch had fully intended on going home after leaving the tree, but something had caught his attention in the woods. A small carving embedded in the chest of a tree. He examined it under the light of a finger-sized flashlight he carried with him in his breast pocket.

As the rain began to draw his hair over his eyes and his feet began to sink into the mud, he wondered who had drawn such a symbol. Had it been Reece? Hollie? Certainly not Paisley. She would have giddily brought his attention to it herself. And it had only been by chance that he had caught it out of the corner of his eye.

The symbol was detailed and had been scribbled in with an expert's hand.

It was of a circle with seven twirling conflagrations bursting out of its side. It looked as if the sun was spilling its molten insides into space. At its center lay a row of three crosses just like the ones on Calvary Hill, the ones he had read about in Sunday school.

August was a devout Christian, which he knew irked Paisley. Paisley was very much Hollie's daughter, as much as she would deny such claims. To be honest, August was frightened of Hollie. The older woman was very energetic and kindly, but she had a sharp look to her. She looked as if the slightest misstep would set her off … and she was the kind to hold a silent grudge. August didn't want to ever upset her, so he walked on eggshells when she was present.

*It's her eye.* August found himself thinking about her. *She wears that goofy eye patch, like a pirate, and you can't help but think about how her eye must look under there. Is it sealed shut? Is it milky white? Is it inflamed and pus-soaked? Does it leak tears? You don't know. You probably never will. It creeps you out that you'll never ever know.*

August decided the thoughts weren't very polite, so he shuffled them like a deck of cards and buried them at the bottom of the stack. He returned his attention to the three crosses at the epicenter of the pictogram.

The center cross bore a round halo at its head. The halo, like the circle, was bursting at its seams.

August stepped away from the tree and let his flashlight's beam fall away from it. How long had he been standing there, staring at the odd artwork? He shook his head and became dimly aware that he was soaking wet and would leave a muddy trail up the latticework of his house if he tried to climb back into his bedroom.

Maybe his mother was already asleep … or maybe he would get caught and wind up grounded. He didn't like the thought of having to skip his date with Paisley on Saturday …

But he couldn't pull himself away from the drawing just yet.

He shined the light on it once more.

As he did, the downpour became a deluge.

"Who put you there, little fella?" August asked aloud as if he was addressing a stray kitten. "Who put you there?"

Above his head, a bolt of lightning cracked through the sky.

# CHAPTER TWO

Hollie Karkoff always woke up earlier than her children. And she *did* think of Reece as her own child. After all the trauma, Hollie's sister was no more Reece's mother than her left sock was.

If it wasn't for Hollie's knocking on their bedroom door, the two girls would sleep the whole century away. They hibernated like bears every time they curled up under their covers.

"Reece! Paisley! Wake up! Breakfast!" She trilled her knuckles against the door again.

There was no response. Hollie sighed, rolled her eye, and shook the knob.

"It's a school day, girls."

"Uhhhh." She wasn't sure who said that. It sounded like Paisley, but sometimes Reece could be just as grumbly. "Coming!" Yes, it was Reece.

Hollie stepped away and descended the stairs. Reece would shake Paisley awake. Hollie's job was done.

In the kitchen, she had breakfast prepared. Three boxes of cereal sat at the center of their round dining table. Three bowls orbited the boxes like ceramic planets. Each bowl was cherry red and decorated with painted ladybugs. They had been made by Reece in pottery class only three years ago. She had insisted they eat from those bowls every morning. It was a habit that Hollie was now accustomed to, so accustomed to that she assumed her hands would shake if she tried starting her morning with a dull, regular, uninspired, white bowl purchased from a chain store.

She poured her healthy cereal—which she knew her girls would ignore—into her own bowl and followed it with a stream of almond milk. She dipped her spoon in and took a long, savory bite.

Today was already off to a good start, Hollie Karkoff thought. It was a misty Friday morning. The sun was shining, but the wind was blowing. She had stuck her hand out the front door and was happy to report that it was neither too hot nor was it too cold. It was *just right*.

Hollie found herself knocking her fingers against the patch resting over her left eye. It was an old habit. One that refused to die.

She sighed and forced her spare hand into her lap as she took in another spoonful.

She had lost her eye over a simple and stupid accident. It had been when she was in her early twenties. Hollie Karkoff had chosen to work at a movie theater after dropping out from college. She had spent the day down the hallway, cleaning cinemas. She would use a cumbersome broom and dustpan set to scoop up popcorn and candy wrappers. After filling the trashcans outside the theaters, she had to pull the bags and bring them to the dumpster outside and toward the back of the building.

She remembered it like it was just yesterday … She had been walking with both of her hands full when she had slipped on the coke spilling out of the sides of one of the bags. She righted herself easily and tried to move forward, but her legs had become tangled.

As she fell, Hollie remembered throwing her bags of trash ahead of her. She thought, with hindsight, that she hadn't wanted to be coated in stale soda and sticky candies. If she had fallen on those bags, it probably would have cushioned her and kept her safe.

Instead, her head banged against the corner of an air conditioner. The big units sat beside the exit doors to each theater, and they often roared to noisy life unexpectedly. They had scared Hollie once or twice on her trash runs. But …

They did more than scare her this time around.

This time, they took a bite.

A manager had found her after a customer complained about the noise coming from outside. She was curled up behind the building, holding her blood-streaked face in her hands and screaming.

The damage had been done, and it had been done efficiently. The sharp metal siding had torn her eye right out of the socket.

Bizarrely, her life seemed to take a turn for the

better after her eye was removed from her skull!

Becoming unexpectedly pregnant with Paisley only five years after that had been a blessing atop other blessings. She didn't care that Paisley's father had been a stranger she had met in a bar—or that he had never called her back. He had given her a wonderful gift, and she was thankful that it had come at a time when she was *ready* to have a child. Was she surprised? Yes ... but she was, nevertheless, ready.

Her mother and father had passed in a car accident before she had gotten the job at the theater, and so the land became hers. Her sister had had little to no interest in the farm.

Hollie was happy here.

Endlessly happy.

Reece was, predictably, the first one down the stairs. She took her steps harshly, the sound of each footfall reverberating through the house. Paisley was behind her. She was using her fingers to scrape the crust out from her eyes.

"Paisley," Hollie said, "can you drive Reece to school today? Malcolm and I were thinking of having coffee—"

"Yeah, Mom. No problem."

"Thank you, dear."

Paisley had only started driving on her own a month ago and was secretly thankful whenever Hollie asked her to run errands.

"Take the van," Hollie said.

"Why can't I take the Cadillac?" Paisley sniffed as she took her seat at the table and chose a sugary cereal.

"Because the Cadillac is nice, and I don't want it vandalized."

"No one's going to touch it, Mom," Paisley retorted.

"Someone keyed Mrs. Worship's car last week," Reece piped in.

"That's because Mrs. Worship is a prude, and no one likes her," Paisley stated. "C'mon, Mom."

"Why would you even want to take the Cadillac?" Hollie took a long draw from her spoon. She clicked the silver against her sharp teeth.

"Because." Paisley poured milk into her bowl.

"Malcolm wants to drive it, Paisley. You'll have to take the van."

Malcolm Ansell usually did all the driving for the Karkoff family. After losing her eye, Hollie hadn't trusted herself to get behind the wheel of a car and take her two young ones out into the dangerous road. She could drive comfortably around the farm, but outside of her property ... it was too unpredictable.

Malcolm hadn't minded being a chaperone. In fact, he had generously insisted on it. He turned up at their door at eight in the morning, every morning, and was welcomed in for his usual breakfast—buttered toast, a cup of black coffee, and a banana—before he drove the girls to school.

Now that Paisley could drive, Hollie had made Malcolm bow out from most of his responsibilities. Instead, they spent their mornings on the porch with their coffee and a few words of conversation. It was much more relaxing.

Malcolm was a pleasant, astute, and unobtrusive gentleman, and Hollie very much enjoyed his friendship. Reece had once blithely asked if Hollie and Malcolm would ever get married. Hollie was sure that if they did, it would be out of convenience and the merging of their two properties instead of love. As close as they were, their relationship was strictly platonic. They had disastrously tried fooling around one night after sharing a bottle … and had ended up resolving to keep their clothes on and their hands to themselves.

Hollie wasn't too sure if she was keen on finding a husband. That had been her sister's district … and look how she ended up!

*That's an awful thought, Hollie!* a little voice spat in her ear.

She shook her head. The fate of her older sister was a trauma she had to combat with humor. Otherwise, she was sure she would cry until there was no moisture left in her body.

She returned her thoughts to Malcolm. As kind and as loving as Malcolm was, he wasn't too painfully interested in women.

Or men, for that matter.

Malcolm liked his friendships. That was enough love for him. He was too folksy to refer to himself as an asexual, but Keegan had diagnosed him after citing their own queerness as qualification enough to make the call.

*Speak of the Devil and he shall appear.*

Malcolm knocked at the front door.

"I'll get it!" Reece announced and dashed away from the table.

"It's unlocked, Reece! He can just walk in!" Paisley smirked and turned back to Hollie. "How about tonight?"

"What about it?" Hollie asked as she chewed.

Paisley gave her a look that said: *You should be able to read my mind at this point.* "Can I take the Caddie out on Saturday?"

"The Caddie? What are you … a fifty-year-old golfer?"

"Okay. The *car*. Can I take the *car* out?" Paisley stuck out her tongue.

"Yeah. Wait … who are you seeing?"

"Keegan, for sure, and maybe Ron … and I think August ... if he's free."

Malcolm came plodding into the kitchen, being tugged along by Reece. He was a large man with heavy paws and a black beard. Malcom's dusty hair was broken by a widow's peak. He wore a pair of circular spectacles that made his eyes look bigger than they actually were.

"Whoa! How long did it take Hollie to make breakfast today?" Malcolm joked when he saw the boxes of cereal.

"You got any better ideas?"

"Let me come over and make pancakes tomorrow."

"No!" Hollie declared. "No one wants shrimp pancakes!"

He tousled Reece's hair. "Reece liked them."

"Reece is too nice to tell you she washed her mouth out with soap when you left—"

"Everyone liked my shrimp and grits."

"Yeah, because that made sense!" Paisley

interjected.

Malcolm put his hands on his hips and stood in mock protest. "Well, what if I made omelets?"

"As long as they are regular, normal, actual omelets." Hollie waggled her spoon at him.

"I'll make them right. Don't worry. So, breakfast tomorrow? How's that sound, girls?"

"Yay!" Reece shouted supportively.

"You want butter or jam today, Malcolm?" Hollie asked.

"I'll get it." He went to the fridge and began to dig through it with familiarity. "You know, Paisley, I almost killed your boyfriend last night."

Paisley sat in silence for a moment. "What do you mean?"

"He came running out in front of my car last night. I don't know how late it was, but ... It was raining, and I was coming back from work, and he bolted right in front of me."

"Oh god." Paisley rolled her eyes.

"What was Auggie doing in the woods?" Hollie asked Paisley.

"I don't know." Paisley's voice was too defensive. She cast a quick *don't tell* look at Reece. "He takes walks sometimes."

"He was running like there was a snake at his heels." Malcolm stood upright, examining a jar of peach jam. "He stopped right in front of me. I had to crunch on the brakes. Then he was gone. He ran off. I mean, I hope I didn't give him a heart attack, but he almost gave me one!"

"That's weird," Hollie muttered.

"Well, I'll ask him about it," Paisley said.

"Give him my regards." Malcolm moved the jam from hand to hand as if he was about to toss it across the room. "I don't know what he was doing in that rain. Did you hear it last night?"

"It kept me awake." Reece moaned. "There was lightning too."

"Yeah. It started right as I was leaving work." Malcolm worked at his brother's bar. His older brother, Wylie, had an apartment in town. The great outdoors had done little for him, so, Malcolm had inherited the family estate much the same way Hollie had. Still, Malcolm and Wylie got along well, and whenever Wylie was short staffed at The Hopping Frog, he was quick to ask for Malcolm's assistance.

Malcolm never needed the money; he just liked to help.

Hollie suspected he refused to let his brother pay him for his labor.

Hollie also suspected he was thankful for any excuse to get away from his lonely house.

Malcolm Ansell's farm was a smaller bit of land at forty acres, but it was more profitable than the Karkoff residence. Malcolm raised goats and chickens there. The girls had spent many hot days playing with the animals, casually ignoring the fact that most of the chickens would eventually wind up on their dinner plates.

Hollie, being a vegan, had refused his offer for weekly deliveries of goat's milk, but she had never wanted to force her beliefs on her daughters. And so, they ate chicken, and they ate shrimp, and they ate omelets. Whatever Malcolm made, they ate gladly.

Even when his meals verged on the experimental.

"Oh, I need to get ready for school." Paisley stood and glanced impulsively at her bare wrist. "You too, bean-sprout."

"I'm not finished." Reece took a soggy bite of marshmallow cereal.

"Hurry." Paisley bounded up the stairs and toward her room.

Malcolm took her seat after toasting two slices of wheat bread and spreading an obnoxious amount of jam on them.

"So, Reece, how's school?" Malcolm sounded like a surrogate father, Hollie noted. He had a way of doing that, of stepping into vacant roles. She hoped he didn't feel obligated to interact with her children some days, but she was also happy for the relief.

Hollie began to wash her ladybug bowl at the sink. She listened to Reece's response.

"It's okay."

"Just okay?"

Genuine concern. How did he pull that off so effortlessly? They weren't his kids. Malcolm had never even given a thought toward having his own children, as far as Hollie knew.

"Yeah. It's no prison, but it's no award-winner." Reece scowled.

"Ouch. You're a harsh critic."

He was so goofy too. Just like a dad. It would have infuriated Hollie if he wasn't so damned likable. She looked out the window just above the sink, and toward the woods.

The visual of August Patch racing out from the trees and almost colliding with Malcolm Ansell's car sank in. *What was that boy doing in the woods so late?* She didn't suspect him of any tomfoolery, but still …

Had he and Paisley gone for one of their midnight strolls, the ones Paisley thought were covert? Had he climbed up the tree and talked to her on that dangerous plank that she was hoping to convince Malcolm to remove? She had heard that those visitations had been going on for a few nights now but … Paisley and August hadn't done anything other than chat and kiss. Another thing Paisley had wrongfully assumed was that Reece wasn't a tattler.

What was August doing? It was dangerous to be in the woods during a storm. The land was uneven and filled with pits and gullies. And if he was running, then he risked slipping and hitting his head against a tree. Hell, maybe if he lost an eyeball, then he and Hollie would match! *Twinsies!*

She realized that she was genuinely concerned … just as Malcolm had been when he had received a vague answer from Reece. She *liked* August. It was a blessing to have her daughter date a boy that didn't leave her wringing her fingers with worry. August had been a friend of the Karkoff family for years, and he had been nothing but sweet and sensitive.

What had he been thinking as he bolted in front of a moving vehicle?

Reece hadn't said anything about last night, but until now, she hadn't been outside of Paisley's sight.

"Do you know anything about August being in the woods last night?" Hollie found herself asking the question before she could really formulate her thoughts.

Reece took a reluctant moment before responding. "He swung by to say 'hi,' but … I don't know what would've scared him."

"Maybe he ran into an animal or something." Malcolm spoke through his first mushy bite, a little jam running out of the corner of his lips.

"He really looked scared?" Hollie asked Malcolm.

"Yeah." He wiped his mouth with the hairy back of his massive hand. "He looked terrified."

# CHAPTER THREE

Paisley was quick to pull her phone out from her pocket and send a message to August. As she hurriedly brushed her teeth, the little device dinged with his response:

"Hey. Sorry. Should've told you. We'll talk at school. Tell Malcolm I got lost and didn't even realize I was coming toward the road. Okay?"

Paisley sat on the closed toilet. Her green toothbrush hung limply from her mouth, its bristles lodged into her molars. She ignored the coagulating paste as she wrote him back:

"Are you okay?"

"Yeah." His response was fast. "Don't worry, Paisley. I'm fine. Got a little spooked. I'll tell you the whole story at school. And Mom didn't even hear me come in so I'm not in trouble. We're still on for Saturday."

Paisley smiled, stood, returned to the sink, and

spat her toothpaste into the basin. Her heart could rest a little easier now. Still, she wanted to know what had scared him so much.

"Want me to pick you up for school? Malcolm and Mom are hanging out today, so I've got the van."

"Sure. See you in a few?"

Outside the bathroom window, another storm was brewing. Raindrops dotted the window, and thunder grumbled in the distance. Paisley needed to get dressed for school, but she found herself briefly transfixed by the noise. The thunder sounded almost musical. Like the beating of a drum building up toward something more cacophonous. She looked down at her phone once more and decided to check the weather forecast.

It looked like it was going to rain all week.

Last night's storm had been torrential. Paisley wondered if it would be any worse tonight. If so, she doubted that she or Reece would get any sleep. She also worried that they may be in for a tornado. It wasn't too uncommon for tornados to pass by, but Hollie insisted that their land wasn't flat enough to attract them. She assured both of her children that if worse came to worse, all they would have to do was hang out in the basement for a few hours until there was nothing to fret about.

Still, Paisley couldn't help but be a little paranoid. She had had nightmares about a tornado appearing outside her window and gobbling her and Reece up into its swirling belly.

She had once heard of a tornado striking a house in the neighboring county. Rumor at school had it that the winds had torn the clothes off of the residents' bodies and had shot nails through them like bullets. The mental image was harrowing, to say the least.

And so, Paisley looked out the bathroom window and sighed heavily.

*Just one more thing I'll be putting too much focus on. What if a tornado comes whirling out from those trees? What if it assaults our house with branches and stones and whatever debris it can grab?*

Paisley decided she was being dramatic. She almost stepped away from the window when an errant shadow caught her eye. She froze and scanned the trees, trying to see what had stood out to her even before she could truly formulate any thoughts.

Something had moved. Maybe it was whatever had scared August. An animal?

She looked from one narrow tree to the next. Her scrutiny was pointless, considering the length of the field between their home and the woods. The drizzling rain was clouding over the window as well, making a clear visual impossible.

Whatever she had seen … it was gone now. Gone before she could even hazard a proper guess as to what it was. All she was left with was a head full of dull speculations.

# CHAPTER FOUR

Malcolm sat down with a heavy grunt. Hollie could hear his knees popping beneath his weight. Such were the woes of the middle-aged. Your joints began to ache and creak like the foundations of an unsteady house. He sighed and sank into his rocking chair and began to gently drift back and forth. His left hand rested just above his knee, massaging it softly. His right hand held a mason jar filled with iced tea up to his pink lips.

Hollie had her own tea filling a smaller cup. She argued that he drank too much of the stuff and that it would wreak havoc on his guts. He also used too much sugar. He always dismissed these arguments with a wave.

"What do you think?" Malcolm asked.

"About what?"

"I don't know." He looked out from the porch and across the field where Kurt Karkoff had once grown Christmas trees. The grass bordering her manicured lawn was thick and knee high. Huge stalks wafted in the wet breeze.

The rain was pattering down steadily. Hollie hated to admit it, but she worried about Paisley driving in this kind of weather. She hoped August's presence in the vehicle wouldn't prove to be too distracting.

"I think ..." Malcolm took a swallow of his cold beverage. "I think it's about time we got some rain."

"I suspect you're right." Hollie sighed and sank into her own chair. She hadn't expected to be a "rocking-chair" lady, but now here she was ... in her late thirties, sitting next to a forty-five-year-old, drinking tea and idly rocking back and forth. The cushion beneath her slid forward so that her tailbone rested uncomfortably on the seat of the chair. There was no use scrunching the pillow back up. It would only slip down again.

She realized that she was employing some Paisley logic there—*Why should I make my bed? It's only going to get messy again.*

Well, there was nothing wrong with unchecked hypocrisies. She was old enough to have earned it. Hollie snickered through her teeth.

"I tell you what, Hollie," Malcolm moaned. "It's gonna be weird when it's just you and me in the morning."

"Oh, c'mon. Paisley has a year left at school, and she's probably going to take a year off before going to college." The truth was that Paisley was woefully ambivalent toward continuing her education. She was a smart girl, but she stirred up enough trouble to be a bad conductor. "And Reece is yards away from graduating."

"Time flies," Malcolm intoned gravely. "They're young women now. Soon … they'll be all grown up and we're going to be left behind. We'll have to break all our habits."

"Do you think we'll learn how to sleep in?" Hollie asked.

"Nah. I reckon not." Malcolm took another slurp. "So, I gotta milk the goats. Then do you wanna hit the town? Maybe swing by the thrift store? We could meet the girls for dinner after school … in town."

"Yeah, that sounds nice." Hollie took her first sip of tea. "I'm not going to the goat barn today, though. It's going to be musty."

"That's okay. I'll run off and do all of that. And then I'll pick you up."

"Yeah. Sounds good."

The two sat in comfortable silence for a moment.

"Got anything to smoke?" Hollie asked.

# CHAPTER FIVE

Reece was sprawled in the very back of the van. She wasn't listening to August or Paisley as they drove. Her ears were plugged and blaring loud pop music. From their distance, Paisley couldn't even begin to guess which artist her little sister was listening to. It was excessively clear that Paisley and August were being left to their own devices, and so … Paisley asked him outright about the previous night's events.

"I still feel bad about it. Malcolm looked shocked." August glanced out the window at the passing trees.

"He said you almost gave him a heart attack."

"Geez. Tell him I'm sorry."

"What were you running from?" Paisley pressed.

"Oh." It seemed all August had prepared to say. He took a deep breath between his crooked teeth. "I … I wish I knew?"

"What does that mean, Auggie?"

"It means I kind of … can't remember. Well. I can't remember all of it."

Paisley was having a hard time concentrating on the road ahead. August's evasiveness was becoming infuriating. She hadn't been worried since he had promised to explain everything to her on their drive to school, and now he seemed to be backing out.

"You're gonna have to tell me the whole thing," she insisted. "Otherwise, you're gonna be the reason I go bald."

"Sorry. Sorry." August pinched his brow. "I'm composing my thoughts, okay?"

"Boy, whatever it was it must have really spooked you."

August let a smile play at his lips. "I don't think I saw anything. I wish it had been something I could put my finger on, you know? It was more like … a feeling."

"A feeling had you running into the road in the middle of a dark and stormy night?"

"Yeah. It was weird." August seemed to wait a beat before he asked Paisley a question that had obviously been wriggling around in his brain for a while. "Did you carve something on one of the trees in the woods?"

"Carve what?"

August popped his tongue against his bottom lip. "I don't know. Like, did you try drawing something on one of them?"

"I don't even have a knife to carve with." Paisley laughed.

"Maybe Reece did it, then."

"Did what? August, you're stressing me out. Use your words. Tell me what it was."

"I think I just have to show it to you," August stated. "After school, can we hang out a bit?"

"I don't see why not."

"It's like a symbol or something. I can't describe it very well, but I caught it out of the corner of my eye, and I just couldn't stop looking at it. Even when it started pouring down rain, my feet just felt like they were bolted to the ground." August visibly shivered. "And then I started to think about things."

"What things?"

"I started to remember being scared of the dark. Like I was a little kid again. You know when you get up at night to use the bathroom or get some water and-and you've just come back in your room? Like, I remembered turning off my light and dashing toward my bed … and, when I was a little kid, I always did that because I felt *pursued*. By the darkness itself. Like there was something in it, and if I didn't get to my bed in time, it would drag me somewhere scary. I felt like that last night. The lights had been turned off in those woods and *something* was in the shadows."

Paisley wasn't sure whether or not to take her boyfriend seriously. As they bounced over a pothole, she reached out and clasped his hand. It was sweaty.

"I sound foolish, don't I?" August asked.

"You sound scared. I just don't know what of."

"Neither do I," he admitted. "I damn near wet

my pants. I think Malcolm almost hitting me was what woke me up from the nightmare I was in."

"What did it look like?" Paisley asked. "The carving?"

"It was like …"

"Hey." Reece spoke up from the back of the van, startling both of them. "Mom just texted me. We gotta meet her in town after school. We're going to dinner with Malcolm."

"Where?" Paisley asked, but Reece had popped her music back into her ears and could no longer hear her.

"Well, there goes that," August said. "I'll show you tomorrow—"

"No. We'll come back to the house afterwards. Show me then, okay?"

# CHAPTER SIX

Chief Chilton Farnsworth wasn't too happy.

He didn't like the prospect of combing through the Patches' dense forest, but he saw no alternative. And he didn't really envision seeing Charlotte Patch calming down until he did exactly what she wanted.

He swirled his phlegm from one cheek to the other before spitting it into the gravel and stamping it beneath his boot.

"You said it, boss," Tobin Marks stated. "Damn."

"That's life, kiddo." Chilton shrugged. "Just a big ol' shit-sandwich."

They were standing on the shallow ditch between the road and the forest. They hadn't seen any cars pass by, except for Malcolm Ansell and Hollie Karkoff, who had stopped by for a brief conversation.

"What's going on, Chief?" Malcolm had asked,

leaning toward the open passenger window. Hollie Karkoff was seated in the passenger seat, staring nervously with her one good eye. The two ex-hippies smelled like sweat and marijuana. Chilton took no notice of the stink. He knew they were potheads, but they never caused any trouble for him or his boys. Besides, pot was almost legal anyways. He didn't even give the kids much fuss over it nowadays. What would be the point? As long as they weren't drinking and driving, Chief Chilton saw no reason to drag them down to the office and fill out a ton of paperwork. Still, something about Karkoff and Ansell bothered him. They were insular folks, and yet they became nosy busybodies the moment they saw an opportunity.

Chilton turned his chin toward Malcolm and said: "Spot of bother from Ms. Patch. Said she saw someone in her property. Probably a vagrant or a poacher."

"Oh, man. I've had that issue. People poach on my land without asking ..." Hollie started. She was wearing a sleeveless top, exposing the black tattoos running in waves down her tanned arms. Chilton wondered what those tattoos were of. He had never been given an opportunity to look too closely at them. They just looked like inky threads to him.

Chilton was a tall man and obliquely round. His cheeks were bright red, and his hair was blond and wispy. His sallow green eyes were tight and beady, conveying no expression and giving his features a frog-like hue.

Chief Chilton was only a few years older

than Malcolm. He had been in the same class as Malcolm's brother, Wylie. He and Wylie had remained close; he even frequented the bar—The Hopping Frog—and had gladly been served many a whiskey from Malcolm.

"Well, let's hope it's just a drifter. We see 'em coming off the highway and looking for a spot to bed down every now and then," Chilton said. "You guys can move on. Enjoy your day."

Chilton stood upright and walked away from the Cadillac. He listened to it roar back to life and trundle away, and then he went to stand by his officer. Tobin was a little green around the gills. He had his hand placed firmly on his gun, and his eyes darted ecstatically back and forth. His red hair looked like a pale orange flame in the drizzling weather. It wasn't raining too hard, but it would be pouring again in a few hours.

"Poacher my ass," Tobin mocked.

"Yeah, well, what can you do? Tell 'em the truth?" Chilton scratched his meaty throat. "Let's go in."

"What was it Ms. Patch had said?" Tobin asked.

"Said to come right away. Said she saw … a group of people in her backyard. Said she came out with a shotgun, but they didn't move." Chilton coughed into his elbow. "But what did I say about Ms. Charlotte Patch?"

"She's been one to exaggerate."

"Yup. I did. That's what I said."

Charlotte Patch was trigger happy when it came to dialing 911 and asking for Chilton to come and take a look at something on her property. Only a few weeks ago, she had claimed to have seen a man hanging outside her window. Come to find out it had been her son crawling down the lattice work on the side of the house. Seemed August was keen on late night visits to his girlfriend across the road.

But even Chilton had to admit that her tone had sounded more worrisome today than usual. She had been speaking in a whisper when she talked to Sweet-Anne in dispatch:

"This just happened a few minutes ago. Chilton. You gotta send Chilton. I don't know … these people didn't even blink when I pulled my gun out. I didn't even fire at them. They just stood there … then walked backward into the woods. I'm so glad August had already left for school!"

"How many of them were there, Ms. Patch?" Sweet-Anne Sawyer asked into the emergency line.

"Oh, I don't know. Only about five or six."

"Can you describe them to me?"

"They were all male, I think. Some was hard to tell. They were dressed normal. Blue jeans. One had a polo shirt. Another had this awful t-shirt that was all stained and dirty. He looked homeless."

*Maybe,* Chilton thought, *it was a caravan of homeless folks.*

"Were they armed, ma'am?" Sweet-Anne asked.

"No. They didn't have any weapons. They were just standing there. They looked like they were lost."

*And maybe they were,* Chilton reasoned.

Maybe they were just bunch of homeless men, lost in the woods and needing directions out of town.

He was thankful for his gun at his side. Chilton didn't like going into situations like this one empty-handed. Not that Chief Chilton had been in too many situations that had required him to draw his firearm. In his last five years as Chief, he could count the number of times he had even pointed the weapon at someone on his hand.

There had been that time Ryes Chambers had drunkenly thrown a bottle at him after Chilton had followed up on a domestic disturbance call at the boy's trailer. Ryes had been soused and had apparently gotten into a passionate screaming session with his girlfriend. He hadn't taken kindly to the legal interruption. And he especially didn't take kindly to the idea of remaining silent and steady for longer than a few seconds so that Chilton could cuff him. He had been much more submissive and compliant after he realized a gun was being pointed at his chest.

The other two times had both been at the Quick-Serve Gas Station. One had been a disruptive homeless veteran who had decided to brandish a knife at a cashier when his lottery ticket hadn't paid big enough. The other had been a robber. Chilton had been swinging by for a pack of cigarettes and a sweet tea when he saw a man leaving the station with a bag full of cash and a gun in his hand. Chilton had quickly drawn his pistol and aggressively demanded the punk get down on his knees.

Come to find out, the punk's weapon had been a squirt gun painted black. Chilton had been in no real danger. The dude had a swastika tattooed on his tongue. Chilton didn't feel too bad getting that guy off of the streets.

But still, his wife had cried that night and said: "You didn't know that. What if he had turned and shot you with a real gun?"

"Jules, he was just a kid. Seventeen years old—"

"What if he had, though? What if he had shot you and made me a widow?"

"Then," Chilton took her hand and sighed, "I know you'd avenge me, Charles Bronson."

There wasn't much cause for concern, Chilton thought. Kissing-Brooke was as small a town as America had. Their students had to travel to Oaks just to get an education. There were some farms and a smattering of apartments downtown, but they had only need for four cops to be on duty at a time. And that included Sweet-Anne Sawyer at dispatch.

Right now, their other officer was taking a day off to be with his daughter. She was nine years old and was celebrating her birthday. Officer Butler had promised to bring leftover cake to work the next day.

Chilton had never learned to say no to free cake.

Nothing bad ever happened at Kissing-Brooke, and on the off chance it did, Chief Chilton Farnsworth felt like he could just about handle it.

Tobin and Chilton began to walk into the woods. They were going to do a quick sweep around the Patch property, and then they'd swing by and get Charlotte's statement. Charlotte had told them that she was going to lock the door and stay seated until Chilton gave her his word that there was no one on the property.

And so, Chilton and Tobin were going to lumber through the brambles and bushes in the untrimmed woods, and he hoped that they would find a harmless group of vagrants chilling by a makeshift bonfire.

*"Sorry, officer. We didn't mean to spook her. She came out with a gun and we just … backed off. To be frank, we were just going to go through their trash and find some food."*

*"Well, gentlemen, trespassing is a crime. But I'll make sure Charlotte doesn't press any charges or give you any grief as long as you all promise to leave these woods tonight and go to the shelter here in Kissing-Brooke. It's not too far from here. Officer Marks and I would be happy to give you a ride if'n you're game to leave now."*

*"Oh gee. Thanks, boss."*

*"No problem, boys. Let's get you a hot and a cot, okay?"*

Chilton sighed and allowed himself a smile. He always engaged in more charitable conversations in his head before confronting people who were up to no good. He liked to think that there would be some kindness and understanding to be found in the world.

Tobin coughed loudly.

"You okay?" Chilton asked.

"Yeah. Cripes. I … I swallowed a cloud of gnats."

"Gross." Chilton rumpled his chin "Don't do that."

"Ten four." Tobin moaned clownishly.

The two shared a laugh and trudged onwards.

"What if it's a gang of bank robbers? What if they stored their loot here ages ago and are just coming back for it?" Tobin really should have been a spy. He had a lust for the theatrical and the bawdy. He was always hoping that they would get called in for something headline worthy. "We'd be heroes!"

"If they are bank robbers, then they'll probably kill us before we can say 'Freeze'." Chilton hoped he could crush this fantasy before Tobin turned it into a whole ordeal.

The rain was coming down again.

Chilton sniffed into his heavy paw and brushed past a tangled thatch of poison ivy. He hadn't even given any thought toward that when he had entered the woods. "Watch your step there, Tobin. Don't want you turning your baton into a back scratcher."

"Hardy-har." Tobin sneered. "Have you had breakfast yet?"

"Yeah. Jules has got me eating grapefruit every morning. Says it's good for me. I don't know. It's really tart."

"Want an egg muffin after this—"

Tobin's voice stopped in his throat. Chilton glanced through the trees at the officer, who was standing stock-still in a clump of knee-high grass.

"What's up, Tobin?" Chilton asked.

"Hey, boss. Come over this way. Slow."

Chilton drew his firearm and began to shuffle through the forest toward Tobin. He tried to quiet his breaths, but they came out in thick grunts. He had been working on getting over a slight cold this last week, and he was certain that the humidity wasn't helping. His throat was clogged with sticky green paste, and his nose was mossy.

"What is it? Do you see them?" Chilton asked.

"No. But maybe they left this." Tobin pointed toward the tree in front of him. "And maybe that means they're close."

Chilton looked at the tree. He felt his mouth go dry.

"Oh my …" He put his free hand against his hip and tilted his head. "Is that what I … is that what I think it is?"

"Yeah." Tobin nodded. "Yeah, I think so."

In front of them, stenciled into the tree, was a diagram.

It was of an angel posed with its arms outstretched and its seven wings overlapping its back. Atop its round head sat a beaming halo. Its face was sweet and puffy, like a cherub. Its hands were soft bulbs of light.

The tree's bark had been scraped away, and this drawing was about the size of Chilton's face. It was so detailed and intricate; he was certain it belonged in a church-window.

"It's an angel." Tobin confirmed his thought.

"That's not all." Chilton pointed toward the angel's feet, where a piece of faded paper had been tacked to the tree. The paper was wet. If they had been even fifteen minutes later, he was sure the rain would have torn it loose, and it would have become lost in the mud.

Chilton pulled the paper down and studied it.

"What's it say?" Tobin asked expectantly.

"It says … it's written in cursive. It says …"

*Say a Prayer.*
*God is still punishing his angels for their rebellion.*
*Satan was the first. Not the last.*
*The Fallen One is here.*

"Geeze." Tobin mused and ran a hand over his sweaty brow.

"Get some pictures of … this." Chilton indicated the artwork in front of him. "Let's go have a talk with Charlotte. Okay?"

"What are we gonna tell her?"

"We'll tell her that maybe she should stay with her sister for a while."

"Do you think those folks did this?"

"Who else?"

"Do you think they're dangerous?" Tobin asked.

Chilton took in a lungful before he spoke. "I'm a God-fearing man, but, Tobin, anytime people start talking about this type of stuff"—He held up the paper and pointed the snout of his gun at the word *punishing*—"it's usually trouble."

Tobin's eyes grew wide.

"What is it?" Chilton asked.

Tobin quickly drew his firearm like he was a cowboy in a western. His expression said it all. Before he even got a chance to say, "Chilton… right behind you!", Chief Chilton Farnsworth knew that there was someone in the woods, and whoever it was, they clearly meant them harm.

*It's like wildlife. They're probably more scared of you than you are of them.* Chilton thought this as his hips began to swivel. *Just gotta assert your dominance.*

*Show them who the boss is—*

An arrow pierced Chilton through the throat. It came out of nowhere. One moment, Chilton was standing upright, and the next, he was on his knees gagging and hocking up blood. The paper had become a crinkled ball in his large hand.

The arrow was inordinately long. The length of two arms. Its end had been whittled—assumedly by the same hand that had carved the angel into the tree—into an icicle-white point. Chilton grasped at the arrow's shaft with his left hand. He hadn't realized that he had dropped his gun. Where had it gone? Into the bushes? He had to get it back … good cops didn't lose their guns …

An ejaculation of red blood spluttered out from his mouth.

*Oh,* Chilton thought unemotionally. *There's no coming back from this, is there?*

Tobin fired without aiming. The bullet sailed through the woods, skimming against leaves and low hanging branches. It struck no assailant. He couldn't even see the perpetrator.

"Stop!" Tobin shouted. "Freeze! This is the police!"

Somewhere in the woods, an adult voice laughed.

"I mean it!" Tobin tried to sound big and grown up, but his effort was a failure. "Come out with your hands up!"

Another arrow slid through the woods. Maybe it was Chilton's imagination, but he thought that the arrow was moving slowly, as if it had been shot underwater. He wanted Tobin to see it and to step out of its way, but the officer was blinded with terror. He didn't notice the arrow until it had slammed into his right leg.

Tobin's knee buckled, and he bowed, gasping anxiously as he went.

Tobin's gun went off again. Chilton was barely able to follow it, but the bullet had seared upward and taken off his partner's nose. Flesh, smoke, and blood exploded out of the sudden pit that had grown in Tobin Marks's face.

Tobin was out. He tumbled backward and stopped screaming. Chilton saw his partner's chest heave up and down, assuring him that Tobin was not dead. He had merely fainted from the shock. The arrow that was screwed above Tobin's right knee was slimmer and smaller than the one lodged in Chilton's throat.

*They didn't want him dead. They didn't want him dead. Just me.*

"Guh!" Chilton collapsed onto his belly. The arrow speared into the earth and forced him to hover just above it. He felt the wood slide through him.

More blood was squirting out of his mouth in thick ropes. His eyes had rolled into his head. "Guh."

*I should've never been a cop …* Chilton thought as he filled the back of his pants with liquid shit.

# CHAPTER SEVEN

August was having trouble focusing in class. His fingers drummed relentlessly over the surface of his desk. He had received an alarming text from his mother, which was adding to his worries from the previous night's surrealism.

"Don't come home until I tell you to, okay?"

"Why?" August had replied.

"Just do as I say, sweetheart."

August was sure Hollie and Malcolm wouldn't mind him joining along for their dinner in town. They would probably be going to The Hopping Frog. August tried to think about hanging out with his girlfriend's family, eating burgers and drinking root beer floats. The thought of it brought him sparse seconds of warmth. Otherwise, his head was clouded with bad vibes.

After last night's shenanigans in the woods, August had felt a strange sense of guilt curled up in his ribcage. His heart was thumping rhythmically in his ears, and his breath felt hot and worried.

*I'm in trouble. Mom knows I was out late, and she doesn't want to even look at me until she's calmed down.*

That wasn't even his main concern. He was still struggling to place his finger on the nerve that had been struck in the forest. What had it been about that symbol carved into the tree that had frightened him so much? It wasn't as if he had found a swastika, or a pentagram spattered in blood, or even a death threat! It had been an abstraction. Nothing more.

And yet … the very memory of it drew cold water down his bones.

He was sitting in algebra. He was supposed to be watching the board, where his teacher was drawing an elaborate formula. He couldn't pay attention to it. All the numbers looked like mulched peatmoss. He investigated his fingernails, noting that they had grown a bit too long and a little too yellow around the undersides.

Even that couldn't distract him. His mind was off to the races.

*Who put that on their tree? Who? It wasn't Paisley. It was too high up for Reece. And if Hollie had done it, she would have shown it off proudly the moment it was done. Could it have been Malcolm? But why? And if it wasn't anybody I know, then who could it have possibly been?*

The carving hadn't been too far into the woods. That had also been troubling. The person that had done it could have easily been standing a short distance away from Paisley's window.

He had a horrific thought of a shadowy man lurking outside the shared bedroom. He saw sharp claws scrabbling up the tree, hot breath fogging against the closed glass.

Even worse, he envisioned this loathsome person pushing the window up and sneaking into their bedroom—

*Stop it, Auggie. You'll worry yourself sick, and you'll end up just as paranoid as your mom.*

Charlotte Patch—August's mother—was a worrywart. He wondered if she had been that way before his father had passed. He had been too young to remember clearly.

Jack Patch had died when his tractor had rolled over on top of him. August was five. The loss of a parent had given him and Reece a small bond. They never spoke about it, but the familiarity of grief and trauma was always present. Even though Jack Patch's death hadn't been nearly as gruesome as Stewart Brampton's.

August couldn't stop thinking about his mother. Conspicuously, he pulled his phone out and checked for new messages. Nothing. He wrote to her:

"Hey, is something wrong?"

Almost immediately, he saw an ellipsis rotate at the base of his screen. She was writing back to him. His tongue flicked against the back of his teeth, and his legs jittered nervously.

"Everything's fine now. Just need to do some cleaning. Don't really want anyone in the house until it's done."

August sighed with relief.

*Your mom is gonna kill you with all this anxiety, Auggie.* Paisley's voice rang in his head. *You really gotta stop all this overthinking.*

He tried to refocus his attention back on algebra.

August hated inviting himself to anything, but he didn't really have a choice here. After algebra, he met Paisley in the halls and took her hand in his.

"Hey, my mom says she's kind of busy today. You don't mind if I tag along—"

"No. Of course. Feel free."

"You sure it wouldn't be rude of me?"

"Absolutely not. You know my mom. The more, the merrier." Paisley grinned and bumped her hip against his. "I just wish we could get some color back into your cheeks."

"Do I look that bad?" August sighed and rubbed the space between his eyes with his thumb. "Really?"

"Really. Really. Really."

"I don't have a cold or anything. I probably should after running through the woods like I did. What was I thinking?"

The hallway was congested with students. Some were jovial and noisy. Most seemed dour. They dragged their feet and talked in huddled clumps. Everyone was feeling the effects of the dreary weather, it seemed.

They stopped by Paisley's red locker, which she furtively began to fiddle with. Paisley could never keep her combination in her head. She had written the numbers down on a cheat sheet early in the year, but she had lost the little slip of paper only a week into their first semester. It always took her some twiddling before muscle memory took over and released the lock. August leaned up against her neighbor's locker and tilted his head back as if he was waiting for a nosebleed to subside.

"I don't know, Paisley."

"Neither do I. So, let's have dinner with my family and forget about it for a while, okay?"

August grinned. "That sounds like a plan, Stan."

"I swear to God; I'm going to take an axe to this piece of shit." Paisley slammed her agitated hand against the door and groaned. "Ow."

"Do you guys ever get poachers on your property?" August asked.

"Once or twice, but they stayed far away from the house. Mom called the cops on them."

"My mom is always saying that there are people in the woods around our house. Poachers, vagrants … you know. It used to give me the heebie-jeebies when I was a kid—"

"Did you just say 'heebie-jeebies'?" Paisley jeered.

"I'm being serious." August chuckled. "It scared me. Like, a lot."

"You scare easy, you know?"

August paused, taking a moment to press his tongue against his teeth. "Yeah. You're right."

"That's what's up." Paisley's locker clicked open just as the one-minute warning bell went off overhead. "I kind of want to bail." Paisley glanced down the hall. "I'm not feeling school today."

August rolled his eyes. "Okay, smart-one.

Should've probably thought of that before you drove all the way over here."

"I had you in the car … and Reece—"

"Honestly, I'd have bailed today. I need to relax."

"Oh. Gee. It must've been bad if it's encouraging such a deviant streak." Paisley smirked.

"I'm not going to act up or anything. I could just use a break. I could barely focus on class."

"I like this bad side. Why haven't I seen it before?" Paisley reached out and plucked at his fingers. Her sarcasm was helping ease his troubled heart. August was glad that his girlfriend wasn't taking this too seriously.

"Let's do it." He glanced around nervously. "Let's play hooky. I don't even care if they call my mom. I wanna run out and spend the day with you."

"You're sweet." Paisley pecked him on the nose. She had to stoop down an inch to reach him. "And you're going to be late for class. See you at lunch?"

August frowned. He had meant every word he said, but Paisley had only thought he was joking. He was half disappointed and half relieved. "Yeah," he mumbled as she walked off. "See you at lunch."

# CHAPTER EIGHT

Tobin woke up in a daze. His face was thumping with pain. The front of his pants was wet and sticky, and his leg was numb. It was still raining, but only lightly. Tobin briefly recalled an instant from his childhood wherein he had been playing with his friends in the backyard when a storm had hit. The children had obstinately remained in the yard, assuring themselves that a little rain wouldn't hurt. All had returned to their homes with sniffles and had ended the week with aching colds.

Tobin took a deep breath. He realized that his nose wasn't working properly. He tried to sniff but found his nostrils obstructed. There was a dull pain in the center of his head, a rhythmic thump of agony that would not subside.

Tobin tried to reach a hand up toward his face, but it wouldn't budge. Something was holding it back.

*What had happened? Try to remember. Oh ... yeah ... I got shot. And Chilton? Well ... Chilton got shot too.*

Tobin tried to open his eyes, but they were immediately overwhelmed by the effort. They snapped shut despite his protests. While they were briefly open, he saw a fuzzy shape standing right in front of him. It was thin and muscular, and obviously male. He had also seen an excess of foliage. They were still in the woods.

Tobin wiggled his hands. They were bound behind him, snapped together with his own pair of handcuffs.

"They'll ... they'll send help." Tobin's voice seeped weakly through his teeth. He noticed a thread of drool leaking out between his battered lips.

The man standing in front of him laughed. The tone wasn't humorous. It was a mocking, nasty sound. More like the snuffling of a pig.

"Does that hurt?" The man flicked a hard finger against the hole where Tobin's nose had once been.

Tobin lurched backward, hitting his head against the snout of a handgun. Was it his own gun? Plucked from his unconscious hand and now turned against him? He assumed so. If these people had had a gun, they wouldn't have wasted the arrow on Chilton.

He realized that his injuries had been bandaged. The arrow through his leg had been uprooted, and his nose has been wrapped. Still, the flick of his assailant's finger had stung like a wasp.

"It wasn't as bad as it looked," the assailant

assured Tobin. "You're just a heavy bleeder. It's gonna leave a mighty fine scar, though. That's cool. Right? Chicks dig scars."

"They'll … send someone …" Tobin repeated, trying to pinch his eyes as tightly as he could. He didn't want to look at the man. He was sure that looking at him would make this whole situation real, and if he kept his eyes shut, then he'd just wake up and this would be a crazy nightmare.

The man vocalized. It sounded like radio feedback. Then he spoke in an unassuming voice. "Yeah, dispatch? This is Officer Marks … we didn't find anything out here. Chilton and I are gonna stick around and help Charlotte clean out her shed. Call me on my cellphone if you need us. Over and out."

Tobin sighed. This wasn't a dream. He couldn't sleep through this. He had to open his eyes. He had to see what he was up against.

The man in front of him would have been handsome had it not been apparent that he had been living in the woods for a considerable amount of time. His hair was dusty blond and knotted into a tail. The man's strong jaw was dotted with stubble. His nails were long, curved, and yellow. His teeth had gone gray with calk, and bits of meat were blackening along his gums. Tobin couldn't smell, but he imagined a grimy odor wafting from the man. An ill manicured, unwashed, and uncivilized animal. He was wearing a frayed tank top and a pair of baggy jeans that had white gaps over his scabby knees.

The man wiped the back of his hand along his

nose. "Hey, pal. Glad to see you're waking up."

"Fuck you," Tobin growled.

"There we go. That's the spirit." The man pressed his tongue against his cheek and leaned back on his hips, crossing his arms over his skinny chest. "Officer Tobin Marks … I guess you're the chief now, huh?"

The gun nudged Tobin's neck. He twisted his head around to see the man threatening him. Tobin had been set up on an old wicker chair. Aside from his handcuffed arms, he was unrestrained. But the gun was a formidable hazard, and he made sure that his movements were slow enough to be deemed unthreatening. He didn't want to be shot out of reflex. It was best not to pluck at an exposed nerve.

The guy behind him was bigger and burly. He had a thick beard and wore a Hawaiian shirt. His round belly flopped out over his waistband, white and squishy. His wiry chest hair was dotted with perspiration. His khakis had holes in them; one was just beside his groin and was leaking pubic hair. The guy grinned foolishly. He was missing several teeth.

"That's Chuck," the scrawny man said. "I'm Moby."

Chuck seemed uninterested in talking. He just smiled happily and waved the gun in a semi-circle toward Tobin's bandaged nose.

Tobin turned back toward Moby.

"Is it just the two of you?" Tobin asked.

"No. There's more."

"What if Sweet-Anne calls Charlotte … to check

up on your story?" Tobin inquired.

"Oh. We killed Charlotte Patch hours ago." Moby smirked. "Shot her when she stepped out with her gun. She was so busy looking at us, she didn't even see me in the woods with my bow. That was my girlfriend that your Sweet-Anne talked to on the phone. Tanith has a knack for voices. Sweet-Anne didn't even suspect that something fishy was happening, did she?"

After a beat of silence, where Tobin was sure Moby had expected to hear an inquiry, Moby began to speak again.

"Tanith's my girlfriend. She's with the others right now. Light of my life. Do you have a girlfriend, Tobin?" Moby hunched down into a squatting position with a strained grunt. Tobin realized that his captor wasn't wearing shoes. His bare feet were rough and hairy.

"What do you want with me?" Tobin asked hoarsely.

"What do we want from you?" Moby scoffed. "Man. Can you spare some change?"

Chuck guffawed behind Tobin. The laugh irritated him. Chilton was dead. That was irreversible. And these two buffoons had the *balls* to laugh about it. Tobin found himself impulsively rubbing his hands up and down against his steel cuffs. The metal bore into his skin. He would end up with a rash running along his wrists after this was over.

"Wanna know how many of us there are … right now?"

Tobin managed to squeak out a reply. "Yeah."

Moby held up six fingers. "Me, Chuck, and Tanith, we run the show."

"What type of show?"

"You'll see." Moby grinned cryptically.

"I-I don't have anything to offer you. I'm sorry." Was Tobin bargaining? If so, he was doing a shit job of it, he reckoned.

"You've got plenty, Tobin. You've got a whole lot to give." Moby sneered. "Why don't we take you to the rest of the crew? We could introduce you to Tanith."

"I don't want to," Tobin sniveled.

"Sure you do." Moby leapt upright and shuffled toward Tobin eagerly. "You'll wanna meet all my friends. Because if you don't, then that means we can't use you. And if we can't use you, then you'll end up just like Chilton and Charlotte." Moby pouted. "Do you wanna end up like them?"

"No." Tobin remembered Chilton's panicked expression as he fell to the ground, the arrow shooting out of his throat like a mosquito's proboscis. He could only imagine how Charlotte Patch had looked when the wooden projectile slammed into her skull.

"Let's go meet them." Moby took Tobin by the arm and hefted him out of his seat.

Tobin's leg immediately ached. He had almost forgotten about the wound above his knee. With a whimper, he slumped onto the ground.

"Oh, fuck. That's right. Chuck … get him." Moby stepped aside. "Give me the gun."

Tobin looked up and watched as his handgun was slipped into Moby's skeletal grasp. Moby stepped back, unsure where to point the weapon. He chose the ground. Chuck knelt down and gathered Tobin up in his burly arms.

Tobin was sure that if his nose had been working properly, he would have been overwhelmed by Chuck's pungent odor. As it was, what was left of Tobin's nose had clotted over and dried up. Still, he could taste onions and sweat on his tongue, and his eyes began to water the way they did when he had had to clean vomit out from the drunk tank at work.

Chuck must have smelled horrendous.

Tobin blinked. His eyes were wet with tears. His teeth chattered together. While his leg had been wrapped with a blue bandage, it had done little to spare him the effects of blood loss.

Tobin felt almost giddy. His body was hollow, and his bones were made of jelly. He was sure that if Chuck wasn't careful, Tobin would melt right out of his arms like an octopus through a doorjamb.

He was thankful that Moby hadn't clipped an artery. As it seemed, all Tobin suffered from was a puncture wound. It left him immobile, but it wouldn't kill him.

Unless it became infected.

*You're about to lose your mind, Tobin. Keep it together. Push through the pain. Bite down on your tongue if you have to.*

Tobin realized that he was crying. He really wished he was at a hospital, rested and repaired. He hoped that this would all be over soon.

*Sweet-Anne will know something is wrong. She wouldn't fall for a phony voice over the radio. She wouldn't ...*

Chuck began to walk forward in jumpy strides. Tobin shook between Chuck's perspiring arms. Each jolt drew a thump of pain from his leg and nose. His ruptures were leaking profusely. He needed help. He couldn't stand this for too much longer.

Moby was talking. "We've set up camp over here. We'd take Charlotte's house, but ... we got someone that needs it more than we do. Right here! Just through these trees." Moby held a lean branch aside and allowed Chuck entrance into their campsite.

Tobin was surprised by how clean it all looked. There were four tents lined up in a neat little row. Each tent was scarred and decorated with patches, but they looked sturdy and homey. Only one was open, displaying its interior.

It looked like a little church. Paper crosses, drawings of angels, and a clay sculpture of Jesus Christ filled the little structure. It looked like a miniature shrine, complete with candles. At the foot of the tent sat a bowl filled with a red liquid.

Was it wine? Tobin hoped it was, but he could easily envision Moby slitting Charlotte's throat and squeezing the back of her neck, issuing a jet stream of blood into the clay bowl. Tobin's guts roiled with anger at the thought.

Tobin made a silent promise that if he was able to put his hands on his gun again, he would use it to kill Moby. The thought of putting a bullet in between the bastard's eyes gave him a moment of joy. It was enough to help him swallow his agony.

He returned his attention to the shrine. The statue of Christ was three feet tall. It was chalk-white, except for two red lines trailing out from his open eyes. His arms were stretched out in the stance of crucifixion, but there was no cross behind him. He was naked, and his chest looked emaciated where the sculptor had taken the time to sketch in each individual rib bone. He had also endowed Jesus with an erect penis. The penis was veiny and thick, and Tobin could almost envision it throbbing with lusty energy.

Tobin was offended by the sight of his God's sex organ. Especially by its obscene length and sturdy position. He was even more offended by the dewdrops that rested along it like pre-ejaculate and vaginal mucus.

Then Tobin saw that Christ didn't have a crown of thorns on his head. Instead, he had two curved horns perched above his brow. They were heavy and curved like a ram's. The horns were—like his body—as white as snow.

"Do you like it?" Moby's question was genuine. "I used to dabble in the arts. All I really made that I was proud of was that and a few bowls. Everything else … I threw out what I couldn't sell. Yeah, I mostly just do drawings and carvings now." Moby kicked awkwardly at a pile of crunchy leaves.

Tobin didn't know what to say. Apparently, his silence was enough of an answer. Moby frowned and pointed the gun at Tobin's head. "So, do you like it?"

"Yeah." Tobin moaned. "I like it. I just … don't get it."

Chuck huffed deliberately and bounced Tobin in his arms. Tobin winced as a lightning bolt of pain raced up his leg.

"What's not to get?" Moby shrugged. "It's pretty self-explanatory."

Tobin looked around the campsite. He saw a woman standing behind one of the other tents. He could only assume that this was Tanith.

Moby's girlfriend was thin and rat-like. Her teeth stuck out inelegantly from between her pink lips. She was wearing a pleated skirt and an oversized t-shirt. The shirt was stained and patchy, just like the tent she was hiding behind. Her hair was long, stopping just above the backs of her knees. It was tangled with burrs, sticks, and twigs. She looked like a mound of hay.

Three other figures stood nearby. They were all male.

No one was saying anything. They all wanted to hear Tobin's defense.

"Maybe you need to explain it to me. Why … why does he have horns?"

"Because Jesus and the Devil, they're the same guy, right?" Moby espoused. "Both are creations of God … sent to Earth to communicate to Man. To us. One taught us evil, and the other taught us good. Two sides of the same coin, man."

"Yeah!" Tanith squawked.

"See, Satan wasn't the only angel God kicked out of his Heaven. And do you think Jesus died at the cross for being a goody two-shoes? No. God sent him to Earth as punishment. Don't know what he did, but it was bad enough to warrant the cross.

But the Devil? We know exactly what he did. He dared to ask questions. He dared to call God out for his tyrannical hypocrisy. And so, what does God do with thoughtful fuckers like that? He puts them on a fucking cross!" Moby clicked his teeth together. "You know what separates an angel from a demon, Tobin?"

Tobin shook his head.

"Loyalty," Moby stated. "Set him down, Chuck."

Chuck squatted down and laid Tobin on the ground. Tobin didn't have the energy to sit up, so he looked toward the sky. The trees provided good coverage here, but the rain was still coming down. Big thunderclouds rumbled overhead.

Chuck gripped Tobin by the nape of his neck and hefted him up. He was then dragged backward and put against a tree.

Now he could see the other three members of the gang. One was a finicky looking teenager. His head was shaved bald, and his lips were so chapped they looked like raw ham slices.

"This is Liam." Moby grabbed the teen by the shoulder and shook him. "Liam's a runaway. Like me. Like all of us. He was raised up to fear God."

"God is love." Chuck's bellow was the first time Tobin had heard the man speak. The sound made him jump.

"That's right, Chuck." Moby nodded. "And this here is Hurwitz."

Hurwitz was older than any of them. His hair was white and wiry, his gaunt face pock-marked and liver-spotted. He was dressed in a thick sports jacket and a pair of tight black jeans.

"And this is Sam." Moby clapped hands with a slender looking man with light skin, a hawkish nose, and fearsome eyes.

Sam grinned at Tobin, and the expression chilled his blood. Sam looked like the kind of guy you crossed the street to avoid if you were the judgmental type. His neck and arms were coated in tattoos, and he had heavy piercings on his lips, thick rings that gave the illusion that his mouth was stitched shut whenever he closed his lips. He had a dangling cross hanging from his left ear. His fingers were decorated with rings. His fishnet shirt did little to hide the gruesome drawings on his skin. Tobin could see a conflagration of demons, skeletons, and naked people suffering in eternal agony. He also saw, much to his chagrin, a swastika in the pit of his throat. It lay right between his collarbones.

He didn't like any of Moby's friends.

Not one bit.

"Tobin," Sam growled. "Nice to meet ya."

The older man scoffed and returned his attention to a frayed book. Of course, Tobin wasn't surprised to see that the man was holding a copy of the Holy Bible. Hurwitz had the look of a backwater preacher, the kind of guy that claimed he could pull cancer from people or the type of guy that dangled venomous snakes over his head—*They will not harm me! God is my shield*! Hurwitz's eyes were judgmental and cruel. His clothes were the nicest of the group's. They were muddied and soggy, yes, but they didn't have the wear and tear of the younger folks'. Tobin was willing to guess that he stayed at the camp while the rest left to … hunt?

Overhead, a rumble of thunder tore through the rainclouds. Tobin was shivering in the cool air. He wondered briefly how these barely dressed folks could stand it. But they had probably thrived in worse conditions.

Tanith took a brave step toward Tobin. "You wanna be our pal, Tobin?"

"I …" Tobin didn't know what to say. He looked at Moby for aid. He wasn't sure why, but his exposure to Moby had made him seem like less of a stranger. He at least had some familiarity with him, if not comradery. "I don't know."

"We wanna be your friend." Tanith knelt down and let her hands hover over the wound on his leg.

"You … you said that someone's using Charlotte's house?" Tobin suddenly recalled what Moby had told him. He looked beyond Tanith and toward the rest of the group. "I'd like to know who … as long as we're making introductions."

Sam guffawed, reminding Tobin of a hyena. His laughter exposed his teeth. His dental hygiene was even worse than Moby's and Chuck's. His teeth had become rotten barbs. They hung from his black gums like stalactites.

"I don't know." Tanith whinnied. "Is he ready?"

"You gotta be patient, man," Liam moaned. "Careful you … don't get ahead of yourself."

Hurwitz scoffed again and turned away from the group. Apparently, he had little constitution for their coyness. He crouched down and crawled into the "shrine." Tobin could hear him praying in a low rumble.

Praying to what God? Surely not the cocked-up Jesus that Moby had sculpted.

Tobin was angry at their audacity to carry the Holy Bible with them while they mistreated some of God's very own creations. This band was a sorry excuse for Christianity as Tobin knew it. Not that he was too devout, he just expected more kindness and compassion from the followers of Jesus.

But then again ... *Their Jesus wears horns.*

He looked into the tent and at the kneeling old man. Hurwitz had his hands clasped over his head, which was dipped down between his knees. His voice was rising in intensity. At the foot of the tent, the clay bowl still lay. The stagnant waters had congealed around the rim, developing a pudding-like skin. Tobin took note of the clay bowl itself. There was something inscribed in its sides, but he couldn't read it from this distance.

His scrutiny did not go unnoticed. Tanith asked him, abrasively, what he was looking at. Before Tobin could answer, Moby spoke up:

"He's looking at the bowl."

Tanith smiled, apparently pleased by this.

"Do you know what's in it?" Moby asked. Moby slipped the gun into his waistband. A dangerous place to put a loaded gun, Tobin thought. He hoped it went off and took his balls.

"It's blood. Isn't it?" Tobin said.

Liam chittered. His voice was high-pitched and nervous. He was quieted when Sam laid a hand on his shoulder and squeezed. But no one stopped Chuck from laughing. The goon released a few hiccupping chuckles that overtook the campsite. He laughed as if Tobin had passed gas midway through a recital of the *Ave Maria*. It made him feel hot cheeked and ashamed.

"Well?" Tobin asked, anger boiling in the pit of his throat. "Is it?"

From inside the tent, Hurwitz was growing louder. Tobin could hear a few of his words. "Let us be good followers, God. Let us be divine worshipers. Let us know there is no difference between good and evil. Let us experience both."

Moby scooped up the bowl of blood. The dim rain dotted its surface, making the coagulating liquid ripple. It looked less like wine now and more like jelly.

*Whatever is in there, it's real bad news, Tobin.*

Moby stood upright and held the bowl at his eyes so that they were shadowed by the frothy contents. "Angels are meant to serve, Tobin. It's literally written in their blood."

Tobin felt his spine shrivel and his toes curl.

"Do you know Reece Brampton?" Moby asked suddenly.

The surrealism of the question threw Tobin off guard. "What?"

"Not 'what.' 'Who.' Do you know Reece Brampton?"

Tobin swallowed a mouthful of spit. "Uhm ... she's Reece Karkoff now."

He immediately felt a pang of regret. Reece Karkoff was a child, and somehow, these monsters wanted to involve her in whatever this was. And he had just told them he knew her. Not only that, but he had given them her new name. Whether they had known how close to her property they were or not, that was not information he should have divulged.

And yet, all he could do was look upon the mark and fear it.

"Whose blood is that?" Tobin asked. "Is it Chilton's?"

"Moby, tell him!" Sam whined. "Tell him!"

Moby stepped forward. "It's not human blood, Tobin. This blood isn't even from Earth."

"What is it?" Tobin demanded, growing impatient.

"It's the blood of the Lamb!" Liam bleated and was rewarded with a smack on the back of his bald head. Sam hissed at him.

Moby continued, undeterred by Liam's outburst. "We have a message we want you to deliver for us. We want you to tell the world the good news."

Tobin struggled against his restraints. The handcuffs bit into his wrists, drawing blood. "You're fucking crazy! I'm not helping you or your *cult*!"

"You don't have a choice." Moby flung the bowl toward Tobin. It smacked him just beneath the chin, splashing its contents upwards. The blood filled his mouth and his eyes. It even slipped through his bandages and filled the furrows of his damaged nose.

And as soon as it touched him, it burned.

It burned like acid and hot oil.

It burned like the very fires of Hell.

Even the droplets of rain that slipped through

the overhanging branches did little to stifle the pain. It was as if the blood had seared into his flesh, tattooing itself where it had splashed.

Tobin released a scream and began to writhe viciously.

His legs popped out and began to jump against the ground.

His elbows bent as far forward as they could go.

His teeth ground down on his tongue, mashing it to a pulp.

He turned his face toward the sky …

… and let loose a cry so horrible it was barely lost in the clash of encroaching thunder.

# CHAPTER NINE

Hollie and Malcolm were already hungry. The cravings brought on by their smoke were undeniable. They stopped by a fast-food restaurant so that Malcolm could gorge himself on a greasy burger, while Hollie ran across the street to a little café that served whole-wheat muffins. She and Malcolm finished their respective meals on a park bench set across the street from the local thrift store.

Both of them had been raised in Kissing-Brooke, and both of them were well adjusted to its minimalism. Hollie and her sister had made big plans to move out the moment they turned seventeen. Becca had been successful … for however briefly.

Malcolm had been content. Even in high school, Becca had once sharply chided him and asked: "What do you even want to do, Malcolm?"

Malcolm had shrugged nonchalantly and said: "I'd like to raise goats."

Becca had rolled her eyes and spat, "Lord."

Hollie had thought she had been on Becca's side back then, but now she realized that even then, Malcolm had had it all figured out. In a laissez faire kind of way.

And Hollie was now happy to have stayed in Kissing-Brooke, even if she had only one true friend here.

She looked at Malcolm admiringly. He had one arm draped over the back of their bench. The other was squeezing the end of his burger so that its contents wouldn't drip out onto his flannel shirt. His legs were spread obscenely. His glasses and cheeks were freckled with the oncoming rain—only a drizzle now, but soon it would be a collateral storm, the type that tore limbs from trees and shingles from houses.

Hollie shook her long black hair out from her eyes.

"Wanna go shopping?" Malcolm asked around his mouthful of food.

"Yeah." Hollie stretched her arms. "What are you thinking about?"

"I think this burger could have used some more ketchup." Malcolm shoved the last rim of bread into his mouth and swallowed it whole, a habit that always drew a shiver of revulsion through Hollie's spine. It was bad enough that he ate meat … did he have to do it in such a horrible way?

"I was just thinking about Becca," she blurted.

Malcolm paused. A dewdrop of mayonnaise

rested between his thick lips. "Yeah? What kind of thoughts?"

"Nothing heavy, man. I was just remembering … how much she wanted to leave."

"Yeah," Malcolm said. "I think about that too. Sometimes."

"Ugh. Sorry." Hollie tossed her hair over her shoulder. "Sometimes she just pops into my head."

"That's to be expected." Malcolm furrowed his brow. "It isn't like you can just forget her; you know?"

Malcolm always had such a simple way of looking at things, Hollie reflected. He saw things in "of courses." Of course Becca had popped up in Hollie's mind. She was her sister, after all. And of course those thoughts were never easy to deal with. Becca had done some terrible things. And of course Hollie wasn't going to just "get over it." Becca had left a wake of unanswered questions behind her.

Malcolm had barely known Becca in the end. He hadn't stayed in contact with her after she left Kissing-Brooke. Sometimes, Hollie was sure he only stayed so close to her because of their proximity. It wasn't that Malcolm didn't care; it was just that the world tended to move a bit too fast for him. And before inheriting Reece—after Stewart Brampton's folks had rejected her—Hollie had kept a few too many secrets from her best friend. She hadn't told Malcolm about the weird phone calls or about Becca's flighty tendencies, which had begun to truly alarm Stewart.

Stewart had once cried about it to her over the

phone. "It used to be every once in a while, but now I'm not sure whether or not she'll be next to me when I wake up. And I don't know where she goes or who she's with. She's never gone too long, but she's gone often."

"She never did that before," Hollie said. "She never ran away from home, even when she hated it here."

"Jesus, am I that lousy of a husband?" Stewart asked, trying to sound like he was joking and failing miserably.

"No. Sorry. I just mean … that doesn't sound like Becca."

"Reece is too young to notice, I think. Christ, the kid's only five and as gentle as a lamb. I worry that she'll already have abandonment issues. You know? Is that insensitive?"

"I'll try and talk to her. I'll figure out what's going on," Hollie had assured him.

The truth was that Hollie was scared to initiate a conversation with her sister. The last few times Becca had called her, she had rambled about some pretty weird stuff. And so Hollie had put her intervention-style phone call off a few days.

And in that time, Becca had killed Stewart, and herself, and left Reece behind as an orphan.

Hollie had shouldered a fair amount of guilt from the situation. She told herself that if she had only taken the time to call her sister, things may have worked out for the better. Maybe, just maybe, Becca could have gotten the help she needed. But there was little Hollie was capable of doing now, other than grappling with her memories and trying to enjoy her day out with Malcolm … and, soon, her children.

Because Reece was *her* child now.

And if August Patch was nice enough to Paisley, then maybe he'd count as one of her own too one day.

It was the marijuana that had loosened up her emotions, she decided. She had been a real demon with the stuff in high school. Now, she only partook every once in a great while. Not on special occasions but on average days. The type of days that slipped through the cracks. Days like today, which would be filled with *things* but not excitement.

Malcolm put a hand on Hollie's bare shoulder. He squeezed it comfortably and gently, reminding her of his loyal presence.

They stood and crossed the street. As they did, rain began to fall heavily behind them. As they stepped under the awning overhanging the shopfront, Hollie counted her lucky stars that they hadn't waited a second longer.

"God's really pissing today, huh?" Malcolm laughed. "Ho-lee shit."

Hollie Karkoff laughed. But as she did, she remembered Becca's voice, garbled over the distance, speaking through her telephone—

*I'm holding my heart in my hands, Hollie. It's right in my hands. Oh God … can you hear it?*

Hollie had to shake her head and bite into her lower lip just to rid herself of the awful sound of her sister's voice.

*I pulled it… right out of my ribcage.*

Malcolm held the door open for Hollie and ruffled her hair as she walked past him. She yipped and pushed him away. The two were as incorrigible as teenagers.

The old lady at the front desk—a woman who had worked at this store for ages and yet Hollie had never directly spoken to—shot them a mean glance from behind her newspaper. It was as if they had spoken aloud in a library.

Hollie and Malcolm began to peruse the shelves. They were looking for nothing in particular. This was just a time waster for them. They habitually shopped when they were bored, even in their youth.

Hollie approached a stack of dusty DVD cases. "Maybe we should watch a movie after dinner?"

"Why not?" Malcolm began to parse through the cases. "Rom-Com … Rom-Com … Eww." He held up a case with a blood-stained face on it. "A horror movie."

"Sounds fun."

"No thanks." He put it back.

"C'mon. I remember you dragging me to the drive-in when they did a back-to-back *Creature from the Black Lagoon* marathon."

"Hey." Malcolm held up a finger. "The Gill-Man is cool. I just can't do the blood and guts stuff."

# CHAPTER TEN

Sweet-Anne Sawyer was just about to get concerned when Tobin Marks pulled up to the front of the police station, which was less of a station and more of a tiny office equipped with a cinderblock holding cell at its back. The dispatch desk was a quiet place. In a town like Kissing-Brooke, the worst thing Chief Chilton ever had to worry himself with were a few rowdy drunks and chaperoning the school dance in their sister town. So, Sweet-Anne spent a lot of her time reading blustery mystery novels, filing her nails, or just talking to whoever decided to pay her a visit.

No one had come by today, which made Sweet-Anne sad, since she had taken great care to doll herself up before coming to work. Her frizzy blonde hair had been pulled into a bun, and her eyes were shadowed heavily. She wore a checkered shirt and a comfy pair of jeans—"Mom Jeans" she had heard people call them in a derisive tone. She didn't care. They looked nice on her rump.

Sweet-Anne was thinking of asking Harrison Folger out on another date after work. She was tired of his politeness. The man was so old fashioned he seemed to insist on a long gap between their first and second date. Well, Sweet-Anne was in her forties, and she wasn't getting any younger. She was sure that if she showed up at his front door and winked at him, it may undo his modesty. Unless he was a silent celibate.

When Tobin walked into the office, she barely gave him a second glance. "Hey, Toby," she said smoothly as she finished up the current paragraph of her latest novel. In this one, a teenage boy had been present during the murder of his schoolteacher. The only problem was that the boy was mute and blind, so he couldn't communicate what he had heard. It was a fairly gripping read, but nothing all that new or exciting. It helped her pass the time.

"Hey," Tobin responded with a nasally snort.

"See. I told Chilton you two would catch a cold running around Charlotte Patch's property."

"Yes." Tobin sniffled.

Sweet-Anne snapped her book closed and gave Tobin a quick smile. His back was turned to her. He was rustling around at the coffee counter. He probably needed something hot to drink.

"Make sure there's enough for all of us, Officer." Sweet-Anne smirked.

"Sure."

"Where's ol' Chilton at?" She looked out the

front window. The car that Officer Marks and Chief Farnsworth shared was parked askew. The front left tire had hit the edge of the walkway.

The town looked almost deserted, save for the thrift shop and the café across the street, and their only business had been those hippie reprobates, Hollie and Malcom, both of whom had left the thrift store with their plastic bags less than ten minutes ago. Sweet-Anne had watched them depart with narrowed eyes. She was scornful of their vitality and appearance. Hollie was wearing a thin shirt and didn't even care that it was raining … which meant that anyone who dared to glance at her could see she wasn't wearing a bra!

Sweet-Anne was no prude—she was hoping to get dicked herself tonight—but she believed in public decency.

Sweet-Anne had clicked her tongue and shook her head. Those two had always been ne'er-do-wells. And she really wasn't sure whether they were even dating or not. For as much time as they spent together, they never even held hands or looked at each other with any affection. They were more like a brother and a sister than a man and a woman.

It confused Sweet-Anne that two people of the opposite sex could just be friends … but that wasn't any of her business. And so, she had returned to her book.

But she did hope that someday Chief Chilton would take their habits a bit more seriously. Malcolm Ansell *always* stunk of weed. It was like he sprayed himself with skunk-powder every morning.

Tobin hadn't answered her question, so she prodded him. "Is Chilton still with that loony, Charlotte?"

"Yeah."

"She's got him doing all kinds of housework, doesn't she?"

"Yeah."

"Okay, Mr. Talks-A-Lot." Sweet-Anne laughed. "Let me get a word in?"

Tobin didn't even chuckle. He said nothing. She realized he wasn't even fiddling with the coffee machine. He was just moving napkins around. He was trying to look busy, as if he wanted to avoid scrutiny.

Sweet-Anne set her book on the desk and crossed her arms over her chest. She tucked her chin into her neck and raised an eyebrow. It was the same look she gave to rambunctious teens and misbehaving animals.

"Okay, Tobin. Something's on your mind? Wanna talk?"

Tobin's whole body seemed to tense. Still, he kept his front hidden from her. He didn't speak. He just shivered a little and put a hand to his face.

The thought suddenly came to Sweet-Anne that her humble officer was in shock and was too embarrassed to say anything. What if something bad had happened at Charlotte's? What if there had been an intruder on her property and he had gotten rough?

Scenarios flitted through Sweet-Anne's head. She envisioned Tobin drawing and firing his gun.

She saw a raggedy monster bound in handcuffs and bleeding from a wound on his shoulder. She could almost hear Chilton kindly saying: "Hey, let me handle this. I'll call the hospital; you just go take a breath and get yourself some coffee, okay?"

Tobin released a quiet whimper. It was the sound a mouse makes beneath a cat's paw. Sweet-Anne felt her chest swell with pity.

"What happened, Toby?" Sweet-Anne cooed. "Did something happen?"

Tobin spun around.

The first thing Sweet-Anne noticed were his tears. She was right; he had been crying. And until he had turned around, he had been trying to keep it under control. The moment they locked eyes, it all came blowing out of him. Tears and snot …

… and blood.

It took Sweet-Anne a second to become accustomed to the many things that had happened to Tobin's innocent face since she had last seen him. For starters, his nose had been ripped out. All that remained was a black hole sealed tight with coagulated blood and growing scabs. But the redness on his cheeks wasn't blood; it looked more like a burn. It was hot pink and lined with pustules. Even his eyes were stained, and a yellow fluid was dripping out among his tears.

He stepped forward, limping on an injured leg.

"Oh, good lord." Sweet-Anne leapt out of her rolling chair and rushed to his side. She caught him just as he started to lose his balance. "Toby? Toby, speak to me! What happened?"

"They killed me!" Tobin cried aloud.

"No, no. You're okay, hun. You'll be fine. Come here." She dragged him toward his desk, which was decorated with office-toys and untouched reports. Tobin was kind of lazy when it came to the nuts and bolts of his job. He had joined the force looking for excitement, despite Kissing-Brooke's docile reputation.

Sweet-Anne pushed him into his seat and started toward her phone. His hand snatched her sleeve and held her by his side.

"Toby, hun, I've gotta call you a paramedic or … I gotta get help."

"I'm dead!" Tobin shouted in a state of pure panic. "I'm *dead*!"

"No! You aren't! Hey! Hey!" Sweet-Anne took his hand and squeezed it. There was dirt and gore buried beneath his fingers.

She heard something thump against the window. Sweet-Anne quickly turned her head to see a long-haired man staring agape into the police station. She shouted at the rough-looking stranger. "Call for help! We've got a hurt kid in here!"

She turned her attention back to her coworker. A long stream of snot hung from the hole in his head. He sputtered horribly, releasing black gobs of blood across her shirt.

*Oh, Lord, Tobin. You better catch my dry-cleaning bill for me.* Sweet-Anne ushered the thought out of her head and squeezed his hand again.

"Hey, what happened?"

"I'm dead. I'm dead … and … and *He* tells me what to do now." Tobin moaned.

"What?" Sweet-Anne heard the door open. She

turned and saw the blond man stepping into the office. His jeans and face were dirty. "Use my phone to call an ambulance!"

"Whoa, Lady," the dude sneered. "He's pretty fucked up."

Sweet-Anne didn't have time to focus on the newcomer. She kept her eyes trained on Tobin. Another gout of blood sprayed onto her chest.

"They … they killed Chilton." He howled. "They murdered him … and then … and then they washed me in *His* blood. Not Chilton's blood! No … *His* blood! The blood of—"

Something hard struck Sweet-Anne's head. She stumbled forward, knocking Tobin out of his chair. Both of them crashed onto the floor. Sweet-Anne cried weakly and put a blood-soaked hand against the back of her head. A bump was already rising, but the skin hadn't been broken. She looked upwards and saw the assailant leaping onto Tobin's desk.

With a whoop, the blond menace kicked Tobin's papers into the air. He hooted like a drunk on last-call and took a swing at Tobin's computer with the object he had beaten Sweet-Anne with. It was a large wooden bow. Its ends were knotted bulbs, blunt instruments meant for beating!

It must have been slung over his shoulder the whole time. She hadn't even noticed it when he had walked into the station.

He had a secondary satchel drawn over his shoulder as well. It was filled with hand-carved arrows, thick shafts of wood that ended in a hard notch. She wondered how sharp their points were.

Did they end in whittled blades, or had the boy taken the time to place genuine arrowheads on them?

Tobin seized her throat and whispered in her ear. "You don't ... want to be ... what ... I've become. But ... it *has* to be this way. I'm so sorry. *I'm so sorry*!"

"Wait-wait-wait-WAIT!" Sweet-Anne shouted.

Tobin dug his nails into the soft skin below her chin and then tore his hand downward. His strength was preternatural. No one could possibly do what he was doing—not without at least a blade and some effort. Her throat opened all too easily, exposing the flexing muscles just beneath her skin. Sweet-Anne felt her mouth and nose fill with blood in an instant. It had happened way faster than she had anticipated. Tobin raked his fingers into the open pit, pulling out a handful of sinew and snapping tissues. Blots of blood fell out of her in a roaring rush. She could hear it splattering across the tile floor beneath her.

Sweet-Anne reached toward the florescent lights overhead as if they could offer her some aid. As if there were angels in their beams.

"This ... is ... *servitude* ..." Tobin groaned.

His fingers wormed around her wind pipe, pushing the hard chute to the side. She felt her breath turn raspy, then cut short. Before she could suffocate, he'd grabbed the soft tissue of her esophagus—

—and pulled it out with a twist and a yank.

The tube flopped out obscenely, draped against Tobin's clenched fist like a wilted stem. Sweet-

Anne's eyes darted back and forth, watching as he pulled her esophagus free from her throat with a second tug. More blood sluiced up and filled the air around her. Her mouth turned into a hot oven, and her chest was heavy with stones.

*Oh, God. Oh, Jesus! IT HURTS!*

One more yank, and her esophagus was almost totally free. Strands of tattered flesh clung to it.

*IT HURTS!* Her brain revolted against the pain, but there was nothing she could do. She helplessly watched as Tobin dropped the organic pipe. It lay across her clavicle like an empty garden hose.

She wasn't allowed to die … not completely. While the blond man trampled over to Sweet-Anne's desk and began to beat her computer with his bow, Tobin started to work on her corpse. Tobin bit his lower lip and spat a bloody ball of phlegm into her open wounds.

Sweet-Anne found herself fading in and out of life. It was as if the station was lit with a strobe light. There were painful, vacuous flashes of darkness followed by overwhelming sound and color.

Sweet-Anne dropped her arms to her sides. She looked as if she was going to make a snow-angel in the gory puddle surrounding her.

*"You will serve … you will serve me …"*

A voice rang in the base of her skull. It took the pain out of her the moment it arose. It was deep and guttural, yet it soothed her like a warm bath.

Sweet-Anne listened closely as it spoke:

*"Worship me … and me alone."*

Sweet-Anne found herself awash in a sudden sea of calm and lethargy. *Yes …* She tried to say it out loud, but the hole in her throat stopped the words short. They came out in a wet blast, followed by another trickling expulsion of blood.

Tobin stood and stared down at the new monster he had created. Half of him was proud of his work. He had done as he was commanded, and he had done well.

Another portion of him screamed in agony. It was this part that was slowly drowned out by the voice in his own skull, the voice that he had been listening to ever since Moby had sprayed him with the poison in the clay bowl. The voice sang to him:

*"You're only the beginning. Spread the word. Spread the word."*

Sweet-Anne began to crawl to her feet. Her back and front were decorated in sappy clots of blood. Her mouth hung dumbly open. Her throat looked like a tube of moist licorice.

"Guuuuuugh." She said it with a cough.

*She looks the part,* Tobin couldn't help but think. *She looks just like …*

*… a zombie.*

Whatever parts of him that were still left rattling around in his head took humor from this. Inside, he laughed deeply and sickly. He laughed as his soul shriveled up and died, and all that was left was a beast fit for nothing more than burden.

Sweet-Anne and Tobin both turned and looked to Moby for instruction.

*"Serve … serve … serve …"* The mantra rolled through their heads as the storm began to overtake the world outside.

Tobin and Sweet-Anne didn't even notice the

bumps growing beneath the skin on their backs, just beneath their shoulder blades.

# CHAPTER ELEVEN

Reece looked out the window and at the dreary day. Recess had been canceled due to the rain, so all of the kids had been let loose in the common room to make small talk, play board games, and laugh way too loudly. Reece was sitting on one of the ratty bean bags by the exit doors. Her friend, Julia Coffey, sat opposite her. The two had decided that it would be more fun to sit down and judge the other kids than to actually join them in their games. The boys were full of rambunctious energy, and the girls were unstoppably chatty today. The rain had riled up their baser instincts, it seemed.

Tommy Claymore was pushing Franklin Pits whenever the teachers weren't looking. Franklin made a great show of landing on the ground and rolling frantically as if he was a fallen spin top.

Cellphones were not only discouraged, they were illegal. They had to be placed in a little kiddy-cubby at the beginning of class and could only be retrieved at the end of the day. Reece wished she was in high school. Sure, the big kids weren't allowed to play on their phones during school either, but nothing and no one stopped them from checking their messages in the hall, playing music while they ran laps in gym, or congregating around their devices to watch videos during lunch. None of the ten-year-olds had such privileges. It made Reece bitter.

"The rain keeps coming and going." Julia tugged at a curly lock of hair hanging between her eyes. "I wish it would just make up its mind, you know?"

*God's really pissing.* Reece remembered Malcolm Ansell's favorite bad-weather phrase. She considered repeating it as if it was something she had merely come up with on the fly. But Reece knew that her delivery would be stilted and that Julia wouldn't catch the joke as well as it deserved.

Instead, Reece looked up at the exit door, which led to the playground. The playground was a small square of black top. On one end sat a basketball hoop, and on the other stood a tetherball. The basketball hoop had seen better days. Its rim was malformed, its net was frayed and grungy, and the backboard had a massive crack scuttling across its center. The tether ball was a little too high and stout for Reece and Julia to enjoy. They were, after all, the smallest girls in their class.

Behind the blacktop was a jungle gym and a slide. No one in Reece's grade used that equipment without some shame. They were ten to eleven years old; they weren't babies.

Still, herds of kids would crawl up the jungle gym and dangle their legs through its interlocking pipes. They would balance themselves precariously and pretend to have important conversations.

"Who is your favorite superhero?"

"Who would win in a fight? A T-Rex sized chicken or an army of chicken sized T-Rexes?"

"What do your parents do?"

"Which teacher do you think has the worst farts?"

Really important, life altering debates took place on the summit of that jungle gym.

Reece wished they could go outside today, but even now she could hear thunder roiling in the distance. The overbearing clouds made it look like it was already nighttime.

Every half hour or so, the sky would open up and the rain would fizzle out into a gray mist. Then, just as quickly as it had calmed, the storm would raise its temper once again. Thunder clashed like an angry array of impatient cymbals. Lightning zig-zagged across the sky.

"I heard," Julia had once said, "that if lighting hits the ground and you're talking on the phone and it's plugged into the wall ... the lightning will go through your cord and zap ya!"

Reece had glowered dubiously. She took everything Julia said with a fine pinch of salt. The girl got most of her "facts" from the internet ... and never from reputable sources.

But the next week, a storm had come through town, and Reece had watched in horror as Hollie Karkoff ran through the house unplugging every electronic she could find.

It had scared Reece then, even though no one had been *zapped*. And now, she found herself unplugging her electronics by habit whenever a storm was approaching.

Reece sank into her bean bag and huffed grumpily. "What are you doing after school?"

"Taking shelter." Julia looked toward the watery window. "Or getting some inflatables. Just in case."

"We should all be wearing life-jackets." Reece laughed.

"Yeah." Julie smirked.

"My family and I are all going out for dinner."

"In this?" Julia pointed out the window.

"I hope so," Reece moaned. "I don't know. Mom may get nervous and just take us home. Then all we'd have to eat is leftover mashed potato. Yuck." Reece had decided recently that the only way she'd eat potatoes was if they were fried. "We don't even have beef gravy. It's all vegan food. I hope Malcolm comes over to cook."

"Malcolm?" Julia asked. "Is he your mom's boyfriend?"

"No. They're just friends. But he comes over a lot. I think he's lonely."

"Oh." Julia looked at her palm, where earlier she had used a marker to try and draw a star. "Do you think you'll get a tattoo when you're older?"

"Probably." Reece shrugged "My mom has a bunch. All over her arms."

"Neat," Julia said. "My mom would freak."

"What would you get?"

"I don't know. Something cool. Something I'd

never ever get rid of."

Reece put her tongue against her cheek. "I … kind of already have a tattoo."

Julia stared at her with an open mouth. "What?"

"Sorry. I don't talk about it much," Reece muttered with embarrassment. "I don't even think my sister knows about it. Mom does, though. It came from my first mom." She had grown out of the habit of referring to Becca Brampton as her real mom. Thankfully, most everyone had forgotten about the spectacle that had taken place early on in Reece's life. Julia only knew that Reece was an orphan and that Hollie Karkoff was not her biological mother. But Julia had only moved to Kissing-Brooke last year. She hadn't heard about the murder/suicide or the shrine.

The shrine that Becca had set up in her gardening shed.

Reece bit into her lip. "She put it on me when I was a baby. My dad didn't even know about it until a few days after she did it, apparently. They got in a really big fight about it."

Hollie had told Reece about that fight. Reece had been sitting in the bath and had asked about the little symbol etched into her skin while Hollie brushed her teeth.

"Your mom did that." Hollie had said it in a very serious voice. "She did that when you were a baby. Used a needle and some ink and just …" Hollie sighed. "It's hard for me to remember your mother for who she was … instead of what she became."

Reece had shivered at that. Even now, sitting on her comfy bean bag, she felt a tremor crawl up her spine.

"It's on my left foot, right between my big and index toe."

"What is it?" Julia asked. "D-Do you wanna show me?"

Reece felt her face go red. She didn't know why she had even brought the tattoo up. It was nothing now, just a weird blur of ink. Reece had let it fade and was sure that it would be nothing more than an irregular color between her toes by the time she was a teen. She didn't think it was worth showing off. And even if she did, she knew there would be no pride with it. It was just a permanent reminder of Becca Brampton.

"It's really nothing," Reece intoned. "It's … well … it was supposed to be an angel. It just looks like a stick with a V running through it. It kind of just … looks like a person raising their arms up, you know? My … my first mom said it was supposed to protect me. Like, it's a marker, so that my Guardian Angel will always know where I am."

Julia wasn't even Reece's best friend. That title belonged to her older sister. She didn't even feel *close to* Julia. They were just pals. They swapped food at lunch and ran around in circles outside. And yet, Reece was opening up to Julia. Of all people.

"An angel," Julia said. "That's kind of beautiful. It's like your mom knew she wouldn't be around, you know? So, she left you an angel!"

Reece went pale. Julia didn't know about Becca Brampton. How could she?

Reece remembered the pale arm stretching out

from underneath her bed. She remembered the weird atmosphere that had taken over her once-familiar bedroom. And she remembered the little voice in her head that had told her to leave, to lock the bathroom door and stay there.

She remembered the sound of her mother killing her father … and the sight of blood pooling in from beneath the door.

"Yeah. It's like … she knew."

"What happened to your mom?" Julia blurted and then seemed to regret it. "If you don't mind—"

"She died," Reece said. "I was really young. I don't remember it. But … she died."

Reece couldn't help but wonder if it was the storm that had triggered these memories of her past. Had it been raining the day Becca Brampton had killed her husband? She did recall wetness on her window, just over her bed. But … those details seemed insignificant.

*Yes, it had been raining. Not as badly as it is today … but it had been raining.*

"What type of tattoo do you think you'll get?" Reece asked aloud. "For real. Right now. Gun to your head … you have to get a tattoo. What would you get?"

"Oh, gun to my head?"

"Right between your eyes." Reece scowled.

Julia pinched her brow pensively and thought for a long moment. "I dunno. Probably a seahorse or something. I'll get it on my finger so it looks like it has its tail wrapped around my knuckle." Julia laughed. "There's no way I'd get tired of looking at a seahorse."

"Yeah." Reece nodded. "Seahorses are cool."

"We should ask more people what they'd get." Julia stretched her little arms over her head and yawned like a cat basking in a warm spot. "I bet Ronnie would get, like, a tiger ... tearing its way out of his back or something."

"Sure." Reece found her eyes drifting toward the window once more. She wondered just how cold the rain was.

# CHAPTER TWELVE

Hollie couldn't feel her face. Her teeth chattered, and her jaw trembled spastically.

"Oh, fuck." She took a deep drag from her joint.

Malcolm had parked the Cadillac in the alleyway beside Wylie's bar. The Hopping Frog was desolate. The rain had scared off most of the casual costumers, which meant that the only patrons would be stone-cold day-drinkers and a few sad sacks. Just the type of folks Hollie didn't really want to have her daughters around. She was reconsidering the whole *let's get dinner in town after school* thing. She was sure she could blame it on the rain. But all she had at home were a few frozen vegan patties and a couple of potatoes, which she knew her kids would be less than pleased with.

After driving aimlessly for a while, they had decided to park by The Hopping Frog, take a couple tokes, and then make up their mind over what to do with their time until the kids were out of school. So far, the plan was still to have Paisley drive Reece and August over with the van.

Hollie sipped at her joint before passing it to Malcolm.

"It's cold," Hollie muttered. "God. It's cold."

"Yup." Malcolm inspected the yellowed joint before taking a drag. "We could stay here at Wylie's tonight if you're worried about driving through the rain."

Hollie pursed her lips. The problem wasn't exactly the rain itself. It was the gravel road stretching between the highway and her farm. The gravel gave easily, and sometimes cars would wind up in the ditches or, worse, up against a tree. Hollie had never had any such troubles, but the idea of it made her nervous.

Unfortunately, Wylie's place was less than ideal.

Wylie lived in the loft above the bar. It was a stinky pad, littered with ashtrays, nudie posters, and one of the grubbiest bathrooms Hollie had ever had the displeasure of using. The whole place stank of bong-water and dirty sheets. She couldn't believe that his girlfriend lived comfortably with him amid his filth.

Staying at Wylie's for the night was *not* an option.

Malcolm and Hollie were both stoners, but at least they were hygienic.

"No," Hollie said. "We'll be fine. Just gotta drive carefully."

"We probably shouldn't be smoking then." Malcolm blew a mouthful of smoke in Hollie's direction.

She swiped at the air and laughed. "We'll sober up by the time we finish eating." She said it more to herself than to him.

Malcolm held up his hand and pantomimed turning on a flashlight. "Ma'am, *wut* have you been smokin' tonight?"

"Is that supposed to be Chief Farnsworth?"

"He arrested me in high school once." Malcolm leaned back into his seat and thrummed his free hand against the steering wheel. The joint bobbed between his lips as he spoke. "You remember that? I pulled an all-nighter in the drunk tank?"

"I remember … because you sacrificed yourself to save the rest of us."

"It was a dank summer night. Not wet … but, you know, just humid." Malcolm rolled on. "We were having a bonfire on someone else's property. Who? Whose place where we on?"

"I don't think I ever learned. I had assumed it was Darcy's because he was the one that suggested a party that night. We didn't know we were trespassing."

"Well, we found out when Farnsworth came plodding out of the woods."

"If you hadn't have jumped toward him like you did, none of us would have gotten out of there alive! You're a hero. A goddamn hero." Hollie sniffed and reached her fingers out.

Malcolm handed the joint over. "You know what's funny? I think that kid was with us that night. Yeah, he would've been a freshman! Tobin Marks?"

"Oh, Officer Toby was there?"

"Maybe that was the night he decided to become a cop."

Hollie laughed, and then recalled the very serious look on Chief Farnsworth's face when they had accosted him on the road by the Patch property. He had a good relationship with Malcolm, it seemed. Apparently, standing up to him and then accepting your punishment like a good sport was a fast way to get into his good graces. And aside from the bonfire, Malcolm had proven to be a law-abiding stoner. There was no ill will between the two. Still, cops made Hollie nervous … especially when they spoke in a patronizing tone.

Farnsworth had *definitely* been patronizing them when they asked why he was at the Patch residence.

"Welp. If God wasn't pissing before, he's really pissing now," Malcolm wheezed.

Hollie rolled her eyes and watched the windshield wipers drift back and forth. They scooped armloads of water and tossed them aside. It did little to improve their view. The glass was blurring with air-conditioned heat.

"Want to go in and see how Wylie's doing?" Malcolm asked.

"Yeah." Hollie took one last toke. "Why not?"

The interior of the bar was—thankfully—a lot cleaner than Wylie's loft. Hollie reasoned that that was mostly Malcolm's doing. Malcolm was good at holding Wylie accountable when it came to keeping customers happy.

Just as Hollie had predicted, there were only

two patrons at the bar. One was a hard drinker named Cliff, who always sat by himself and had unsuccessfully hit on her a few times. He was round, hairy, and unappealing. Then, sitting at a booth was Wylie's girlfriend.

Krystal looked up at Hollie and Malcolm as they entered. She smiled and waved. "Oh my gawd, Hollie!" She leapt to her feet. "Wylie didn't even tell me you were coming over!"

Before Hollie could protest, Krystal had her in a rib-cracking embrace. Hollie felt like a wet towel being wrung loose. Her hair was sopping from the rain-drenched run from the Cadillac to the bar.

"Where's Wylie at?" Malcolm looked toward the empty bar.

"Oh … he's upstairs switching out the buckets." Krystal released Hollie and strolled back to her seat. She had set up camp at the booth. There was a biology textbook, a pad of legal paper, a thermos, and a set of pens. Krystal was studying at the community college in Oaks—Kissing-Brooke's bigger sister city. Hollie could never remember what it was exactly Krystal was studying to become.

"Switching the *what*?" Malcolm asked.

"Wylie hasn't told ya yet?"

"No, I haven't seen him since I left work last night." Malcolm took a seat across from her.

"Roof sprung a leak. Wylie woke up last night and heard it dripping. In this rain, it's been like an open faucet. The carpet is *ruined*." Krystal rolled her eyes. "He's been putting buckets beneath it and trying to seal it with electrical tape but—ugh!—it's just a mess."

"Oh lord." Malcolm rubbed his hairy chin. "Did he call—"

"He called *everybody*. No one wants to work in this weather."

Hollie took a seat beside Malcolm and nodded sympathetically. She didn't know the first thing about roof repair. Usually, when something was broken at her house, all she had to do was call Malcolm. He'd fix whatever it was while she watched TV, and she never had to ask him too many questions.

"Tell him not to call anybody after the weather clears," Malcolm said. "I'll take care of it."

Krystal's painted brows popped up as if someone had just yanked on her tail. "You'll fix it? Now?"

Malcolm's face went red. His eyes darted toward the window. "Well, not ... *now*. But once the weather taps out, I'll get it fixed lickity-split." He slapped his hand on the table.

"Thanks, man. Jeez, I hope you weren't planning on eating or anything." Krystal frowned. "Lenny left early. We've been dead all day."

Hollie's face fell. There went their plans for supper.

Krystal returned to her book, letting her pen trace along the undersides of a paragraph. Hollie could see her tongue imprinted against her left cheek, a motion Hollie impulsively imitated.

Krystal had jet-black hair, a nimble frame, and long, painted nails. She had come to Kissing-Brooke from New Jersey and had obstinately held on to her accent. She and Wylie had started dating when they were in high school, and they had only gotten stronger as time went on.

Malcolm always said that if it wasn't for Wylie's "not believing in the institution of marriage" and Krystal's reluctance to lose focus on her classes, the two would have tied the knot a long time ago.

Krystal had started taking classes right before moving in with Wylie, Hollie recalled. Krystal had never had the opportunity to go to school after her mom had gotten sick. Wylie had reassured her that he'd take care of the money so she could focus on being a full-time student. He wanted Krystal to be happy, even if that meant she devoted more time to her books than to him.

"We're gonna close as soon as jackass leaves." Krystal indicated Cliff—who seemed to be falling asleep on his barstool. "No reason to stay open. No business."

This would have been an unusual statement in a bigger or rowdier city.

Hollie thought that the leaky roof had more to do with Wylie's decision to close up shop and pack it in than the rain. The real drunks of Kissing-Brooke and the young folks weren't even out of their houses yet. There was plenty of trade to be made.

Hollie glanced out the foggy windows facing the street. The rain was coming down in buckets. Maybe it had drowned the whole community.

Well, if people *really* wanted to drink, she was sure that they would risk the short drive over to the competition—a little bar called Moon Finger, which worked on the outskirts of town.

"Welp ... shucks," Malcolm said. "Why don't you guys come over to my place tonight?"

Krystal looked up from her book. "Huh?"

"It's gonna rain all night, and I don't want you guys to have to deal with it. You guys can just come over and take my spare room."

"Oh, honey, thanks." Krystal reached across the table and gripped Malcolm's heavy hand. "But I've been behind on my schoolwork, and I won't be much for company."

"You don't have to be," Hollie stated. "How's this sound? We go to *my* place instead. Uh ... I don't have too much to eat, but Malcolm and I will make dinner. Wylie can take a nap in the guestroom, and you can study at my writing desk? Hell, you can take my room for the night!"

"Sounds like a deal." Wylie slammed into the seat next to Krystal, making her jump. "Plus, there won't be any"—Wylie pantomimed taking a toke—"medicinal *distractions* at Hollie's with the little ones running around."

Krystal batted her eyes. "Aw, that's so sweet. Thank you, Hollie. I think we'll take you up on that!"

"Speaking of distractions." Wylie took a big sniff through his bulbous nose. "Did you guys run over a skunk?"

Hollie laughed and shucked her shoulders. "Maybe a little rainwater will clean up that pigsty you call a room."

Krystal went red, but Wylie slapped his knee and hooted with laughter. "Okay, so it's settled. Party at the Karkoff house."

"Sounds good to me. We could have a sleepover." Malcolm laughed. "We could set up a pillow fort for the kids!"

"Oh, Christ." Wylie looked over his shoulder and at Cliff. "Hey! Get going! Last call! Fuck off!"

Cliff threw them the middle finger and nestled into his arms. He wasn't ready to move just yet, it seemed.

Wylie laughed and slapped his knee once again. He turned toward Hollie and smiled, jerking his thumb over his shoulder. "See what I've gotta deal with?"

"Too cold." Cliff grunted. "Too wet. Don't send me out."

Wylie seemed to agree with the older man's sentiment. He scowled and looked over Hollie's head and toward the window. "It's been a while since it's rained this much, hasn't it?"

Wylie was a round Black man with a furry beard and olive-green eyes. He was older than Malcolm by five years. He had been adopted by Mr. and Mrs. Ansell when they had thought themselves incapable of having children. Only they found themselves surprisingly pregnant shortly after signing the adoption papers!

Wylie always looked slightly contemplative, like he was a little smarter than he would ever let anyone know. His arms were tree trunks, and his legs were solid stone. He always smelled of sweat and spices.

Krystal snuggled up to him, and he wrapped an arm around her shoulder. "Yeah. It's really coming down."

Hollie snapped her cellphone out from her purse. She began to text Paisley to let her know that there was going to be yet another change in plans. This day had switched directions so many times, she was getting dizzy.

"Hey, this guy isn't gonna budge for a while." Wylie grunted, indicating Cliff. "Why don't you guys go ahead?"

"What?" Malcolm looked aghast. "No, it's really no trouble."

"Nah, bro. Seriously. I'm too old for pillow forts. Plus, you know all I'd do is distract Krystal. You take care of her, and I'll take care of the bar."

"Are you sure, darling?" Krystal asked.

Wylie chuffed like a horse and rolled his fingers on the table. "No. But if I go, then the whole place might flood."

Hollie shrugged. Wylie was probably right. She could already imagine Krystal losing focus from hearing his uproarious laughter rolling up the stairs and into her make-shift study hall. And Malcolm would be no help either with his cooking and his pillow forts. At least Malcolm would be more subdued without his brother's company.

# CHAPTER THIRTEEN

"God," Paisley moaned. "Another kink in the plan." She tossed the cellphone across the table and into August's palm.

August took a second to flip the phone upright and stare at the message.

"Hopping Frog not an option. Krystal needs a quiet place to study. Gonna do dinner at home. Auggie still welcome. Malcolm promises Reece a pillow fort. Get hyped. Love you."

Outside the cafeteria, the thunder roared. It was like living next to a subway track. Every time the thunder bellowed, the whole school shook in its frame.

"No one has it worse than Paisley," Keegan yipped. "No one on the *entire* planet."

Paisley smiled and snapped her fingers between Keegan's emerald eyes. "I'm the queen of sorrow."

"The queen of hyperbole." Keegan and Paisley

laughed.

Keegan and Paisley had been thick as thieves since grammar school. Jessica, Ruth, and many others had come and gone, but Keegan had remained a consistent and constant source of love and support. They always sat right beside Paisley at the lunch table, and August had always sat across from them. It was his designated spot. Even becoming Paisley's boyfriend hadn't changed the hierarchy like he had expected it to.

Sometimes August was jealous of their relationship. It seemed that Keegan always knew exactly what Paisley was thinking, while August still had to *ask*. He was also irrationally upset that Keegan was as tall as Paisley was. Both of them towered over him easily. He knew his little complaints were nonsensical ... but they persisted.

Keegan had pulled their purple hair into a bun, and their glasses sat on the bridge of their sharp nose. They rolled their acrylic nails along the surface of the lunch table and pursed their lips together. Their snaggletooth stuck awkwardly out of the smile that suddenly flashed across their face. They had only recently *come out of their shell,* as it were. August thought that had something to do with their dad retiring from the police department. As soon as Walter Peterson was just another dad and not a gun-toting lawman, Keegan had come out as non-binary, dyed their hair, and smiled a lot brighter than they had ever been able to smile before. Even if they still got called "she" or "miss" by the teachers—who seemed set in their ways and refused to change despite the current climate—

Keegan had been accepted with openness and consideration by their friends.

It had taken August a few weeks to get used to the new pronouns, but Paisley had picked them up within the blink of her eyes. August found his heart thumping with pride that his girlfriend was so quick to have Keegan's back.

*You keep mooning after her and you'll start drooling.* August tried to draw his attention back to his cold sandwich but to no avail. His mind was already lost in Paisley-Land.

Keegan stabbed their sharpened finger at August. "Hey, I wanna see it too."

"See what?" August asked, knowing exactly what they meant.

"The *whatever-it-was* that you found in the woods!" Keegan's eyes were giant. "What if it's, like, a curse or something? Paisley, do you have any old flames that would want to put a hex on you?"

"I don't know." Paisley studied her fingernails, which she had been chewing at earlier. "I'm sorry, I'm just trying to think about dinner. We already have Malcolm, August, Krystal ... we don't have that much food in the house."

Keegan blew a raspberry. "Text your mom. Tell Hollie that Keegan's coming to the rescue. We'll swing by my place and grab snacks and ... I mean, my mom has bags of frozen tater tots that she wouldn't miss. Tater tots are vegan, right? Hollie can have that, and we'll eat—Oh! I've got frozen pizza as well! We could make it a feast! And I'll bring my sleeping bag, so you guys won't even need to worry about making sure I get home safe."

Keegan cracked their knuckles. They were an expert at inviting themself to parties.

"Also, tell your mom I'll bring a little"—they mimed licking and sealing a joint—"something extra!"

"Thank God we never get drug tested here." August anxiously looked around to see if any of the teachers were watching. He got paranoid every time marijuana was brought up.

Paisley laughed and said: "You don't have to do that. She only smokes at Malcolm's."

"What would she do if I dropped a bag of weed on her lap?" Keegan tilted their head curiously.

"I think she'd shriek. She likes to pretend that none of us know she's a *total* pothead."

"I should do it."

"Just bring the tots." Paisley laughed and took a bite from her peanut butter and jelly sandwich.

August looked down at his own tray. His belly grumbled. The lunch ladies had been lazy today. A cup of fruit, a cold peanut butter and jelly sandwich, and a small salad. He had hoped for something meatier. Especially considering that Fridays were usually pizza or burger days.

He sighed and looked across the table and toward Keegan Peterson. They had brought their own lunch. A thick cut turkey sandwich, dripping with spicy mustard. A yellow stain bloomed in between their lips and their cheek.

"You wanna trade?" He offered his fruit cup.

Keegan laughed, took an egregiously large bite out of their sandwich, and said through a mouthful of turkey: "God, Auggie. You gotta try better than that."

"I feel like your mom snuck into the kitchen today." August smirked at Paisley and tossed her his fruit cup. She caught it and began to peel its top away.

"Hey, you still have my phone, dummy." Paisley smacked her lips.

"Oh." August passed it across the table. He took a second to admire his girlfriend. Her short brown hair seemed to shimmer in the dull light of the cafeteria. He caught himself and looked away, back toward his dismal lunch tray.

"I can't eat this." He pushed it away.

"Jesus," Keegan moaned. "Aren't you worried your arteries will clog up? All you eat is hamburgers and pizza."

"I'd rather die happy than skinny." August laughed.

Underneath the table, Paisley Karkoff tapped August Patch's foot with the steel tip of her fashionable cowboy boot. He blushed.

Keegan grimaced and then returned to their hypocritically slobby sandwich. "It's been ages since we've had a sleepover. August, do you wanna spend the night? You could tell your mom I'm going to be there, so … there'll be no funny business."

August blushed even harder. His throat felt warm. Once more, the tip of Paisley's boot grazed his leg.

"I don't know. She kinda … oh, damn, I think she'd freak out regardless."

"Well," Keegan pouted, "you snooze, you lose."

# CHAPTER FOURTEEN

Hurwitz stood at the mouth of his little church.

The tent was waterlogged.

The sides had drooped down tremendously so that the shrine felt even more claustrophobic than usual.

He patted his bloodied hands against his knees and looked over his flock. The idiot, Moby, was hard at work converting the townspeople. Liam was sitting under a branch, trying to hide his bald head from the sheets of rain that poured between the trees. Even a cold blast of wind would draw sniffles from that weakly little boy.

They had found Liam behind a bar in Springfield only a few weeks ago. He had been beaten up and left for dead by a bunch of preppies after he had attempted to pick their pockets on the dance floor. Moby had been the one to call their attention to the boy.

Hurwitz remembered it like it was yesterday. Moby had come running up to their makeshift camp and beat on the side of Hurwitz's tent.

"Hey, boss!" Moby shrieked. "I got another one! C'mon!"

Hurwitz had been instantly excited by Liam. When he helped him out of the dumpster Liam had been crammed in, the boy had been quick to speak. "I'll kill them! Fuckers outnumbered me. But give me the chance and I'll kill them!"

"Okay." Hurwitz looked Liam in the eye. "Here's your chance."

Hurwitz always carried a gun with him. It was a heavy revolver, and it sat in the inner pocket of his tattered jacket. When he pulled the gun out and dropped it into Liam's pale hands, the boy had almost screamed.

But then a serene expression took hold of him. A strange calm only known to people who are absolutely sure of themselves and their actions.

Hurwitz—being a good Samaritan—had given him a gun and told him to take revenge, and Liam had become indebted to him.

"Show them you're the man." Moby patted the boy's back. "And afterwards, come and hang with us, yeah? We'll keep you safe."

That night, there had been fire in the boy's eyes.

After the deed was done and a blond jock had received a devastating—but nonlethal—shot through the cheek, Liam was a glad member of their gang.

But unfortunately, Liam's had been nothing more than a crime of passion. He could only vent his anger toward those that had done him wrong … which meant he was incapable of grasping the bigger picture.

He couldn't see things the way Hurwitz did.

Even now, Hurwitz could see a complaint bubbling out of his pink lips. He shouted across the camp: "Hey, Grandpa?"

"Hmmm." Hurwitz shot a glance at Sam. Sam was picking his yellowed fingernails with the corkscrew on his Swiss army knife. Hurwitz felt a lump of frustration form in his throat. *There's a nail filer and a cleaner on that knife. Why in the world are you using the fucking corkscrew? Why?* Sam had a habit of using that knife in all sorts of inappropriate ways. Hurwitz had once witnessed him scoop a booger out from his nose with the blade. He had hoped that he'd accidently pick too far someday and lobotomize himself.

Sam looked up at Hurwitz and grinned. His mouth was repulsively long.

"Grandpa?" Liam asked.

"I ain't your grandpa!" Hurwitz barked.

"Sorry. Jeez." Liam looked over Hurwitz's head and toward the woods. "Hey, do you think we could spend the night at that lady's house? It's getting kind of chilly."

Sam snickered and spun the corkscrew around the tip of his middle finger.

"What do you mean, Liam?" Hurwitz asked.

"I mean, *He* wouldn't mind if we slept downstairs, right? It's a pretty big house. Why should He get the whole place to Himself?"

"We don't share the house with Him." Sam

sneered. "It's the Holy of Holies, right, Gramps?"

Hurwitz cringed. He hoped this nickname wouldn't catch. He deserved more reverence than these clowns ever offered. As idiotic and as charismatic as Moby was, at least he really knew who wore the pants in this outfit. Moby took the front stage, but he was nothing more than a puppet. He spoke so Hurwitz didn't have to.

"What's that mean?" Liam had to shout to be heard over the rainfall. His voice was so grating.

Hurwitz's tongue rolled lethargically around his mouth. He wanted to take the boy by the mouth and drag him through the woods. He wanted to find a deep enough puddle of cold rainwater to drown him in, like a kitten that won't stop mewling.

"What do you think it means?" Sam snorted.

"I dunno." Liam looked down at his dirty hands. "I jus' think there's enough room in that house for all of us."

"If you think that … then go ahead." Hurwitz's voice was low and flat. "Walk into the house."

Liam perked up. His cheeks flushed red. "Really?"

"Yeah. Why not?" Sam instantly knew what Hurwitz was getting at. "Nothing's stoppin' ya."

Everyone was present now. Tanith looked afraid. She ran her hands furtively through her hair and bit down on her lower lip. Chuck looked like he was about to give the whole game up. He was probably going to grab Liam by the shoulder and warn him about the trap Hurwitz had just laid out for him if Liam didn't get a move on soon.

*Don't go in there, Liam. You haven't seen Him*

*without His mask on … you don't know what He's like … you don't know what He is capable of.*

If only Chuck was capable of stringing so many words together. Chuck was a happy laborer, and he did whatever was asked of him, but he had a mind that seemed to be fighting a constant concussion.

"I'll race y'all there!" Liam stood and stretched. "I call the couch!"

"No, no, no …" Sam hissed. "You gotta go in alone, brother. I ain't entering the Holy of Holies."

"Yes," Hurwitz stated. "I'm a lot more comfortable outside. Even in the cold. Even in the rain."

Liam's mouth hung agape. "Okay … Tanith, you wanna come?"

"No!" Tanith said, way too defensively and uncomfortably. "I … wanna stay out here and meet Moby when he comes back."

"Okay." Liam looked Hurwitz up and down. "Are you sure it's okay? He won't mind … will He?"

"As long as you're very quiet and very polite, I'm sure He'll understand. Hell, maybe you should take a shower, shouldn't you?" Hurwitz intoned gravely.

Liam blanched. His body odor was not the worst of the group's, but still he smelled like rancid bread. His teeth had grown especially foul, being neglected long before he had become a homeless drifter.

"Yes, a shower and a good afternoon's rest should treat you nicely, shouldn't it? Just promise me something?"

"Yeah, Gramps. Whatever you say."

Hurwitz cringed once more. He hoped that no one would call him that after Liam died.

"Just promise me that you'll say a little prayer before you sleep, okay?"

"Okay." Liam unceremoniously began to walk past the tents and into the woods.

Hurwitz didn't bother to watch his departure. There was no point in it. Instead, he crossed his arms behind his back and began to hum beneath his breath. He heard twigs snap and brambles part as Liam left.

"He's gone now!" Sam shouted over a thunderclap. "Think we'll see him again?"

"Of course we will," Hurwitz declared. "The Fallen One never lets good meat go to waste."

"Hmmm," Tanith mumbled. "I don't really … I don't like that we did that."

"Why?" Sam scowled.

"It's one thing when it's that cop or people we don't know. It's another when it's … one of us."

"He wasn't one of us, dear." Hurwitz pursed his lips. "He didn't have the stomach for the work ahead of us."

"Bye-bye, li'l Liam," Sam sang. "Bye-bye."

Liam stepped out of the woods and into the backyard of Charlotte Patch's house. Her home looked no different despite her absence. He shivered spontaneously at the memory of her death. The arrow had slammed into her head with all the force of a bullet, but it hadn't quite killed her. She had been lying in a puddle on her porch, gasping rhythmically … until Moby broke her neck for her. In Liam's very short life, he figured he had done his fair share of rotten shit before, but he had never killed anyone. He had shot that dude at the bar a few weeks back, but he hadn't *killed* him. Liam had put the gun into the preppie's mouth and blew one of his cheeks open. The guy would be scarred for life, but at least he wasn't dead.

And yet, Moby had killed so easily. He had killed Charlotte, the Chief, and, in a way, he had killed Tobin. Liam didn't know much about the blood, but what he did know was that if it touched you, there was no way you returned to "normal." And it didn't wash off either. It stained you like a tattoo. And those who were touched by His blood became a …

*Zombie.* The word struck him like a slap to the rear. *No … not quite. Close, but no cigar. "Zombie" is too simple. "Zombie" just means your body moves after you've left it. No. This is something else.*

He shivered. He didn't like thinking about it. Of course, it had been one thing when it was all just talk. But the moment Moby had poured that shit on Tobin, it had all solidified around Liam.

*This is real, and we are messing with it.*

Liam approached the house cautiously. The upstairs lights were on, meaning that He was still awake. Their weird, unnamed shadow. The man that wore a potato sack over His head and always kept His distance from the gang. At first, it had really creeped Liam out. He would catch snippets of Him standing just outside of his peripheral vision. But after only a few days, he had become accustomed to their solitary bandmate.

"Do you want to know who He is?" Sam had once asked.

"Yeah." Liam had licked his lips expectantly.

"He's something else, man. I caught a good glimpse of Him once before … without the mask. He was trailing us in Arkansas and He had stopped to get some water. His back was to me, and He was kneeling down beside a creek, scooping up the water in his soft little hands." Sam looked toward the Heavens. His eyes seemed bewildered. "He has horns. Hurwitz wasn't lying about that. Two horns just sitting on His head. And His hair was jet-black and stringy. But I didn't see any wings or anything. Maybe He only pulls them out on special occasions. But those horns … they looked … they looked ornate. They looked … beautiful. I looked away before He could catch me rubbernecking."

"Whoa," Liam muttered.

"I think when they fall, their halo gets turned into their horns. I think that's why it was so beautiful; you know? Because it had been a halo once … a long time ago."

"Whoa." It was all Liam seemed capable of saying. "Whoa."

What if Liam got a better look at Him than Sam had seen? He was excited to spend a few hours in the same house as Him. Liam could feel his tummy rumbling and his heels becoming sweaty. He imagined sitting down across from Him at Charlotte Patch's dinner table and asking Him questions.

"What's Heaven like? Have you seen God? Is he

really a big old man with a white beard, or is that bullshit? Why did you leave? Do you miss Heaven, or is it overrated?"

Liam burped and wiped his brow with the back of his hand. The first order of business was he had to attend to his hygiene. Hurwitz had been right; his stench was unforgivable. Of course, the same could be said for everyone in the gang. Chuck especially had a bad habit of picking at his sores, and his breath stank of infection. Sometimes, Liam felt like gagging just by walking near the lumpy son of a bitch.

*Think about it, Liam. You may get to see Him! You may get to see Him up close! Sam will be so jealous.*

*You need to make sure not to embarrass yourself in front of Him.*

*Don't ask Him anything stupid.*

*Don't ask Him anything He doesn't want to talk about …*

And then the most demanding question occurred to Liam. "What do you want with a ten-year-old girl? Why is she so important?"

Liam sighed. No one in the gang told Liam anything. Their worshiping was all in private, and their plans were all made in secret. Liam was just there to witness it all unfold. He felt as if this was an opportunity to get *in the know.* Maybe he could even scale the ladder a few rungs simply by being near Him.

Liam slid the back door open and stepped inside.

The house was warm. Liam instantly felt his bones melt in the heat. He sighed in pleasure and stretched his arms overhead. It felt like years since he had last slept inside of a house. Home for Liam had been a broken place with an argumentative mother and an absentee father … and too many siblings for him to look after. He had fled his responsibilities with a backpack filled with chewing gum, canned sardines, a hunting knife, and a few hundred dollar bills he had swiped from his mother's dresser. All of those precious possessions had been stolen from him early on, leaving him destitute and exposed to the elements. If it hadn't been for Hurwitz and Moby, Liam was pretty damn sure he would have ended up dead … or dejectedly returning home to face whatever consequences his parents had in store for him.

Maybe they wouldn't punish him. Maybe his disappearance had been a catalyst for great change. He doubted it, but it was a nice thought.

He was so lost in his thoughts, he didn't notice that he wasn't alone. Charlotte Patch's body was with him.

The dining room was quaint. There was a cabinet displaying ornate china dishes and plates. Liam thought there was no use in owning any plate you couldn't eat out of. He wondered if he would be allowed to trash the house … after their mysterious benefactor moved out of it, of course. He would like to take out some of his anarchistic rage on the dishes.

He honestly found the dishes more offensive than Charlotte's body, which Moby and Tanith had propped up at the dining table as if she was awaiting lunch. The arrow Moby had shot her with had lodged itself through her temple. It didn't break through the other side as Liam had imagined it would have. It was just stuck there, towing her head downward and placing it against her shoulder. The arrow was slender and about as long as a child's arm. Way shorter than the sturdy shaft that had gone through Chief Chilton Farnsworth's throat.

Charlotte's mouth hung open. A long rope of blood dangled between her lips, solidified in the warm air. Her blouse was covered in stains, and her eyes had rolled into the back of her skull. There was a stink of iron around her, undercut by the musty smell of feces.

Charlotte was a wide woman with curly gray hair and a mustache. She would have looked warm and comfortable, like a grandmother, if she wasn't dead.

Liam definitely felt like destroying her plates, her knickknacks, and her awful floral wallpaper ... but he found himself strangely compelled to apologize to Charlotte. They had meant her no *real* harm. She had just ... needed to die. There was nothing she could offer them, as far as Liam knew. Still, it tugged at his heartstrings to see such a—presumably—kindly old woman dead.

He impulsively crossed himself and turned his attention away from the corpse. He had to take a shower. There was no way he could stand in front of their enigmatic sponsor smelling as rank as he did. He had to find the bathroom fast.

But first, a drink. His throat was parched.

Liam walked toward the fridge and popped it open. He ducked down and gaped into its shelves.

There was an odious amount of pickles, a tub filled with assorted cheeses, and a container of lemonade.

"Thank you, ma'am." Liam took the container and pulled it free.

Outside, thunder clattered and rain swept across the barren yard. He felt a smile touch his lips. While his friends suffered in the woods, Liam would be living large and luxuriously. Crotchety Hurwitz might even catch a cold for once in his miserable life.

Liam drank directly from the container. The lemonade was sour and fusty. It filled his nostrils and burned the back of his throat. He sighed heavily after swallowing. A stream of it flowed out from the seam of his lips and trickled down his chin and against his chest.

Liam thought that he had never been so satisfied by a drink before. He took another gulp before returning the container to the fridge.

"Really," he said, "Ms. Patch, you've outdone yourself."

Liam walked from the kitchen into the living room. It was immaculately clean and tidy. The coffee table was littered with coasters. Liam got the feeling that Ms. Patch ran a *shoes off* kind of house. He looked down at his feet. He had tracked mud onto the carpet. Only half of him felt truly guilty about this.

Liam plopped down onto his rear and removed his shoes, exposing his gnarled nails and wart pocked toes. He would have to take care of those yellowed nails soon.

Liam hopped back to his feet and walked toward the stairs. He froze halfway up. He had been so distracted by the lemonade that he had almost entirely forgotten that he wasn't completely alone here. Upstairs, resting peacefully, was their friend.

The inexplicable man that wore a potato sack over his head and apparently had a pair of impressive horns. The man that didn't even have a name, as far as Liam knew. What had Hurwitz said to him only a few days ago when Liam had asked for an explanation?

"He may as well be *God* to us."

It made Liam shiver.

"What do you mean by that?" Liam had prodded.

Sam had responded for Hurwitz. "Grampa means that He is the beginning of *us* … and the end of *them*." Sam pointed in the direction of Kissing-Brooke. "All of them are going to die. That okay with you, Liam?"

Liam gulped. "Yeah. Why not?" He crossed his arms and tried to look brave. He was only trying to fit in, after all. If Sam and Hurwitz wanted to imagine people dying in hordes, then Liam would go along with it.

*And then they had actually started killing people.*

It made Liam's guts feel funny. But it also excited him. He had injured that yuppie prick in the bar … why hadn't he been strong enough to plant the gun in between the jock's eyes?

He wasn't brave enough yet. That was why. He was still hanging on to a tiny shred of himself, the self that didn't believe in horned people and zombies. But that self was dying in slow-motion.

It was no longer shouting in his ear that "this is wrong, and you need to run." Instead, it whispered so faintly that he could barely hear it.

"You're one of us now." Moby had once declared that with a laugh. "You're in the frontlines of His glorious army."

"Hullo?" Liam called up the stairs. "Excuse me. Are you there?"

He wished he had a name he could put to the mysterious man's face. Moby and Hurwitz only called Him "The Fallen One" or "The King of Kings." They spoke of him in reverence and with a touch of awe. They had seen more of Him than Sam could ever dream to.

They had been the ones that had led Him into the house and had filled the clay bowl with His blood.

Liam licked his teeth and wondered what it was like to know Him so intimately. Was He wise and well-spoken? Was He mute?

"Hullo?" Liam called.

There was no response. He stopped midway up the stairs and took a deep breath. He really needed a shower. His body stank so badly it made his eyes water. Liam shook his head and plodded up the stairs, hoping to make enough noise to rouse Him from His silence.

Liam just wanted to make introductions. He wanted to feel welcome in this house. Otherwise, he would feel like a thief.

*Say a prayer*. Hurwitz's voice floated into his mind. Liam sighed heavily. He had never really prayed before. He knew how it was done, of course.

He had watched Hurwitz pray multiple times to the clay shrine Moby had created. But Liam had never prayed on his own.

He clasped his hands together and bowed his head. "Please … bless this house … and bless me?"

"You are blessed," a voice boomed from the top of the stairs. The sound almost forced Liam out of his skin. His back cracked up and his hands struck his sides as if he were a soldier being called to attention.

"Oh, God!" Liam proclaimed.

The man at the top of the stairs snickered lightly at the exclamation and waved His clawed hand.

Liam took a second to really take in the unnatural image before him. The man's shape was familiar, with a tall frame, narrow shoulders, and a potato sack obscuring his face. His hands were soft and white, but the nails had grown repulsively long and curled. They made Hurwitz look downright manicured and delicate. Even with the whole house to Himself, the man hadn't changed clothes, taken a shower, or trimmed His gruesome claws.

He wore a tattered trench coat and a pair of ratty jeans. His chest was bare and disfigured. Liam could see scars welling along His ribcage and dancing between His nipples. His wiry hair was as thick as shag carpeting.

A fresh scar glowed along the palm of His right hand. Liam imagined Him carving the skin open and allowing His blood to discharge into the bowl offered up to Him by a kneeling Moby.

"I'm sorry." Liam acknowledged his staring. "Uhm … Hurwitz said I could come in. Because of the rain."

The man chuckled once more. It was a bellowing noise, like the coughing of a muffler. "Did he now? Well, Liam, what's mine is yours."

"Thank you, sir." Liam didn't know what to do next. He stood at the ready, in case he needed to run down the stairs, out the house, and into the woods ... or in case he was invited up by The Fallen One.

The Fallen One took a languid step toward Liam. It spooked him so badly he almost tumbled down the stairs. Liam steadied himself and held his breath with anticipation.

"Liam." The Fallen One breathed. "You're making me nervous."

"Sorry, sir. It's just—I don't know what to say." Liam began to stammer. "I-I kind of-of—"

"Are you scared?"

"Yes." Liam nodded. "I'm sorry."

"Don't be sorry." The Fallen One sighed. "I am scary, aren't I?"

The joke was enough to force Liam to smile. "What ...?" He hesitated.

"If you're thinking about not finishing your question, boy, I'll send you back into the rain." The Fallen One chided him with a husky tone. "Don't be still. Don't be silent. Ask whatever you feel like asking."

"Okay, sir. I'm sorry, sir." Liam scrunched his mouth closed and thought about his first question as carefully as he could. After a few seconds' consideration, he blurted: "What are you? Sam said you have horns. Are you a—?"

The Fallen One remained silent for a long moment. Liam feared his question had been inappropriate and that he would be banished into the forest once more. He was about to bleat out an apology when The Fallen One released a soft, whinnying laugh. It was a sound his gruff voice had seemed incapable of moments earlier.

"I am … what I am, Liam. I am *God*."

"That's … that can't be," Liam said. "God's a big guy with a beard, and he created the universe. You … have horns. Like the—" *Like the devil.* His brain finished the unspoken observation.

"You're right, Liam. And very brave of you to contradict me." The Fallen One whisked his finger in Liam's direction as if he was scolding a child. "But compare me to a man and you'll find I'm much *more*. I can bring the dead to life … and I can speak without moving my mouth. I can perform miracles, Liam. Doesn't that qualify as Godhood? Am I not unlike Christ in this respect? And isn't Christ one with his Father? And didn't God say Christ would be returned to Earth?"

Liam thought back to the shrine that Hurwitz and Moby had constructed. The statue of Jesus Christ decorated with devilish horns. Was that what The Fallen One was? A twisted … anti-Jesus?

"Are you thinking of testing me?" The Fallen One asked.

"No."

"You should. You should ask for proof."

"Oh." Liam mused. "Okay. How can you prove it?"

"By bringing you back to life, of course." The

Fallen One chortled.

Liam's breath stopped in his throat.

"But, naturally, to do that, you first have to die."

Liam took a step back. "Wait." He held up a defensive hand. "Wait! I'm sorry! I didn't mean to offend you."

"You didn't, Liam." The Fallen One displayed His gnarled hands in supplication. "You would just work a lot better for me as a puppet."

"No! I'm sorry! Let me go. I'll go out and tell them all that … that you're real. That you're a—"

Suddenly, a dull thump drew Liam's attention away from The Fallen One and toward the living room.

Charlotte Patch was standing by the coffee table. She was still very much dead. The arrow hanging out of her head forced it to tilt painfully toward the ground. The coagulated blood had turned a dry pink, and her eyes were still firmly set back into her skull.

In her left hand, she held a butcher knife. It was long and stern, with a mystical shimmer catching against its narrow tip. In her right hand, she brandished a meat tenderizer, firm and blunt.

Liam turned back, pleading with The Fallen One. "Can't I just go? I didn't do anything wrong, did I?"

The Fallen One reached up and took a handful of His potato sack mask. He began to pull it away from His head, exposing His face. "I'm sorry," The Fallen One said, although His mouth didn't move. "I'm sorry, but I work in mysterious ways."

His face was horrific to behold. It was beautiful

at the same time. Liam stared in awe, his mouth agape. "Oh my … God."

Liam heard the creak of bones as Charlotte's reanimated corpse lumbered toward him. He found it near impossible to turn away from The Fallen One's marvelous and disturbing visage, but he did so with great strain.

When he spun his head around, it was only to register the meat tenderizer being swung toward his skull. He tried to dodge it, but the blow had already struck. The bumpy surface of the appliance smacked against his lower jaw, busting apart his teeth and cracking into his cheek bone. Instantly, he felt his mouth fill with bone chips and blood. The syrupy concoction spumed out of his mouth and zig-zagged across the banister beside him.

Liam slumped against the wall and collapsed onto his rear. His hands instinctively shot up to his mouth and clutched both sides of his wobbly jaw. "Guuuuuugh! *Please*!"

He thrust his left hand forward, only to watch as it was cleaved in half by the butcher knife, which was slammed down with preternatural grace. His hand was split right to the center. His fingers twitched spastically, and blood began to pump freely from the injury. Way more blood than he could have anticipated. His hand had become a shattered, swampy mess.

He felt the sour lemonade ascend up his throat and seep between his remaining teeth. It came out with a mouthful of blood.

He was sputtering like a cackling sprinkler. Blood, vomit, and bile was being ejected between his lips in quick bursts.

Charlotte struck him once more with the tenderizer, blowing his head backward and making him cry out for help.

She yanked the knife free and drove it into his chest. The knife easily slid in between his ribs. The bones cracked loudly, and a new spurt of blood issued forth. The blood hosed out of the hole freely.

Liam found himself thinking of every injury he had ever seen in a film. None of them had felt as *wet* as the real thing.

The blood was cascading down the stairs now. It was cloudy syrup mixed with fast running water. It seemed to both ebb and flow all at once.

His legs jittered quickly. He was shivering with pain now. Ice cold blasts of agony slithered up his throat as Charlotte pulled the knife free and plunged it into him once more.

"Okay ..." Liam said. "Okay! You can stop ... it's okay! You can stop now!" Liam looked up at Charlotte's dead face. "You can stop! Please. I'm ready for you to stop. It's okay. Please—please stop."

Charlotte slammed the tenderizer against his open jaw. He heard it pop apart and dislocate. His mouth seemed to suck in his jaw. The skin huddled up above his throat before shrapnel-shards of bone broke through. More blood iced his skin, trickling freely from each new orifice Charlotte Patch rudely opened on his body.

Before Liam had time to even consider the futility of attempting a scream, Charlotte beat him again with the tenderizer ... and again ... and again ...

"No!" Liam moaned. "No!"

The knife slid into his belly, slicing through his cramped organs. He could feel his guts *popping*. A rope of intestines uncoiled from his unsealed belly. The tubing sprawled out between his jittering legs, unfurling like a massive appendage. Its end spurted like a garden hose from Hell, allowing goblets of fecal matter to pepper the sheets of red that descended down the stairs ahead of Liam.

Charlotte's mouth dropped open. She leaned forward as if appraising him, despite her cold, emotionless eyes. Suddenly, her tongue fell out of her mouth. Like a squashed slug dropping out from the fist on an irate gardener, the pulpy muscle landed in the middle of Liam's gore-stew. Liam could feel it moving into the pit of his belly, both by gravity and by its own wriggling. Despite the fact that it had been severed from its host, the tongue moved freely and rapidly on its own accord.

Charlotte smiled, baring her too-white teeth. Blood oozed out from her chompers and dribbled down her chest. She spoke in a stilted tone, the kind usually allotted to drunks:

"Tastes … *good*."

Liam was aghast. He looked toward his opened belly and watched as the tongue bathed itself like a bird in his bloody fluids. Something inside him seemed to deflate, and he watched as crystal clear water sputtered out of his stomach and doused the flopping tongue.

It was too much for Liam. He lay his broken head back and stared up toward the ceiling. Somehow, his blood had found its way high above him.

As he was dying, Liam could hear The Fallen One descending the stairs. The Fallen One was chanting in a language that Liam didn't recognize. He could also hear a blade gliding against cragged skin.

*It's the blood. He's going to give you His blood.*

*There is nothing you can do about it!*

*He's just going to do this, and you have no choice in the matter, Liam.*

*This is His will! Not yours.*

*You'll no longer be a willing servant.*

*You'll be a zombie.*

*You'll be—*

Liam wished he had never run away from home.

# CHAPTER FIFTEEN

Reece looked at the swirling clouds above her. The rain was still pouring down in obscene bursts, but the thunder had quieted. Still, Reece expected a large boom to rattle the ground at any moment. The storm was not even close to its end.

Reece was standing beneath the awning in front of the grammar school, waiting impatiently for Paisley, August, and Keegan to come get her. A few of the younger kids were trying to run into the rain while their teachers' backs were turned. They wanted to soak their galoshes in the mud and catch rain drops on their tongues. Reece sighed heavily and glared at her fingernails. Her nail polish had been gradually chipped away so that all that remained was a crescent of purple along the place where her nail and her skin met.

She heard a horn honk and quickly raised her head, only to be disappointed by a hatchback with a single driver. A kid rushed out to hop into the passenger seat.

The buses had long since departed, and a long row of cars were weaving their way through the parking lot and along the school's entrance. Reece couldn't even tell if Paisley's van was amid the rabble of cars, the rain was so thick.

"Hey." A hard hand nudged her shoulder. Reece spun around and made eye contact with Ben Moskowitz. Ben was a small child with braces and an allergy to citrus, which he ignored on a daily basis. His lip was welted with canker sores. "Hey, someone told me you had a tattoo. Is that true?"

Reece felt her eyes roll. She shouldn't have even told Julia, apparently. "No. I don't know who told you that, but they made it up."

Ben's face fell. "Oh. Sorry. That would've been cool."

"Yeah. It would have." Reece turned back toward the storm.

She was tempted to pull her phone out and call Paisley, just to see if she was nearby. But Paisley had a habit of ignoring her phone when she had a full car. Besides, she probably shouldn't be on it anyways, considering the weather. But at least August would pick it up for her ... or Keegan. Reece sighed and crossed her arms.

"Are you sure?" Ben asked.

"What?" Reece raised her brows.

"Are you sure you don't have a tattoo?"

"I'm pretty sure, dude." Reece realized she sounded exactly like her adopted mother. "I'd be the first to know if I did."

*I shouldn't have even brought it up. Goddamnit, Julia. God fucking damn it.* Reece bit into her tongue, cursing herself. In her head, she imagined the smudge of black between her toes. A small mark that had once been a modified cross but had withered without her care. A neglected mole … nothing more. It thrummed and itched now that she was so focused on it.

Hollie had promised Reece that she would learn more about her biological mother when she was older, but with the memories Reece had in her head, she wasn't so sure she wanted to know more. She wanted to just forget about Becca Brampton. It was almost impossible to do. Twice already today, her mind had wandered to that rocky terrain.

"Come down here and guide me through the cave, Reece," Becca whispered in Reece's ear. "I don't want to get lost."

Reece shivered and wished that Ben hadn't even opened his canker-riddled mouth. He was still staring up at her, waiting for her to give in. She sighed, rolled her eyes, and gave her best Hollie impression yet.

"Okay, Ben. I do have a tattoo. It's of the American flag. It's got a tiger ripping through it with blood-soaked teeth. Happy?"

Ben smiled in a very deluded way that almost made Reece laugh aloud. "Cool! I knew you had one!"

How fast was the American flag rumor going to spread? Reece wondered. Ben had a big mouth, but no one took him all that seriously. Julia, on the other hand … Reece was going to have to have a talk with her "friend" about keeping secrets. If Ben knew, then that meant *everyone* knew.

But it sounded like Julia wasn't handing out a lot of details. All anyone knew was that Reece had a tattoo … and she hadn't been cool enough to share it with everyone.

Reece stepped out from beneath the awning for a quick moment. The rain immediately soaked her hair and ran down her face. She stepped back to shelter. A cold chill skittered through her.

There Paisley was, pulling out from around the corner of the parking lot. Her van moved sluggishly with traffic.

"Bye!" Reece shouted and darted forward, despite her teacher's shouted opposition that she wait for Paisley to get closer. Reece was already accustomed to the rain. She didn't want to wait any longer.

Her foot smacked into the center of a mud puddle, dashing grime against her legs. She ignored it and pressed forward. The wind blasted her face, turning her cheeks red and clamping her teeth together with an audible *crack*.

A few more yards, and Reece was pounding at the side of the van. She could see Keegan struggling to unlock and slide the door open from inside. "Hey, sport!" Keegan called as Reece climbed aboard.

"Hey." Reece shook her head, spraying droplets against the musty seats.

"Fuck, Reece!" Paisley bleated. "Drip dry! Drip dry!"

"Sorry." Reece slammed the door shut before taking a seat by Keegan.

"What's up, little dude?" Keegan ran their hand through Reece's hair before ruffling it forcefully, as if they were petting a dog instead of a child.

Reece giggled and knocked their hand away. "Nothing. Just looking forward to those tater tots."

"Me too." Keegan gazed between the front seats and out the window. "It's a cats and dogs type of day, huh?"

August was in the passenger seat. His hand was laying mildly on Paisley's knee. He wasn't gripping her, just touching her in a familiar way. Reece felt an odd smile cut into her cheeks.

"You know what Malcolm would say?" Reece stated.

"Don't!" Paisley laughed.

"What?" Keegan demanded.

"He'd say …" Reece scrunched her lips together and tried to speak with Malcom's low drawl. "'God's really pissing today'!"

"I think Malcolm's kind of dreamy," Keegan noted. "In a grandfatherly type of way."

"Gross," Paisley stated. "Stop it. He's basically my dad at this point."

"Is your mom ever gonna date him?" Keegan asked.

"No. Neither of them is interested in dating anyone." This was something both Reece and Paisley had to explain a lot. Even to someone as non-traditional as Keegan, Hollie and Malcolm didn't make a whole lot of sense.

"Well, they should get married anyway." Keegan shrugged. "You know, for taxes. They could combine their property or something. I don't know."

"That would actually be a good idea." August flicked at his nose with his knuckles.

"Right? I only speak the truth, Paisley … you know this." Keegan rolled their eyes at Reece, causing her to giggle once more.

Reece was already happy to be far away from her peers. She had decided, after today, that she liked Paisley's friends a lot more.

# CHAPTER SIXTEEN

Wylie already missed the company.

When Krystal, Hollie, and Malcolm had left, The Hopping Frog had turned gray. Now, with no one else but Cliff and the dripping rain for company, Wylie regretted choosing to stay behind and keep the place open. What was the point of it all? He would barely make enough money to justify keeping his doors open anyways with this storm.

Cliff sat up at the bar and presented his empty glass. "Another?" The man burped through his stringy beard. Cliff smelled repugnantly unwashed.

Wylie pinched his tongue between his front teeth and sighed. He would just have to hold his breath and serve the bastard. "You're a stereotype, Cliff," Wylie said from behind the bar as foam sluiced over the brim of Cliff's glass. "Are you proud of yourself?"

"Yes. Fuck … I don't care. Should I care?"

"A little. Yeah." Wylie placed the drink in front of Cliff and slipped aside. He wasn't interested in watching the old man slurp it down.

Cliff was a lot more subdued than usual. Normally, he was brash and abrasive, spewing racist jokes and sexist remarks while laughing like a hyena. But with no one other than Wylie present, it seemed as if all the steam had poured out of his engine. Cliff had become a more reflective and somber individual. He had gone from an ecstatic lush to a sad drunk. Either way, Cliff was poor company, and Wylie wished he would leave.

The door whooshed open. A long-haired youth stumbled in from the rain. He wasn't dressed appropriately, Wylie noted. His long, blond hair fell in clumps over his oafish brow. His tank top was sealed to his skin, and his pants hung heavy on his hips, bogged down with water. The boy looked as if he had just crawled out of the river. He smelled of it too. A really earthy and mucky smell.

Wylie sighed internally. This kid would make good pals with Cliff. Maybe their odors would cancel each other out.

"Fuck, man." The kid shook his head, exposing his face from beneath his long hair. He was a lot older than Wylie had initially assumed. Definitely able to order a drink but not old enough to hold it with any grace. "It's wetter than sheee-yit out there!" The boy's proclamation proved that he was old enough to swear but not old enough to do so with any dignity.

"Yup." Wylie nodded. "Got an ID on ya, sport?"

The boy rolled his eyes. "I just want water, man."

"Thought you woulda had enough o' that today." Cliff snorted, finding his joke funnier than it actually was.

Wylie's eyes were getting a real work out. Rolling them had become a pretty bad habit at The Hopping Frog.

"One glass of water." Wylie went to the tap and began to fill a cup. "Where'd you blow in from, sport? I haven't seen you around here."

The kid sat at the bar and tapped on the mildewed wood with his slick knuckles. He sneezed into his elbow and settled into his stool in one motion. "Let me have that water first."

After gulping down the glass, the boy tilted his head back and stared up at the ceiling. "I got a couple friends … they'll be here in a minute."

"Okay." Wylie's face didn't move.

"Hey. You know what a legless woman and a snail have in common?" Cliff was already becoming jovial and offensive now that there was a new body in The Hopping Frog. Wylie felt his teeth grit together. He knew he was doing Krystal a favor by staying behind, but he really wished he was anywhere but here.

"I'm from out of town." The boy seemed as uninterested in Cliff as Wylie was. At least they had that in common. "Traveling with … a preacher."

"Oh." Wylie felt his jaw shift involuntarily. "Selling Bibles? On a mission?"

"Just spreading the good word where we can. Don't worry," the boy held up a defensive hand, "I'm not here to preach at ya. I just wanted to get out of the rain."

Wylie felt his shoulders relax. "Well, you and your pals are welcome to shelter here for a bit. I wish my cook was still here; I'd offer you the dinner menu."

"No bother. I'll happily take water, though. Maybe a soda? Cherry?"

"Yeah. No problem." Wylie went to work.

Cliff's lower lip looked like it was about to collide with the bottom of his nose. He was upset that no one had taken him up on his joke. He delivered the punchline—"They both leave a wet trail"—in a whisper to himself and returned to his drink.

Wylie again felt like declaring to Cliff that he was a stereotype. It was only the truth. And besides, Cliff wouldn't remember such insults by the morning. And even if he did, what would he do? Fight the only bartender that was willing to serve him?

Wylie looked Cliff up and down from the corner of his eye. Cliff's beer gut was slopping over his jeans. He was sure that if there were patrons at the booth behind him, they would be given a full view of his hairy ass-crack—a sight that Wylie had unfortunately taken in a time or two before. Cliff's lips were ragged and crusty. The flakes looked hardened and white. His teeth were rusty, and his tongue was pale with calk.

He smelled ripe.

The Jesus-Kid didn't smell any better, but at least he was courteous. "What's your name?" Wylie inquired.

"Moby." The kid grinned.

"I'm Wylie."

"Nice to meet ya." The kid reached into his pocket and fished out a toothpick, which had already been chewed at. He plopped it into his mouth and rolled it from one cheek to the next. "So, Wylie … you God-fearing? I'm not gonna preach at you but figure it wouldn't hurt to ask."

"No worries." Wylie pursed his lips and gave it some thought before he said: "I believe in God, but I'm not very religious. My brother and I went to church as kids, but I think the whole thing felt creepy. No offense."

Moby grinned. "Yeah. That's kind of how I felt. That's what I like about traveling with Father Hurwitz. You know, he doesn't try and sit you down in a dusty old room with a ton of old folks. We're on the road a lot just talking to *normal* people. You know, like regular folks?"

"Yeah. That's the way to do it right, I imagine." Wylie picked up a glass, just to give his hands something to do.

"The nation is pretty divided and a lot of folks see religion and politics as the same thing. I just think that it's sad. Sad that Church has failed the American people. You know?"

"You sound like you're getting pretty close to preaching there, buddy." Wylie laughed pleasantly.

Moby's ensuing smile was slow and methodical. It kind of spooked Wylie, if he was being honest with himself. He was surprised that Moby's teeth looked worse off than Cliff's.

"Sorry, Wylie. Just talking."

"No problem." Wylie looked toward the door,

hoping that more customers would come in out of the cold rain. Had Moby mentioned he had a few friends on their way? Where were they? "Just talk a little more apolitical."

"You see?" Moby slammed his hand on the bar. "There we go. Politics and religion are very unhappy bedfellows." Moby held his arms aloft as if he had made a great point.

"Uh-huh." Wylie nodded with an arched brow.

"I mean we don't do that. Our group is just kind of … all are welcome. You know? Just not the fags, *amiright*?" Moby grinned wolfishly.

"Yeah." Wylie frowned, unhappy with the sudden prejudice. "*Sure*."

"Hey, Wylie," Cliff spluttered. "Should … should I have you call me a cab?"

"Sure thing, Cliff. Why don't you finish your beer first?"

"You got hamburgers?"

"No. Kitchen's closed."

"I could've used a hamburger … you cheap bastard." Cliff snorted and looked at his palms. "I woulda paid ya."

"I know." Wylie was surprised to have his attention swayed so easily away from the snotty Jesus kid. Moby was inched well past weird, and Wylie didn't like weird. Malcolm was about as weird as he could take, and Malcolm was just a hippie pothead. Cliff was a drunk and a fiend, but at least he didn't talk about religion and his hateful jokes were just that … *jokes*.

"Hey, can I go ahead and order some drinks for my friends?" Moby said.

"Yeah. Sure thing, bud. What'll they be having?" Maybe the horrible slur had been intended as an off-color joke. He hoped so, but he also considered kicking the boy out and telling him to take his friends elsewhere.

*They're your only customers, dude. Just grin and bear it.*

Moby stood unexpectedly and put a hand up to his chin. He looked as if he was deep in thought. "Oh, Lord, I really should've asked them what they'd want earlier."

"Well, do you wanna wait for them?"

"No. They'll be wanting something right when they walk in. Let me just think for a moment." Moby was a short ways away from Cliff now. The bar was small, and he had only had to take a few steps before he was standing right beside the grizzled old man.

"I think ..." Moby looked up at the menu board hanging above Wylie's head.

"Hey, if it's more complicated than a jack and coke, I'm afraid they're out of luck today. I sent the cook home."

"Oh, no, sorry. I just got distracted. I wasn't looking at the menu I was ..." Moby looked back at Wylie. "I was wondering how that wall would look in exactly ten seconds ... when everything here changes."

"What?" Wylie didn't like the serious tone that had crawled into Moby's voice. It made the kid sound older than he looked.

"One Mississippi ... two Mississippi ... You wanna count it down, dude?" Moby shouted toward Cliff.

Cliff drunkenly sat up right and looked over to Moby. "Huh?"

"Six Mississippi … seven Mississippi …" Moby goaded him on with a smile. "C'mon! It's almost time! Nine Mississippi … and ten Mississippi!" Moby pulled a gun out from behind his back and placed it on the bar.

Cliff seemed to sober up in a heartbeat. His jaw fell slack, and his eyes curled into beady stones. "Hey. Hey, kid … that ain't funny."

"Best put that back." Wylie stumbled over his words. "Best put that away and walk out of here. I won't worry about charging you, but you shouldn't be …" Where had his nerve gone? He and Krystal had run through every worst-case scenario that could happen in a bar before. Handsy patrons, fights, robberies … but … but nothing that bad had ever happened in Kissing-Brooke. Wylie felt as if he was about to soak his pants and start crying.

*Thank God Krystal and Hollie just left. Thank God they weren't involved in this. Oh Lord, if they were here, this kid would probably have them raped and beaten at gunpoint, good Christ!*

If anything had happened to those two, he wasn't sure if he could live with himself.

Wylie had to bite his tongue to hold back a flood of gruesome "could have" thoughts. It forced his hands to steady and his body to calm down.

"Change!" Moby declared.

"Okay, Moby. I'll get the cash register for you."

"Nah," Moby snarled. "That's not what I meant when I said *change*."

Moby swept the gun up from the bar, placed it behind Cliff's head, and squeezed the trigger.

It happened in a second.

In that second, Wylie had time to make fast eye contact with Cliff before his face exploded and a pound of fleshy matter sprayed across the bar and the menu-board above Wylie's head. It looked like gray hamburger meat with teeth and bone chips, and stringy tissue included at no extra charge.

Wylie tasted iron in his mouth and felt his legs grow warm as his bladder released itself.

"Oh, God!" Wylie shouted and backpedaled into a wall of liquor bottles. Glass smashed and liquid sprayed all around him. It was a cacophony of noise and fluid.

Moby stepped back and watched as Cliff slumped against the bar and then keeled over onto the floor with a wet *thump*. His whole body seemed to disappear completely as it dropped.

Moby flicked a few strands of greasy hair away from his face and released another devilish grin.

"I liked that, Wylie. That was fun." He held the gun aloft and bit into his lower lip. "I kinda want to do it again."

"No! No! God, no!" Wylie's eyes darted beneath the bar counter. He had a shotgun there, but there would be no time to grab it. His movements would be too slow. He felt as if he was pushing through water already. He would move one step at a time, and in that time, Moby would fill him with as many holes as his gun pleased.

"I can't kill you, though." Moby was obviously dismayed. "That wouldn't be very hospitable of me. I can't have all the fun. Right?"

Moby stepped back.

Before Wylie had time to speak, the door to The Hopping Frog blew open. There was a moment of hope wherein Wylie imagined he would look toward the door and see the police standing there.

*I'll be okay. I'll go to Hollie's place after they take Moby to jail, and I'll cuddle up with Krystal and cry in her arms … and everything will be okay. Everything will be okay.*

Wylie was delighted to see that the person stepping into the bar was in fact a police officer. It was Officer Tobin Marks. Toby was young, but he was steadfast and good hearted. He would right this horrible wrong.

Wylie noticed that something was very different about Tobin.

Tobin's body had changed. His face was bulging, as if tumors were vying for attention just beneath the surface of his skin. Two horrible curved structures had erupted from his back. They took no real shape; they were simply growths that had appeared without warrant or cause. They looked like defeathered wings ending in knobby bulbs.

Tobin's skin had gone beet red, and his eyes had been sealed shut. A viscous gray fluid welled up along his eyelids, but they refused to cry. Instead, his skin looked unnaturally dry, as if all of his moisture was held up inside the polyps under his flesh.

And even worse than his malformations, he was carrying something heavy in his hand. Something sharp and vicious.

It only took Wylie a second to recognize the instrument. It was a scythe. The same scythe which sat in the window at the antique store in the downtown area. A scythe which had never been sold and that Wylie had once considered purchasing to hang in the bar before Krystal convinced him that farm equipment and drunks rarely made good pals.

*What's Tobin thinking? A scythe is no match for a gun!*

As Tobin lurched forward, he made room for another visitor. Sweet-Anne Sawyer, the homely dispatcher. Just like Tobin, there was something wrong with her body. Protrusions jutted out from her back, but worse yet, her throat seemed to have been peeled open like half of a banana. Her esophagus hung out and dangled between her blood-soaked breasts. She, too, held a farmer's instrument, a dull, dirt-caked rake.

As the two began to advance into the bar, Wylie realized that they hadn't even so much as glanced at Moby. They were looking at Wylie.

Right … at … Wylie.

Wylie wondered when he would begin to scream.

Would it be after the first blow, or right before? It made little difference when it happened. No matter what, it seemed screaming was inevitable.

# CHAPTER SEVENTEEN

Hollie, Malcolm, and Krystal entered the house in a rush. Hollie was thankful for the warmth and familiarity of her house. She sighed happily and threw her wet hair over her shoulder.

"If I ever get caught in a storm like this again, then fucking kill me, Malcolm." She proclaimed this as she fussed with her messy locks.

"You're gonna have to do that yourself." Malcolm squeezed his beard, draining out the rainwater it had collected.

Keegan, August, Reece, and Paisley were already in the living room. The TV was turned on, and Hollie could smell tater tots cooking in the oven. It was a horrible, greasy smell. She had never been so enchanted by a smell in her whole life. Her munchies had almost grown intolerable. On the drive home, Hollie had felt her stomach gnawing at her throat. She was hungry beyond description.

"Hey, Ms. K!" Keegan chittered with a grin.

"Hello, Keegan." Hollie refused to acknowledge how weird "Ms. K." sounded. It made her feel like a teacher. Or even worse, a prudish church lady.

"Paisley wouldn't let me bring you any weed." Keegan frowned.

Paisley's face went red, and she batted her friend on the shoulder.

"Hey!" Hollie groaned. "What am I, the resident pothead?"

"Uhm." Malcolm pressed his tongue against his cheek.

"You encourage this … deplorable behavior." She laughed. "What are you watching?" Hollie hunkered down beside her daughters.

Reece was splayed out on the floor. Paisley had brought a set of bean bags from the attic for her and August to snuggle on. August had his hands in plain sight, so Hollie figured it was redundant to complain about their proximity. Keegan had taken a seat beside Reece. Their legs were crossed, and their hands were firmly planted on their knees. They looked as if they were ready to spring into action if called upon.

"It's one of mine," Keegan said.

"Oh … probably something Reece shouldn't see," Hollie chided.

Keegan had a vast library of horror movies on DVD and Blu-ray at home, and their father had given them a 4K television for Christmas. So Keegan was always bringing bloody and disturbing movies over for Paisley to watch. Hollie didn't have a real problem with it, but she worried that some of the violent images would trigger Reece.

Reece was a trooper. She had endured a lot of horror films with her big sister. Sometimes, Hollie worried that Reece's tough exterior was just a front. Hollie never wanted her youngest daughter to suffer in silence.

"It's just *Suspiria.* Reece has seen it before." Paisley smirked. "August hasn't, though. He's jumped more times than I can count."

August snorted and buried his head into Paisley's shoulder. "That's because you keep hitting me when the scary stuff happens."

"I was actually going to take a quick walk soon," Keegan stated.

Hollie was quickly flummoxed. "In this weather?"

"Wanna join me?" Keegan prodded.

"No. I think I've had enough of this shit." Hollie flicked a finger toward the windows, which were being berated with rain.

Paisley's hand snaked out from her bean bag and gripped Hollie's wrist. "You and Malcolm should go. Stretch your legs."

Hollie gave Paisley a look that read: *Are you kidding me?*

Paisley returned the look with a sharp: *No. You'll get it in a few minutes.* It was an expression that Hollie had rarely seen her daughter wear, and the only times she had, had been when something serious had happened ... something that she didn't want to involve Reece in.

*Shit,* Hollie thought, *just when I was starting to warm up.*

Krystal walked into the living room, books in hand. She looked at the screen and nodded approvingly. "I love this movie."

"It's a classic." Keegan stood and gave Krystal a quick hug. "Heard you have homework. That's lame."

"Yeah. It's not ideal but … eh, who am I kidding. I love it." Krystal scrunched up her nose and gave Keegan a quick once over. "Love your hair."

"Thanks." Keegan rolled their eyes. "Grandpa still thinks it's a phase."

"That's what grandpas always say. They're usually wrong." Krystal began to sidle toward the stairs. "Okay. Nose to the grindstone. No one interrupt me, okay? No matter what."

"What about the pizza?" Reece called. "Won't you want some?"

"Just save me a slice, babe. Bye!"

"Masochist." Keegan giggled. "I'm never going to college."

Keegan began to walk toward the kitchen, where Malcolm was furtively attending to the nearly burned tater tots and the half-frozen pepperoni pizza. He was shouting something about how if they had put food in the oven, they should intend on watching it and making sure it didn't catch fire. Hollie was too focused on the mystery ahead of her to notice. She followed close behind Keegan.

Keegan leaned dramatically against the fridge and spoke rapidly. "Okay, we don't wanna freak out or anything, but we think someone has been hanging out in the woods beside the house."

"Hmmm?" Malcolm arched his eyebrows as he

removed his flowery oven mitts. "What is this? What?"

"August saw a carving in a tree last night and thought it had maybe been put there a while back. When we got here earlier, we decided to go check it out and—uh—it was kind of freaky." Keegan grimaced.

"Kind of freaky how? In what way?" Malcolm furrowed his brow. "Is this why the tots were halfway to hell?"

"There were more of them."

"More tots?"

"Jesus, Malcolm?" Hollie huffed "More what? Carvings?"

"Yeah. And it's best if you check it out. I'll guide you." Keegan sounded older than they actually were. Their voice was effortlessly serious, as if they were preparing to scold a wayward child. Hollie felt small under their pensive tone.

Malcolm looked rankled. He indicated the tray of knotted tots with a whimper. "What about—"

"Really. You'll want to see it." Keegan was insistent.

"Can't we wait for the rain to let up?" Malcolm said hopefully.

"No." Keegan shook their head. "We should check it out now."

Inside the living room, a young girl screamed as she fell into a pit filled with razor wires. It took Hollie a dull minute to realize that this was only coming from the television. She did not know why the sounds had startled her so, but her feathers had been ruffled and her palms had gone slick.

"Okay then. Let's go." Malcolm begrudgingly stamped across the kitchen and toward the coat rack. "Hollie, grab us a couple umbrellas, okay? I don't want to get soaked."

She agreed with his conjecture. The whole day had been rainy. She was so sick of water; she didn't even want to take a shower now. All she wanted to do was wrap her hair in a dry towel and sit in front of a heater.

After making sure that they all fit under the umbrella, the three made their way outside.

The walk to the woods was a hazardous one. Hollie found herself bemoaning every step as they went. The mud had become a thick sludge that coated their feet with every step. Even the rain itself seemed coated in a sheet of dirt. The umbrella did them little to no good. The wind passionately blustered beneath their shelter and kissed their faces.

"I'll never forgive you for this." Hollie looked at Keegan. She was only halfway sarcastic.

"Yeah, this is ridiculous!" Malcolm crooned. "Why couldn't you just tell us about what you saw?"

Keegan bit their tongue and glanced back and forth between the two angry adults. "I don't think I could?"

"What is it? A flying saucer? A UFO crash back here? I think we would've noticed that!" Malcolm was bellowing against the downpour.

Keegan apparently couldn't help but laugh. They planted a wet hand against their chittering teeth. "God, no. Just wait."

They meandered toward the woods. Hollie hadn't known what to expect, but it certainly wasn't what she encountered. Right past the brush, there was a tree with an elaborate carving stenciled into it. It looked like a circle with several tears in its sides, leaking rays of … of what? Hollie squinted up at the drawing and pursed her lips.

"Okay. It's interesting, yeah … but not an emergency." Malcolm moaned.

"No. That's what we came out to see, but that's not what scared us." Keegan pointed just beyond and above the carving. "Do you see it?"

"See what? My glasses keep fogging," Malcolm whimpered.

Hollie followed Keegan's crooked finger and tried to make out any abnormalities. At first, she couldn't see what the young person was pointing at. All the trees were drooping with moisture, and the sun was obscured behind storm clouds. There was nothing to see except for mud and twisted boughs and—

"Oh my god!" Hollie saw it and almost soiled her pants.

At first, she thought it was a person. It was six feet tall and humanoid. But then, her eyes were confused by its bumpy skin and malformed back. She was about to turn and run when a thought slapped into her head:

*It's just a statue!*

It was a six-foot-tall statue of a deformed Christ, and it was crucified against the tree. It was made of clay, and its design was sloppy. What were obviously supposed to be wings arching from his back were more akin to the crooked, sinewy legs of a grasshopper. The Christ statue had a crown of thorns—real ones—knotted together and screwed onto his egg-shaped head. But what really surprised Hollie were the corkscrewed ram's horns perched on both sides of Christ's noggin.

Hollie's eyes drifted down to Jesus's pelvis. Instead of wearing a soft cloth, his penis was laid bare, and it was disproportionately long and stiff, like a third arm sticking out from between his legs. The artist had given the penis more definition than any other part of the statue. Even from this distance, Hollie could see his crinkled skin and throbbing veins.

The thing had been tied to the tree with several cords of thick rope. It was slightly askew, looking as if it was holding a terrible amount of weight on its left side.

"Oh my god," Hollie repeated.

"What?" Malcolm barked. "What is it?"

"It's Jesus?" Hollie saw why Keegan had wanted to just show them the peculiar art piece. How did someone describe something so weird and uncanny? What was it doing on her property? Who had taken the time to lug it up the tree and secure it there?

"It's *what*?" Malcolm guffawed. He almost sounded relieved, as if he'd expected something far worse. "Are you kidding?"

"Paisley was the one that spotted it. We were about to head back after looking at the carving when she ... she just screamed. I thought something had bitten her. It took me a moment to even see it."

Keegan gestured with a flourishing hand. "I swear to God, I almost ran away when I saw it."

"I'm still not catching it." Malcolm squinted. "Hold this." He handed the umbrella to Keegan and began to screw with his glasses.

Hollie couldn't take her eyes off of the statue. It consumed her vision and held her in a state of awe. "What the fuck?" She mouthed the words without speaking.

"I thought it was a real person," Keegan continued. "I thought someone had climbed the tree and was watching us."

"Oh, holy shit. I see it now," Malcolm said.

Keegan crossed their arms over their chest and released a husky breath. "I've never seen anything like it. Have you, Ms. Karkoff? Do you know who could have put it there?"

Hollie shook her head. "I have no idea. No idea whatsoever."

She suddenly found herself remembering the last distressing phone call she had had from her sister. Becca had been raving like a lunatic before saying in a pitiful voice:

"The angels will come for Reece soon. They'll be at the door."

"What do you mean, Becca?" Hollie had asked, concerned and frustrated all at once.

"I have one in my shed. An Angel. A beautiful Angel. I've been keeping Him safe, ever since He fell from Grace."

Hollie had paused, sure now that her sister was unstable but unwilling to actually deal with the fact. She had pressed her lips together and looked up at the clock. "Becca, Stewart has been worried about you … the way you talk when you get like this … You gotta cool down, you know?"

Becca had sighed like an obstinate teen. "I knew you wouldn't get it." She hung the phone up.

A few days later, Becca was dead, Stewart was murdered, and Reece was without a mother. And now …

Now, Hollie had her own angel in her backyard.

*Was the angel in Becca's shed also so well endowed?*

"Oh my god. Oh my … god." Hollie wasn't sure if she was cursing or praying, but she said it a few more times for good measure.

# CHAPTER EIGHTEEN

Wylie stepped out from the kitchen. He held a meat cleaver in his blood-caked hand. He didn't remember going into the kitchen and picking the instrument up. His mind seemed to be only available in short blips. He remembered the gunshot that had torn Cliff's face open. He reckoned that he would remember that for as many days as he had left on this earth—

*You're already dead.* Wylie's thoughts had soured. He blinked them away and returned his attention back to the meat cleaver. It was a flat and long tool. He had no idea why he had bought such an instrument for his modest kitchen. It wasn't like they were butchering any animals in the back. Most of their beef patties arrived frozen and were simply reheated for lunch and dinner. But the massive meat cleaver had been a staple of the kitchen, even if it went unused.

Maybe he had bought it just for this occasion.

Wylie remarked that his left eye felt gummy. The lid hadn't been sealed shut, but a voluptuous fluid was inking out from where his pupil should have been. Wylie wanted to raise a hand up and prod the sensitive spot, but his body refused to cooperate. He simply moved forward, shambling ahead like a robot. He was being given a command.

*Walk. Walk. Walk.* It was the urging voice of a hypnotist. He felt utterly manipulated. But he also felt strangely calm. He was no longer allowed dominion over his own body, and that was perfectly fine. Why should he care when it was of no interest to him anymore?

Wylie's throat flexed. A dime's worth of blood oozed out. That surprised him. He'd expected an arterial spray. He'd thought that there would be red mist spritzing out of the hole that had been carved just beneath his chin. What had done that? Surely not the twisted prongs of Sweet-Anne's garden rake. It had to have been Tobin's scythe.

Again, he felt a reflective urge to touch the opening. Maybe his fingers wanted to seal the cut closed and hold back the surely massive amount of blood that would soon drench his front. But he didn't *need* to tend to the wound. He needed to do as he was told.

He needed to keep walking.

Wylie wasn't at all shocked to see Sweet-Anne vomiting a mouthful of red liquid into Cliff's destroyed face. That was how they had attended to Wylie after Sweet-Anne had slammed the rake into his back and held him still so that Tobin could work at him with the scythe.

*As you died, you received the Blood … His blood … the blood of the Lamb … of the King … of The Fallen One. Of Jesus the Redeemer's Shadow … It spilled off the cross and landed in your mouth. We drink of the blood and eat of the flesh every Sunday, all to prepare us for this …*

Wylie was surprised by all the information he was now privy to. Simply by swallowing the fluid that had spurted out of Tobin's unhinging jaw, he had become plugged in to an electric socket. Years of knowledge had flooded his brain. It had been an intensive boot camp that had only lasted for a few seconds.

Engaging with their blood was an act of transference. They had opened the gates, and now he was allowed to swim in their pool.

He had no opinions about anything anymore. He was beyond that. Certainly not a*bove* it. Deep down, he knew that he was nothing more than a shell jangling through a bizarre half-life. He was a fraction of a whole. An ant in a colony.

He was just a vessel for The Fallen One.

Nothing more. He had lost all of his identity, all of his emotions, and all of his bodily autonomy.

*Is this bad?* He tried to think through it as he watched Cliff's body jerk to horrible life. A sputter of wet mucus exploded from the gaping hole in the middle of his head where Moby had shot him. His eyes were crossed, his nose had all but vanished save for a few tattered strips of meat, and the top of his mouth was a pink cave. Cliff had certainly seen better days.

But Cliff was now part of the whole too. He was a cog in the system. He was …

He was one of *THEM* now.

*You should be upset.* A shuddering and quiet voice spoke up in Wylie's ear. *They took you away, and you'll never come back. You should be angry.*

But his commander didn't want anger. His King wanted violence. And he was willing to meet these demands. Like a puppet on his strings, Wylie jostled his way toward the door, hefting the meat cleaver up and down as he went. It was weighty in his padded hand. He took great pleasure watching the muddled lights of The Hopping Frog glint off of its charming surface.

As he stepped out into the rain, he wasn't at all puzzled by the cold. Usually, rainwater bothered him. Now, he had no worries. A blatant sense of euphoria rose in his throat. He was going to be a proud and happy servant.

Moby walked out behind Wylie. He had the shotgun from beneath the bar. Wylie watched as Moby broke the gun open and inspected its insides. Two shells. Wylie always kept it loaded. It had always made Krystal nervous, having a gun behind the bar. She didn't like guns.

Wylie wondered briefly what Krystal would make of his new appearance. Would she scream?

Moby snapped the shotgun closed and slung it over his shoulder. He smirked and flicked his fingers against his nose.

"How do I look?" Moby asked.

Wylie tried to answer, but the hole in his throat made words impossible. All that came out was a seeping mouthful of blood.

"Thought so." Moby looked over his shoulder. "Hey! Tobin!"

Tobin shambled toward the door. His wings were slick with mucus and had grown even larger than before. They ended in dull nubs that reminded Wylie of bedposts. Tobin's beet red skin shimmered in the bar's light. He looked as if he was covered in candle wax. His face had become misshapen with tumorous growths as well. One hung over his left eye, completely closing it.

"Take this." Moby tossed him the shotgun, which Tobin caught in his gnarled hands. "Good job, buddy."

Tobin smiled with satisfaction, like a puppy being scratched behind the ears.

"You're coming with me." Moby clapped his hand against Wylie's shoulder. A spark of pain dashed along his body, but he ignored it. "Sweet-Anne, Cliff, and Tobin are going to take care of everything else here. I've got a special little chore for you, man. You down?"

Wylie couldn't speak, so he groaned approvingly. He couldn't wait to be put to work.

"Hop in." Moby held the door to Tobin's police cruiser open. "Let's go on a little ride."

A willowy appendage broke out from Wylie's back. The stubby, featherless wing flexed back and forth experimentally. Wylie took a seat, being careful not to crush his first wing.

*How did the old saying go? Every time a bell rings, an angel gets his wings.*

Wylie's smile was unstoppable now.

# CHAPTER NINETEEN

Hurwitz was praying once more. His knees were sinking into the mud, and his hands were clasped tightly together. He looked strained, as if he was struggling to breathe. Hurwitz had always prayed intently, believing that The Fallen One wouldn't listen to him if he didn't at least sweat a little.

Hurwitz had grown up with strict parents. His father had been a preacher whose congregation met by the pond on their farmland. The pond had looked massive to Hurwitz when he was a youth. This was back when he had been called Oliver—or Ollie, affectionately. He had been blond haired, blue eyed, and freckle faced. He had always been willowy and narrow, even as a child. His mother sometimes pointed out that he acted too stern.

"Little boys, Ollie, shouldn't be so serious. You should learn to have fun and to play."

But Ollie didn't want to play. Oliver Hurwitz

wanted to be just like his papa.

He wanted to preach.

And so, he had been tutored by his own father into the gospel. He learned at an early age the difference between right and wrong and to fear God, as He was set to return any day.

And by the time Ollie had grown up, he was referring to himself by his last name. He had wanted to be taken more seriously, by his peers and superiors alike.

He was steadfast. An unwavering soldier of God. He never gave into temptation, even when it lay right in front of him. To this day, Hurwitz had remained a virgin and had also refused any alcoholic drink that wasn't served in a communal cup. Not that he had recently been inside any *actual* churches. Not since he had met The Fallen One.

To Hurwitz, the mysterious being that exerted His dominion over the land and its people was as good as God. He had never known a human capable of the things The Fallen One could do.

And Hurwitz also approved of The Fallen One's Old Testament attitude.

Hurwitz recalled the fearsome speeches his father gave by the side of that pond. He often shouted in tongues and sometimes pulled snakes out from a wicker basket. He dangled these snakes like slithery halos over his head and shouted:

"God is protecting me! God will not let the snake bite! God will turn the snake on my enemies!"

Hurwitz ground his old teeth together and thought about his father. As he did, he sent a message to The Fallen One, thanking Him for his bounty. Sure, it was cold and raining, but Hurwitz had everything he needed.

A pang of guilt rocked through his heart. He remembered sending Liam into that house all on his lonesome. Yes, the kid was annoying, but it was still a cruel act. Sometimes, it was hard not to feel bad for the sacrificial beast, even if they were killed in the name of a righteous cause.

But if Abraham could so easily raise his knife above Isaac, then Hurwitz was certain that he could send Liam into the mouth of his angry God.

"Hurwitz!" Tanith squeaked like a rodent caught under a cat's paw.

Hurwitz lifted his head and looked over his shoulder. He was kneeling on the far side of the campsite, right across from the little shrine that he and Moby had set up. The tent was empty save for the bust of their God. The kind, Christly, thorn-decorated face looked peaceable and sweet in the dim candlelight. His twisted horns looked majestic.

Hurwitz almost forgot what had drawn him away from his prayers. He was already becoming lost in the sight of his effigy. Then Tanith stepped into his line of vision. Her hair was drenched and plastered to her scalp. Her dress clung to her skin in a way that Hurwitz did not approve of. He knew that Moby and Tanith rutted like dogs whenever they pleased, despite Hurwitz's insistence that they remained pure. There was no controlling some people ... unless, of course, they were washed in the blood of the Lamb.

"What is it?" Hurwitz asked with as much ire as

he could muster. "I'm praying."

"I think something's wrong." Tanith looked toward the woods.

"What do you mean?"

"Liam's already coming back."

Hurwitz scoffed. "We were expecting this. Does it scare you?" Hurwitz lurched up to his feet and peered through the rain. Indeed, a swollen figure was marching toward the camp on unsteady legs. The Fallen One had made quick work of Liam. Now they would see the profits of their sacrifice. Hurwitz felt bad for only a second longer, but he managed to cloud these feelings out with pride.

This was accredited to Hurwitz. He was adding to the Lord's army.

"Come along, Liam! Come out!"

Chuck and Sam had gone out to meet Moby only a few minutes ago. They had been excited to crawl away from the campsite. Just like Liam, they were antsy youths who had no patience. Chuck was at least pure about his excitements. He was such a simple boy. Soft, really. Like a child in the body of a full-grown man.

Sam was craftier. Hurwitz didn't completely trust the little weirdo, but he didn't really have a choice. The company he kept was limited to those who were willing to believe and cooperate. And Sam was a stout believer in The Fallen One.

The figure limped closer.

"Wait!" Tanith said. "Do ... do you see that?"

Hurwitz didn't. He was too preoccupied by a sudden blast of wind that hit his ear. He felt as if he was drowning in all of this rain.

The figure moaned repulsively. It was a low, wet, and guttural sound, like the dying of a car's engine. The moan disintegrated into a clucking cry.

And then a voice ebbed out from the shadowy figure. "Help … me …"

It wasn't Liam's voice. No. Liam's voice wasn't recognizable … but this one was. It instantly tickled his brain and forced his mouth open. "Sam? Sam, what are you doing? Where's Chuck? Where's Moby?"

Sam stumbled out of the bushes and into the campsite. He wobbled on his heels like a drunkard before collapsing to his knees.

Tanith yelped and clapped her hands over her mouth. Hurwitz didn't even think to go to Sam's aid. He simply stood, rooted in his spot, and watched as Sam fumbled with his words.

"We were halfway there when Liam met us. Liam was … changed. We told him to walk with us, but he didn't even look like he recognized us. He—Something's not right, Gramps."

"What do you mean?" Hurwitz asked impatiently.

Sam fell onto the ground. He was breathing heavily, as if he was suddenly asthmatic. Tanith finally moved toward him and knelt by his side. She slung his arm over her shoulder and tried to pull him into a sitting position. Sam had all the mobility of a discarded jacket. His legs were splayed out before him. Hurwitz noticed a line of blood gushing out from his nose.

"I got away, b-but the bastard jumped on

Chuck." Sam gulped.

Hurwitz felt a smile tinge his gray lips. The Fallen One had promised them immunity, but maybe he had only intended to spare the brains of the operation. Maybe Hurwitz was just going to get to sit back and watch the apocalypse by his master's side and all of these other fools would be converted, regardless of their status.

The superiority that filled his lungs was intoxicating. Hurwitz felt as if he had grown a foot taller.

"Chuck was screaming! I heard his screaming while I ran. And I heard him stop … oh god, Tanith! Something went wrong. Chuck didn't do anything to upset Him! Chuck's been a loyal follower. It doesn't make sense. It doesn't make sense!"

As if to offer his opinion on the matter, Chuck came bumbling out from the woods. They hadn't even heard him approach, and stealth was an impossible feat for Chuck. He crashed out of the woods like a bear on a rampage. His mouth was decorated in white foam, and an ugly tear ran up his left cheek, exposing the teeth behind it. He looked frightened … and frightening.

Hurwitz took a few steps back and watched as their companion wandered closer to Tanith and Sam. Both of them were screaming and clutching each other.

Chuck stopped and looked around, dumbfounded.

"Jesus Christ!" Tanith proclaimed. "Are you okay?"

Hurwitz had no idea if she was talking to Chuck,

Sam, or herself. No one really took the time to answer her, least of all Chuck. The big man raised his hands and showed them to his comrades as if he meant them no harm. He spoke in his own voice, a weak and pitiful sound.

"It's what He wants." Chuck's words were slurred. His mouth was filled with blood from the rip in his cheek. "He wants us to be a part of it! To join the horde! This is what He intended the whole time!"

"No. Fuck that," Tanith shrieked. "That wasn't the goddamn deal!"

"He wants what's best for us." Chuck stepped forward. As he did, Hurwitz noticed something on his back. A weird protrusion. A wing, small and flightless. It had torn through his clothing. A strip of his Hawaiian shirt clung to the end of the limb.

*He has changed … He's becoming one of them now.*

Hurwitz's smile was almost out of control. This was just proof that his beliefs were right. Proof that The Fallen One was indeed everything that Hurwitz had ever thought He was. While Tanith and Sam screamed, Hurwitz decided that now was a good time to celebrate.

"Look." Chuck held his shirt open, baring his chest. "He's working *in* me."

As he held his shirt open, his stomach unloaded. A pound of gut-slop flopped out of the ragged hole that had been seared across his belly and toward his pelvis. One of his hip bones was exposed—like a white bubble.

Feces, blood, bits of semen, and even a quick detonation of piss were all pumping out of him.

A thick tube of intestine slithered out and dangled between his legs like an impressive cock. Even worse, an army of roaches were crawling out. They clung to the ridges of his wounds like mussels on the bottom of a ship. A mound of writhing centipedes and worms made their presence known as Chuck took a jostling step forward.

Hurwitz could imagine Liam thrusting handfuls of bugs into Chuck's open belly, spitting a wad of sacred blood in with each one. The mixture of wildlife and body fluids was poignant, but Hurwitz held his gorge back.

This was what The Fallen One had wanted to see, and so Hurwitz would see it too.

Tanith blasted a throat load of puke into the air and cartwheeled backward, releasing her hold on Sam. Sam fell onto the ground and began to scramble rearward.

But Chuck was too fast. He lurched forward and grabbed Sam by the ankle. Sam began to kick, thrash, and buck like an exasperated bull. He didn't even scream or complain; he only grunted with exertion.

Chuck dragged him forward and released his ankle, only to catch a handful of Sam's shirt and pull him closer to the massive hole in his stomach. At first, Hurwitz thought that Chuck was going to dunk Sam's head into the hole … but he had other plans.

"Take my blood." Chuck dipped his free hand into the pit of his stomach. "Take it. It's holy now."

"Oh my god!" Sam declared as Chuck pulled loose a handful of sooty worms and internal juices.

He squeezed the worms in his fist, reducing them to a mashed paste. Their tails wriggled and slapped between his fingers. "No! No!" Sam didn't even realize that he was opening his mouth in protest, giving the worms a dark and comfortable place to live.

Tanith was screaming now. She was running toward the woods, her arms flailing ahead of her. Hurwitz stood his ground, confident in his own security. He simply watched as Chuck smashed his filthy hand into Sam's open mouth. Sam gagged as the fingers dove in. His eyes rolled upward, and his body lurched. His whole belly seemed to ejaculate into his throat. Yellow fluids coursed out and trickled down Chuck's massive wrist.

Without hesitation, Chuck crammed his hand further into Sam's mouth. Overhead, a beat of thunder canceled out the sound of Sam's jaw breaking under the strain. Sam began to protest more profusely. His hands clawed at Chuck's eyes, dug into his wounded cheek, and scratched at his throat. None of this seemed to bother the large man. He simply rolled his shoulder and then thrust his hand deeper into Sam's mouth.

Hurwitz saw a bulge form in Sam's throat. Chuck's wrist was pushing past Sam's teeth now.

Chuck wasn't making a sound.

Sam made a noise that sounded like a spluttering garbage disposal before falling limp.

Chuck yanked his hand out. It was followed by a splash of blood. Sam fell backward and lay on the forest floor. A single worm drooped out from his mouth, wriggling in the froth forming on his lips.

There was a loud crack as a second wing exploded out from Chuck's back.

Sam began to writhe on the ground as The Fallen One's infectious blood took over his body. In mere seconds, Sam would be nothing more than a puppet.

It made Hurwitz proud.

"Bravo, Chuck. Bravo." Hurwitz took a gallant step toward his compadre. "Now, let's catch Tanith and convert her! She can't be far—"

Hurwitz shouldn't have been surprised, but he was. When Chuck's massive, blood- and dirt-caked hand snapped out and gripped his throat, the first thing Hurwitz felt like saying was:

"No fair!"

This wasn't how the game was played. This was cheating.

Hurwitz pawed at Chuck's hand, writhed against his grip, and began to spit as his windpipe was mashed. His cheeks immediately began to tingle, and his breath came in angry gulps.

"You … let … go!" Hurwitz strained.

"They don't take orders from you." A cruel voice rang out from the other side of the camp.

Chuck turned Hurwitz so that he could see The Fallen One. He drifted out from the shadows. A potato sack was covering His face, and His yellowed fingernails were blood soaked. Hurwitz began to fear his God as he had never feared Him before.

"Why can't I keep serving you?" Hurwitz moaned.

"You'll be humbler this way." The Fallen One

raised His left hand. As He did, Hurwitz felt an awful tug at his sternum. He looked down and saw that his shirt had parted by its own volition. A supernatural force was chaffing his skin now, experimenting with his wiry chest hairs and sinking into the flesh … one finger at a time.

"No!" Hurwitz wailed.

Chuck released his hold on the old man and stepped aside.

Hurwitz collapsed to his knees and placed his hands against his bare chest. The skin had grown red hot. He saw steam rise as rain pattered against it. Boils began to form along his ribs. They popped as soon as they rose, expulsing clear liquids and blood strings.

"No! Please!"

"Please what?" The Fallen One's voice sounded acidic. His right hand moved his mask upwards and aside so that Hurwitz could get a good look at his face.

"Please … Master." Hurwitz moaned.

His chest exploded.

Flaps of skin moved aside, splinters of bone shot out and peppered the ground, and his lungs flopped out and hung from the wound like a pair of Christmas ornaments from a tree. They wetly burped as air hissed out from their tattered sides.

He saw something else fly out amid the bloody chaos. It zipped across the ground and tumbled up and toward The Fallen One. As it smacked into His palm and was immediately clutched between His nimble fingers, Hurwitz recognized the little organ.

It was his heart.

The Fallen One had yanked his heart right out of his chest.

Without even laying an actual finger on him.

When Hurwitz leaned his head backward, his mouth was filled with foreign blood. It was dribbled into him via Sam, who had gotten up to his feet and was already following commands like a submissive soldier.

Hurwitz's wondered if he had chosen the wrong side in this fight.

# CHAPTER TWENTY

Hollie Karkoff caught herself thumping the pad of her index finger against the surface of her eyepatch. It was a habit she had picked up when she had first lost her eye in that stupid accident at the movie theater. When the patch had first been affixed to her, she had had a bothersome time with it. She played with the elastic straps, snapped the bottom of the patch against the curve of her cheek, and thrummed the center of the patch with her finger. Sometimes, Hollie convinced herself that she wasn't even wearing the patch, that she just had one eye closed and the other open. But today, she was intensely aware of it.

Maybe it was just a good distraction.

Malcolm was no help whatsoever. He paced nervously, tracking mud along the surface of the linoleum floor. "Well, I tell you … I'll bring the ladder over first thing tomorrow and take that …

that thing down. Or should I? Do you think Chilton will want a look at it? He might. Maybe we should take pictures. Did you take pictures, Keegan?"

Keegan rubbed their hands together. Their coffee sat untouched in front of them. "No," they stated sullenly. "It was too wet out. We didn't even have our phones with us, I think."

"Well, whoever put that thing out there is gonna feel it. I swear to god." Malcolm was too gentle for threats. It made Hollie chuckle watching him get so steamed up.

"Oh, Malcolm. It's probably nothing." Hollie tried to sound blithe, but her voice was trembling. Was it the cold, or was it fear? "It's probably some weird tactic from the local church ... trying to change our ways. Scare the Jesus into us."

"That counts as harassment." Malcolm snapped his fingers.

"It's fine. It's a little spooky, but it's fine. We'll call Chilton over in the morning, and then we'll take it down. It won't be a problem."

"Why don't we call him tonight?" Malcolm offered.

"No," Hollie stated.

"Why not?"

"Because even after standing in the rain for ten minutes, we still smell like Amsterdam."

Malcolm hesitated and then took a whiff of his arm. "It's not that bad."

"Dude." Keegan had decided to take sides. "Your eyes are bloodshot."

"We could say its allergies."

Keegan scoffed and laughed at the same time, a

sound that reminded Hollie of a hiccup. Malcolm's face broke into a smile.

"Oh. I get it. I'm the clown."

"That's why we like you," Hollie cooed. "C'mon. Go pick a movie for us to watch tonight, okay? And nothing too scary; I'm not in the mood." She realized that her suggestion was just in time. From the living room, the thumping sounds of a synth score signaled the end of *Suspiria*.

"I'm going to go check on Krystal." Hollie stood and started toward the stairs. She had removed her shoes at the door, but her socks were soaked through. They squished audibly as she padded up the stairs.

As she went, she heard Keegan say: "Yeah. It's freaky. I don't really like Jesus to begin with."

"Hey, man." Malcolm took on a surfer dude accent. "Jesus was a socialist. It's the Christians that gave him such bad press."

Keegan squawked. Hollie couldn't help but smile herself. She did feel as if her home was a warm and welcome place for all people of all kinds. She was a surrogate mother, both to Reece and Paisley's friends ... maybe, to an extent, to Malcolm as well. As she went up the stairs, she briefly thought about how brave Keegan had been through all of this. But Keegan was made of bravery. It took a lot of guts for someone to be themselves, especially in a red state like Missouri. She was sure that Keegan struggled to get people to even acknowledge their pronouns, much less use them.

What was school like?

Hollie couldn't imagine.

She walked down the hallway and past her daughters' room. She knocked on the door to her bedroom and heard Krystal chirp:

"Come in!"

"Hey." Hollie sighed as she opened the door. "How's it coming?"

"Good. Fine." Krystal turned around and faced Hollie. She was sitting in the swirly office chair. She had moved some of Hollie's papers to her bed so that they weren't in the way and could easily be placed back where they had been found. Hollie briefly glanced around her room, realizing it was a lot dirtier than she had remembered. It was certainly better off than Wylie and Krystal's apartment, but it still needed tending to.

She was only momentarily perturbed by the plain white undershirt draped over the edge of her bedframe. She was thankful that her bottom dresser drawer had been closed, at least.

"I'm sorry to bother you. I guess I'm just a little spooked," Hollie admitted.

"How come, sweetie?" Krystal said. Her eyes darted back to her mound of homework. Hollie felt guilty pulling her away from it all.

"Keegan found something weird in the woods. A statue of Jesus."

Krystal waited a beat, as if expecting a punchline. When none came, she put her pencil in her mouth and leaned back in her chair. "Okay." She pulled the pencil out of her mouth and made the sign of the cross with it. "Out, spirit."

"Okay. Okay." Hollie laughed. "I'll take you to look at it tomorrow morning."

"God. I wish you hadn't told me about it." Krystal paused for dramatic effect. "Because once I tell Wylie, he'll probably want to put it in the bar."

Hollie barked with laughter and stepped out of the room. Before she pulled the door closed, she asked: "Do you need anything? Cup of water?"

"Bring me a slice of pizza in about fifteen?"

"Sure." Hollie pursed her lips. "I could bring you one now; they're hot."

"No. No. Fifteen minutes. It'll be my little reward for studying."

"Gotcha." Hollie closed the door and gave Krystal her privacy.

Hollie was counting her blessings to combat her jangled nerves. She was thankful her house was full of good people that could remind her that the world didn't have to be a scary place ... even if Jesus Freaks were doing their best to spook her senseless.

She descended the stairs one at a time, allowing the warmth from the living room to seize her as she approached it. Malcolm was putting a comedy in the DVD player. Before it even started, she knew it was *Wayne's World.* Even though they had bought a small stack of DVDs at the flea market, Malcolm was returning to his old favorite.

"I can't believe you haven't seen *Wayne's World*!" He gawked at Keegan, who laughed uproariously.

"I don't watch comedies."

"This isn't *just* a comedy," Malcolm said. "It's art! And it's directed by a woman! Huh? Ladies?"

Paisley gave him a begrudging round of applause. "You're so woke, Malcolm. So woke."

"I'm just saying. It's a little fun fact."

Hollie put a hand over her mouth and laughed while she took her seat on the sofa.

"Wait, wait, wait!" August held up his hand. "I haven't seen this either."

"Malcolm's only made us watch it about …" Reece scrunched her brow and put her hand to her chin as if in deep thought. "A hundred million times?"

"This'll make it a hundred million and one." Malcolm flopped down next to Hollie.

"It's funny. You'll like it." Hollie heard Paisley whisper to her boyfriend.

"I sure hope so," August whimpered. "That last one was a bit too much for me."

Hollie's heart swelled. It was as if she had just found the cutest puppy in the shelter. She briefly grabbed Malcolm's hand and squeezed it, thanking him silently for lifting their spirits. Everything felt, all of a sudden, like it was going to be okay again.

As they started their movie, a shadowy figure began to approach their house from the woods. He walked with a limp and left a slug's trail of blood in his wake.

# Chapter Twenty-One

Moby pulled the Chief's car up to the woods and hopped out. He had dropped Wylie off nearer to the Karkoff residence. Wylie was now shambling toward their house with specific instructions:

"Convert as many as you can but leave Reece Brampton alone! She belongs to our Master!"

Wylie had tried to confirm that he understood, but his ravaged throat only allowed him to cluck like a hen before he gave up and nodded his head obediently. He had lugged himself out of the car and crashed through the woods, hacking at the brambles with his meat cleaver as if he was an adventurer in a primitive jungle. Moby had watched him go until he had vanished in the thickets of trees and darkness.

*Good on you, Wylie. Do as you're told.* Moby backed the Chief's vehicle against the ditch and climbed out himself. He jangled with the keys at the back door for a moment to retrieve his bow. He only had one arrow left, and he didn't really plan on using it until he had to. The zombies were going to do all the hard work now. All Moby had to do was go back to the campsite, put his feet up, snuggle against Tanith in their tent, and wait for the "all clear" from The Fallen One. Then, they would attend mass …

The fruits of their labor would pay off.

Moby smiled smartly and shifted his blond hair out of his eyes. He felt really good, as if he had just received an A on a particularly challenging test.

*I've done my part, and now I get to reap the benefits. I get to sit by The Fallen One's side. I get to earn his gifts and powers. I'll be a king … maybe even a god. Once all of this is over, people will fear me.*

His smile was unstoppable. It fluttered up his cheeks and overtook his entire face. He felt as if he was skipping over the fallen tree limbs and rustling bushes. He was thoroughly soaked by the rain, but this didn't bother him. Moby was absolutely ecstatic.

He couldn't wait to see Tanith again and celebrate with her. Of course, he'd probably have to deal with updating Hurwitz about what all had transpired. The old man could be worse than a suit some days. He wanted reports and transcripts and memos about every step Moby took. Some days, Moby wished the old man would just have a heart attack and save him the lip work. But he could endure the crotchety bastard for now. It was worth it.

So much had been accomplished that evening.

Moby suddenly felt as if his hands were empty. "Fuck." He sighed and turned his head around. He had forgotten to grab any beer. He hadn't made any promises, but coming back with some booze would have been a nice gesture. He briefly considered running back to the Chief's car and driving back to town … but that would take too long. He really wanted to see Tanith again.

And he did. The moment he turned his head around, he saw his girlfriend charging through the woods toward him. A look of joy sparked across her face.

"Hey, honey!" Moby held his arms out. "I'm home!"

"Run!" Tanith shrieked. "Moby! Run!"

Moby felt only an inkling of confusion pass through him. He let his arms dangle at his sides and arched his eyebrow. Surely, he hadn't heard her correctly.

A bolt of lightning illuminated the forest and revealed Tanith's pursuers.

There were a few of them. The first one that caught his eye was Charlotte Patch. The older woman's head was concaved, and her skin had grown deep red, like Tobin's. Huge pockets and blisters had developed beneath her eyes, and her wings fluttered uselessly out from her back. She was the most advanced in her metamorphosis.

Liam was close behind, with wings and a fatty growth beneath his chin that looked like a frog's throat … or a bothersome goiter.

Chuck's wings were stubby and slick with mucus; they had only just sprung forth.

Sam's jaw was broken open and wobbled comically back and forth like a porch swing.

Hurwitz looked as if he had been dissected. His chest yawned open, revealing his hollowed-out insides. His lungs, organs, and even his heart had been pulled out of him and were nowhere to be seen. His legs pinwheeled like a cartoon character, having a hard time balancing his unstable upper half. His head seemed too weighty and flopped from side to side as he went.

"Run!" Tanith screeched once again, spurring life back into Moby. "Run!"

Liam was upon her. He hopped onto her back and coiled his arms around her throat, cutting her scream short. Moby dashed forward and swung his bow toward Liam's head. Liam ducked down, pulling Tanith with him.

"Let her go!" Moby demanded, so blinded by rage that he hadn't even noticed that the others were approaching him, until the glint of a butcher's knife caught his eye.

Moby dropped to his haunches as Charlotte made a swipe at him. The blade skimmed over his head and thumped into a tree. The blade sunk into the swollen wood, and before Charlotte could pull it free, Moby struck her wrist with the end of his bow. The bow thrummed up his arms, shaking him to his ankles. Moby stumbled back and watched as Charlotte grabbed the knife and yanked it free. She hadn't even felt his blow.

Moby whirled around and made quick eye contact with Tanith. She was panicked and whimpering like a rabbit caught in a trap. His heart swelled with pity and rage.

"Hey! Let off of her!" Moby shouted assertively toward Liam.

Liam looked in Moby's direction and tossed Tanith aside. She rolled along the top of a sapling and landed with a hard thud at the foot of a cedar tree. Before she could scramble to her feet, Chuck was looming over her and taking a handful of her hair.

"Stop that!" Moby declared. "In the name of The Fallen One, stop it!"

"They won't listen to you! He lied! He lied!" Tanith squealed as Chuck tucked her under his arm and carried her like a load of laundry toward the group. "The Fallen One wants us too!"

Moby extended a shaking hand. "Listen, Liam! Guys! You don't have to—"

His words were cut short when he was bludgeoned against the head with Charlotte's fist. Moby stumbled forward, and his extended hand plunged into Hurwitz's flayed chest. He felt the nubs of the old man's spine and was instantly repulsed.

"Oh fucking shit!"

He stumbled backward and was beat against the head once more by Charlotte, who released a hissing laugh. He tried to turn around and face her, only to be smacked across the cheek by Sam.

"Watch!" Chuck declared to Tanith, squeezing her chin and holding her head up so that she could watch as her boyfriend was surrounded.

Charlotte struck forward, sinking the butcher knife into the space above Moby's hip. He felt the blade scrape against his bones and poked out the other side. A volley of blood was released like an ejaculation from the top of his pants.

"Hey." Moby sounded more bemused than hurt. He reached down and tested the tip of the blade with his finger. It was sharp and instantly drew blood.

Charlotte pulled the blade free.

Moby dropped his bow. It would do him no good. If they had all been standing a ways away, he could have shot at least one of them. But they were clustered around him. He barely had room to move.

So … The Fallen One had never intended to let His chosen few sit by His side. Like the people of Kissing-Brooke, Moby and Tanith and all of their friends were merely a means to an end. They would become part of the horde … and they would become food for the pit.

Moby wished he was more enraged. Instead, he felt resigned. This was his place now, had been his whole life. He just hadn't been aware of it until now.

*Your fight dies easy, doesn't it?* Moby thought to himself.

"I was hesitant, at first." Hurwitz's voice was a croak. "But it feels good to be part of His congregation. It feels good to be His servant."

"I …" Moby muttered. "I don't want to die yet."

Liam reached into his back pocket and produced his own knife, no doubt scrounged up from Ms. Patch's kitchen. It was thin and ridged. A steak knife. Moby felt his mouth go numb at the sight of it.

Then Sam pulled his own knife from his pocket. A Swiss Army knife. The one he carried with him wherever he went. He carved pieces of wood with that knife. He had even peeled potatoes for the communal soup. He picked at his teeth with that blade, and beneath his nails.

Moby had never thought to fear it.

Hurwitz reached into his open chest cavity and loosened one of his rib bones. With great strain and grunting, he snapped the bone free as if he was pulling a branch from a dead tree. Even the thunder couldn't conceal the sound of his bone crunching out of his ribcage. He brandished the ivory shaft like a weapon. Marrow and blood oozed out of its end.

Moby felt warm water spread across his crotch.

"I didn't think it would be like this." Moby was crying. "I thought we would sit by Him."

"We will," Hurwitz rumbled.

"Don't let Tanith watch me die, okay?" Moby asked.

"Okay." Chuck hefted Tanith up and slammed her face against the nearest tree. She let out a brief squeal of pain as a severed branch impaled her between the eyes. Chuck pulled her back, revealing the wicked puncture wound before knocking her into the tree once more and sliding her down. Her face was shredded by the bark as she went, leaving a red smear along the tree's surface.

"No!" Moby raised an arm. It was met by Liam's knife. The blade sliced through his wrist.

At the first sign of blood, Charlotte's butcher

knife sent the butcher's blade in between Moby's legs with an underhanded swing. The blade seared through the seat of Moby's pants and dug into his anus. The metal explored him like a snuffling groundhog. There was a syrupy explosion of gore followed by wet shit. He could smell his bowels as they were speared and then began to furiously leak. The blood rushed downward and pooled beneath his heels. The pain was immense and indescribable.

Sam's Swiss Army was the next partner to dance with Moby. It sliced through the meat of Moby's chin and speared the bottom of his wriggling tongue. Blood coursed between his bent teeth in swampy rivulets.

Hurwitz skewered Moby's stomach with his rib bone. The arched weapon swept upwards and became entangled in Moby's intestines.

As if choreographed, all four of the zombies pulled their instruments loose at once. More sprays of blood sputtered out of him as if he was a twirling fountain. Moby began to spin on his feet, his eyes trying to focus on one face and then another. Each face was devilishly red now, both with his blood and with the effects of The Fallen One's poison.

"Puh-leeeeze!" Moby sobbed.

The four stabbed him again as he rotated.

Charlotte struck him beneath the arm pit. His arm cinched against his body and froze there, his fingers pointing in different directions. Sam struck between the legs, puncturing his scrotum. He could feel his testicles dripping out and jangling inside the crotch of his pants. Hurwitz's bone slammed into his stomach once more and twisted like a fork attempting to pull spaghetti from a plate. And Liam skewered him through the neck.

Again, like synchronized dancers, they pulled their blades free.

Moby collapsed to his knees, doused in blood. Arterial pathways had opened and were dumping their payloads everywhere he looked. He felt his gorge rise in his throat.

"Uhhhhhhh," he moaned. "I … I don't like this." He spoke with a lisp around the hole in the bottom of his mouth and through his tongue. "I wanna go back! Let's go back … let's start over …"

He fell onto his back.

"I don't like this. I don't like this. This hurts. This really hurts. Guys. Stop it. This really, really hurts." Moby began to shake his head back and forth.

The huddled foursome sank their blades into him for the third time. Liam struck his clavicle, releasing a new geyser of blood. It squirted upwards and arched into Liam's broken mouth.

Charlotte hit Moby in the thigh. His nerves were electrified by the thrust of the blade. It dug in deep, spitting fire against his bones.

Hurwitz plunged his bone-shank into Moby's gut for the third time and yanked it free almost immediately. A low hiss issued from the wound.

Sam's switchblade drove itself into his ribs and popped one of his lungs.

Moby gasped horribly and released a fitful cough. The blades were all reeled away once more. Moby found himself immobile. He simply lay in the mud, looking upwards and wishing this was all over and done with.

"I ... I'm finished." Moby tried the words, but they were blockaded by fluids. All that came forth was a syrupy concoction of blood and mucus. "I'm ... I'm done." He sounded like a growling dog.

From outside the circle, Moby could hear Chuck laughing gleefully. His big hands smacked together for a round of applause. Moby tried to ignore him.

His body was incapable of movement now. All that was left were a few spastic twitches. Moby had never felt so low and only dimly realized he would never be allotted the opportunity to strive for better days. This was it. The game was over.

After all he had done for The Fallen One, this was his reward.

He looked up into the night sky and watched the rain pass through the trees. The droplets were cool to the touch and calmed his nerves.

"That's better." He smiled.

Then Hurwitz's face blocked his view, and his mouth was open. A bouquet of venomous, infected blood filled Moby's eyes.

And just like that, Moby was part of it.

# CHAPTER TWENTY-TWO

Krystal looked up from her homework when she heard the sound of knuckles rapping against glass. She whirled her head around, thinking that she must have been confused. Surely, no one was knocking at the window adjacent to Hollie's bed. They must have been at the door. It could be Hollie with the promised slice of pizza.

Krystal glanced at her watch. It had only been five minutes since Hollie had left her to her studies, and she could hear a movie blaring downstairs. What was it? *Wayne's World*? She recognized Mike Myer's voice and cracked a grin. Malcolm had been watching that movie since he was a kid. Wylie claimed he was sick of it and that Malcolm had made him watch it too many times, but whenever it was on, he couldn't help but sit through it.

*You're getting distracted, babe,* Krystal thought.

The knuckles rapped against the glass again.

The sound was still confusing to her. There was something all too uncanny about it.

Krystal stood and stretched her arms. "Come in!"

There was no response. The doorknob didn't tremble or turn.

"I said you can come in, Hollie. I'm decent." Krystal laughed.

Outside, thunder smacked overhead. The house shook on its foundations. Krystal wobbled on her feet briefly and had to focus to catch her bearings. After reasserting herself with gravity, she huffed and stamped toward the door. Maybe the thunder was too loud and Hollie hadn't heard her call.

Krystal took the door and threw it open.

There was no one on the other side. A quick glance up and down the hall proved that it wasn't one of the kids trying to be funny.

*Goddamn it, Krystal. You're driving yourself crazy.*

Maybe she was subconsciously distracting herself from her workload. Admittedly, all of this should have been done yesterday so that she could have enjoyed the weekend. That was her usual plan. But one thing or another had pulled her away from her schoolwork, and now she was going to spend the whole weekend buried in books.

She was thankful for the solitude Hollie had provided her, but it did her no good when she was throwing herself off course.

Knuckles hit glass again.

It was then that Krystal realized that her brain had drawn her to the door, but the sound was clearly emanating from the window. Of course she had gone to the door. Why would she even try to go to the window?

Maybe it was a tree limb bumping against the window. Maybe it was a squirrel running along the surface of the roof. Whatever it was, she decided it was far too distracting and she had to investigate.

Krystal wandered over toward the window and inspected it. The rain was pattering against it, but there was no hail. And besides, none of the drops were heavy enough or solid enough to simulate the distinct sound of a knocking fist.

Krystal ran her finger over the wet surface of the window. It had fogged up. The line she split through the haze revealed an empty yard. A flash of lightning illuminated the woods.

Krystal felt a shiver run up her back and nestle like a warm cat between her shoulder blades. The woods looked absolutely nightmarish in this weather. And Hollie's horror story about the statue wasn't doing Krystal any favors. She couldn't help but imagine what Christ would look like pinned to one of those trees.

She had made light of it before, but now that she could actually see the trees, it gave her the willies.

What kind of sicko did something like that? Who hung up a statue of Jesus Christ in a stranger's yard? It sounded like the kind of thing teenagers would do to freak the old folks out. If so, it was an effective prank.

Still, it didn't feel blatant enough to have been pulled off by a gaggle of high schoolers. High schoolers would have nailed the damn thing to the front door or left it at the end of the driveway.

Hollie said it was in the woods.

She couldn't see the statue, but she was having a hell of a time imagining it. Christ, covered in blood and sores, looking up to the heavens like a pitiful animal. It was a spooky image, and Krystal didn't want to focus on it for any longer.

She stepped away from the window and began to walk toward the desk again. She had homework to tend to. She had dallied enough. Krystal sat down and picked up her pencil.

Something smashed through the window. It was big and white and came crashing in with a flurry of glass chips and rainwater.

Krystal yelped and leapt to her feet, capsizing the rolling chair. She backed into the corner between the desk and the wall and watched through her fingers as the white thing landed on Hollie's bed. She expected it to lope forward with the same voracity it had intruded with …

But the white thing remained frozen.

Water was trickling in now. A steady current being pumped over the windowsill and down the wall. The bed itself seemed spongey and soaked through. The white thing had become entangled in Hollie's sheets.

Krystal expected Malcolm to come barreling in. Surely a sound like this had alerted everyone in the house.

But when Krystal focused her attention outside of her jackhammering heart, she could still hear Wayne and Garth acting like buffoons on the television downstairs. The volume was loud, and the thunderstorm was louder. No one had heard the forced entry. Krystal was trapped in this room with whomever had come crashing through the window.

"Hello?" Krystal said when the vaguely human shaped blob refused to budge. "Please?"

*Please, what? Girl, run!*

But she would have to cross by the bed if she wanted to run toward the door. She didn't want to be near the thing. Her neck was flexing as if she was a balloon being puffed into shape. Her brow had gone beady with sweat. Even her breaths were haltering gasps.

Krystal lowered her hand and looked at the intruder.

She was almost more alarmed when she realized it was inanimate.

It was Jesus Christ's effigy. Sprawled out on Hollie's bed as if it was anticipating the conclusion to a hot date. His form was nude but without distinct shape. His face was pale and smooth, with two dimples where his eyes should be and a ringlet of real thorns wrapped about his brow. He also had a titanic prick. The shaft was ribbed with stone nodes, and its head was like an arrow's point. It stood an impressive thirteen inches.

Krystal paused and took a dainty step forward. "Hello?"

She could've slapped herself. What did she expect? Did she think whoever had thrown this thing into the second story window was going to poke their head inside and say: "What's up?"

She studied the statue once more. Its back held two arched limbs. They looked like they were supposed to signify wings, but they looked more like spider legs.

And he had horns.

Krystal shook her head, put her hands over her mouth. She breathed through her fingers. The whole room stank of rainwater and mud now. She briefly fretted over the wind blasts, which sent a thick shower onto the desk and soaked her homework and textbooks.

But surprisingly, there were more important things to worry about than homework right now. She couldn't afford to waste a single second.

She needed to get Hollie and Malcolm. What was she doing standing around here?

Krystal rushed toward the door. Her feet left wet tracks across the carpet as she went. Her heart hadn't even slowed its pulsating rhythm. Krystal thought, as she gripped the doorknob and threw it open, that she had never been so scared before in her life.

Then she opened the door.

And Wylie swung his meat cleaver toward her head.

Krystal stared blankly as the world suddenly slowed down. Her head was immediately buzzing with questions. But the questions and their answers didn't matter. The details that stood out to her were plain and simple.

Her boyfriend looked terrible. His face was battered and swollen. His cheeks had developed zit-like growths and tumors. It was unmistakably Wylie, but something was wrong with him. He looked as if he had swum in toxic waste or had suffered radiation poisoning.

And his back was exactly like the statue. Two black limbs stretched upwards and toward the ceiling. Their rounded ends looked like the clubbed feet of a bathtub.

It was all so perplexing; Krystal had little time to focus on the sharpened edge of the butcher's cleaver … until it skidded across her face.

A flash of red overtook her vision. Krystal stumbled backward and flopped onto the bed. Her back arched painfully as she landed on top of the wet statue. Its hard surface prodded her and made her thrash with discomfort.

"Get off of me!" She shoved at the statue as if it had any say in the matter.

*Something isn't right. Something's wrong with you.*

Krystal lifted her hands and padded them against her face. Her mouth was fine … and so were her cheeks … but … her eyes …

Wylie had drawn the blade across both of her open eyes.

Milky syrup squirted out between her testing fingers and immediately filled her palms.

*Eye juice.* Krystal's brain screamed. *That's eye juice! Your hands are covered in eye juice!*

Krystal expected another blow to take her down while she was blinded and incapacitated. She was almost resigned to the oncoming suffrage. But nothing came. It was almost as if, after striking her, Wylie had all but vanished.

"Help." Krystal staggered up to her wobbly feet. She felt like a newly born colt testing her legs with every step. "Wylie … please … we can—we can talk about this." She was speaking in a whisper, as if there was a possibility that Wylie couldn't see her.

Krystal stumbled forward. Her feet overlapped and she pitched downward, slamming into the floor. She lay still for a moment before breaking into sobs. The fall had broken her. The pain of losing both of her eyes hit her like a fist. She gripped her belly and wailed into the carpet.

Wylie's hand clutched her by the hair. Krystal's wail turned into a scream.

It was unfortunate timing. Just as she attempted to let loose the loudest scream she was capable of—

A bolt of lightning and a massive boom of thunder drowned her out. She was almost deafened by the noise herself. When the storm quieted and she had her breath back, Krystal prepared to scream again.

Only now, Wylie used his other hand to cover her mouth and clamp it shut. His fingers pressed her mouth shut. Her teeth cut through the tip of her tongue. The tangy taste of blood immediately rippled through her mouth and leaked between her lips. She whined and bucked and protested as best she could, but her lips were sealed.

Wylie's breath was hot against her ear. His lack of explanation felt like a larger betrayal than the actual act of violence he was perpetrating. Krystal felt as if she was at the very least owed a detailed list of why he thought taking her eyes out of her skull was a good idea.

Wylie pulled her around the bed and slammed her against the wall. He gripped the back of her head and pushed her face into the wall with as much force as he had. She felt her nose *pop* like a water balloon beneath his heavy paw.

"Uhhhh," Krystal grunted and was then pulled away once more. "Wylie, *please*!" She spoke around his fingers. Her words were almost completely lost. They just sounded like broken syllables. Like baby talk.

"Sorry." Wylie's voice was even more disjointed than hers. It sounded as if he suffered from smoker's cough. Or even worse … it sounded as if his throat had been shredded apart. "Have to." It was the only explanation he seemed capable of offering.

Krystal's head was pushed out the broken window. Her face was instantaneously slickened with rain. Her hair clung to her scalp in thick clumps. She opened her mouth to scream and was automatically blocked by Wylie's fingers. He pulled her jaw backward, straining every muscle in her face.

Wylie released her jaw and gripped the sides of her face. Now that she was blind, she couldn't tell, at first, which direction she was facing. All she knew was that she was pointed outside … toward the trees.

"Uh!" Krystal managed. "Guh!"

Wylie drew her slowly back into the room, allowing the broken shards of glass to peel the skin away from her throat.

Krystal's legs began to kick and struggle when the pain hit her. She wriggled against his strong arms and cried helplessly.

Her mind couldn't even form coherent thoughts

anymore. It was frantically collecting as much data as it could. She had been shoved outside, and now she was being scraped against broken glass like a mud caked shoe being rubbed clean against a welcome mat.

She felt and heard the hiss of blood being released. The glass had pricked her jugular. Wylie released her once more. She slumped downward and fell back into the room. A large chunk of glass was embedded in her throat. In her panic, she swiped at the shard and yanked it free. She may as well have pulled the drain from a bath. Blood raced out at a high velocity. She couldn't see it, but she could hear it arching up and landing on the floor in a steady stream. It was as if she was listening to someone piss at a urinal.

She tried to use her finger to taper the flow, but her arms felt useless and drained.

*I'm dying. I'm dying. This is what dying feels like—*

She felt Wylie work her pants down her legs. He hadn't even bothered unbuttoning them. He just ripped them down and then wiggled them loose. Then, he took a handful of her panties and tore them from her pelvis like a sinner ripping a page from the Bible. She felt a patch of pubic hair rip away as well, caught in the fabric and his terse fingers. There was pain, but it was muted by the aching in her neck.

He lifted her easily and then tossed her onto the bed. She felt the thirteen-inch stone cock punch her back. It would have hurt enough to make her yowl if her body wasn't so numb. She lay askew on the body of Christ, whimpering and wheezing.

Wylie repositioned her like she was a life-size doll. He forced her to hover over the statue, and then he pushed her hips down roughly. The stone phallus tore through her cunt. The stony surface of the phallus tore the walls of her vagina, ripping the sensitive flesh like a blown wad of tissue paper. Blood began to fall from the split between her legs in pissy waves.

She gurgled in agony. This pain wasn't so easy to ignore. Despite the blood loss and the fire that roared through her throat, she still felt the full force of the violation. It was as if a hot poker had been screwed through her tunnel and forced into her guts.

*Oh, God.* Krystal's last thoughts echoed in her skull. *Just kill me.*

Wylie obliged by hewing her skull in half with his meat cleaver.

# CHAPTER TWENTY-THREE

Paisley decided to take the pizza upstairs. Like Reece had said, they had watched the dumb movie over a million times by now. Malcolm still laughed as if it was his first time ever seeing it. It was adorable, but it was also a little tiring. August was just happy the film didn't feature any bloodshed or jump scares.

Paisley looked down at her feet as she marched up the stairs. The floor was soaking wet. Had her mother brought so much rainwater up with her after Keegan had taken her to see the statue?

Paisley sighed and continued up the stairs. She wished that her mother would replace their stinking, aged carpet with hardwood floors. That would be much easier to clean and a lot less of a hassle. Thankfully, none of the carpet was shag. Although her mom was such a stoner hippy she wouldn't be surprised if she came home and found a fuzzier carpet and a dreamcatcher at every window someday.

Paisley ran her free hand through her short hair and sighed dejectedly. She loved her mom, and her home, but she was definitely feeling an itch to go away. Not forever. Just for a little while.

Paisley wondered if Keegan and August would be down for a weekend road trip. She immediately began to envision what that would entail. They could sprint for Eureka Springs, Arkansas. Visit the Glass Chapel and walk around the hills to their hearts' content. Paisley had heard there was a hotel there that was rumored to be haunted.

Or maybe they would just find a quiet place to nap and swim. They could sleep in the van. It wouldn't be the pinnacle of comfort or anything, but it would be worth it.

She imagined swimming out to the middle of a lake, with Keegan and August close behind. She imagined dunking her head under the chilly water and swimming as deep as she could go before she burst back to the surface for air.

The thought was calming. She breathed through her nose and allowed a smirk to snuggle into her mouth.

*Do it, Paisley. Ask them as soon as Mom and Malcolm are busy. You don't need her permission or his advice. Just tell her as you're headed out the door.*

It was a fun idea. She needed a break from everything. Yes, even from Reece. Her younger sister had been so clingy lately. Reece needed to make her own friends or learn what to do with herself when Paisley wasn't around. Besides, she and Keegan couldn't smoke when Reece was around.

Not that Mom was doing a *great* job at hiding her habit around her adopted daughter.

Paisley knocked at the bedroom door. It creaked open.

"Hello?" Paisley asked and stepped into Hollie's bedroom. "Krystal?"

She dropped the paper plate. The pizza landed face first on the blood-stained carpet.

Paisley's first thought was that she had fallen sleep in August's arms and was now having a nightmare. She thought that if she pinched her eyes shut and focused really hard, she'd be able to wake up. Or, at the very least, shift to a more manageable dream.

But the steamy smell of death and rot hit her nose and reminded her that she was wide awake.

Krystal was slumped over the bed, on top of the Jesus statue that had been in the woods. Her hands were crawling up and down the statue's shape, testing his bumpy texture. Her head was divided into two halves that flopped open like a crude flower. Her gray brains were leaving a trail along Christ's body. His face and head were soaked. He had gone from pale white to rusty brown.

Krystal had been impaled through the crotch by the statue's heavy penis. She rode it roughly, not seeming to care that the act was like putting a knife through a peach.

*More blood.*

*So much blood.*

Krystal sat up, alerted by Paisley's entrance. Her

two eyes were crimson red and split sideways … and yet they both turned directly toward her. It was as if Krystal could see without seeing.

It was all too impossible. It was a hallucination of the worst sort. Paisley refused to believe what she was watching.

And then Krystal rolled off of the bed. When she smacked into the floor, her head yawned open, exposing the pit of her throat, which was filled with glass shards. The two sides of her head began to clap together rhythmically. The sound of wet meat hitting wet meat was too much to bear, and Paisley found herself backpedaling.

"Oh, God … oh, God … Oh, God!" Paisley shouted.

Krystal began to crawl forward on all fours. Her Venus-flytrap head had become nothing more than a giant mouth. She wasn't Krystal anymore. She was an alien animal.

Paisley turned to run. She didn't like having her back to the Krystal-thing, but she needed to be fast. As she turned out of the room, she collided into a stocky figure.

At first, she thought it was Malcolm, but she was quickly corrected when Wylie reactively shoved her away and then lunged toward her with his meat cleaver.

Paisley feinted to the left and smacked her arm into the door frame. The pain was immediate but manageable. Her balance, on the other hand, was altered. Paisley fumbled with herself before smashing face first into the carpeted floor.

She found herself suddenly happy that her

mother had obstinately kept her fuzzy carpets.

"Get … her!" Wylie shouted in an unhuman tone.

Paisley turned and looked up at him. She was only mildly shocked to see that his throat had been sliced open. She was more shocked by the rapidly developing growths that decorated his face and the two stalks that had been attached to his back.

Krystal came bounding out of the room and scrabbled across the floor toward Paisley.

Paisley screamed and kicked at the Krystal-thing.

She kicked directly in between her bifurcated head and was immediately caught in her open throat. The muscles tightened around Paisley's ankle and sucked her foot down. Krystal had become superhumanly strong, and with two shakes of her whole body, she was able to slam Paisley against one wall and then into another.

Paisley watched helplessly as her shoulders dented the plaster. Her body was already sore and unwilling to cooperate with her. Being slung back and forth like a chew toy had all but drained her. Worse yet, the glass shards were digging into the meat of her ankle and tearing through her shoe. It was as if her right foot had been caught in a vortex of teeth and meat.

*Fuck this*! Paisley slammed her left foot into the side of the Krystal thing. With all her force, she managed to smoosh the side of Krystal's face and pop one of her broken eyeballs out of its socket. The eye landed in the carpet with a soft *plop*.

Krystal began to scuttle backward, drawing

Paisley closer to the looming Wylie-thing. Wylie swiped his meat cleaver once more. Paisley held her arms above her face and watched helplessly as the blade seared her elbow open.

"Oh, God!" Paisley screeched.

Wylie chopped downward.

Paisley's face was suddenly spattered in blood.

When Paisley opened her eyes, she was surprised to see that Wylie's head had vanished. His body wavered on the balls of his feet before pitching forward. It landed on top of the Krystal-thing and crushed her into the ground. Krystal suddenly relinquished her grasp on Paisley and began to struggle against the twitching body of her boyfriend.

Paisley looked down the hall and was overwhelmed with sudden joy.

She had never been happier to see Malcolm in her life.

"Get over here, baby." Malcolm broke his shotgun open. "Get behind me. I don't … I don't think he's dead." He inspected the chamber. "I only got one shell left. Come on, sweetie."

Paisley didn't know if she should laugh or cry. She had no idea where the gun had come from, but she was thankful Malcolm had conjured it. She scuttled to her legs and began to race toward him. She blinked rapidly, hoping to deter the blood that was coursing down her brow and into her eyes.

Behind her, Krystal scratched her way out from beneath Wylie and began to screech unnaturally from her broken throat. The two halves of her head smacked together threateningly.

"Run, girl!" Malcolm bellowed.

"Oh, God!" Paisley screamed and pumped her arms. She could hear Krystal scurrying toward her, her hands and feet spanking into the carpet like a grotesque crab.

"Duck!"

Paisley did as she was told. She hadn't even heard Krystal launch herself forward, but the moment Paisley landed on the ground, she saw a shadow cross overhead.

Krystal had leapt directly into Malcolm's blast. The pellets tore into the insides of her head and sprayed blood and brain matter against the walls. Krystal's body twisted midair, and she landed with a showery *thump* on the ground in front of Paisley.

"I'm out! We've got more in the garage," Malcolm said. "Run down to the basement ... that's where everyone else is." Malcolm sounded surprisingly calm. Paisley was comforted by his voice. It made her blood chill when he added, as if in afterthought: "There are more of these things outside."

"God, Malcolm, what is this—?"

A droplet of Wylie's blood leaked into her mouth and touched her tongue.

And that was all it took.

# CHAPTER TWENTY-FOUR

Malcolm had rushed the kids into the basement the moment he realized what was going on. Not that he quite comprehended it. All he knew was that after sending Paisley up with the pizza, something had seemed amiss outside. He had stood at the kitchen window and scrutinized the tree line. And when the people began to leave the woods and shamble toward the house, his first thought had been that he wasn't actually seeing what was in front of him. He was superimposing an image from an old horror movie over reality. But as their shapes became clearer—each one trailing a tangled rope of organs, each one decorated with bloody gashes, and one with an open chest cavity that would have been impossible to survive with—he realized that this was no hallucination. Something unnatural was happening, and he could either watch it happen or go to work. Malcolm didn't have time to pride himself on his immediate sense of action. He simply ran into the living room, snapped the television off, and turned toward his surrogate family.

"Gang. The storm's looking pretty bad. Let's go into the basement for a bit, okay?"

Hollie was instantaneously concerned. "What is it, Malcolm?"

Malcolm didn't know whether to lie or tell the truth. If he said that zombies were making their gangly way toward the house, he would have prompted them all to go and check for themselves. If he said that a tornado was approaching, he would have felt bad for providing them with a palpable lie and underpreparing them. So, he told an approximate truth.

"We can't panic … but I think the people who hung that thing up in the woods are back, and they're headed toward us. I don't want the children to be in any danger, okay?"

"Oh." Hollie's face was ashen.

Reece was the first to her feet. She was drawn to Malcolm's side like a magnet. She gripped his hand and began to walk toward the kitchen, where the basement door was. As they walked, she spoke in a whisper:

"I'm scared."

"It's okay, baby-doll." Malcolm squeezed her hand tightly. Perhaps too tight. Her knuckles looked white between his fingers. He realized that he was sweating profusely. He hadn't given himself any time to feel his fear.

"Paisley's still upstairs!" August proclaimed.

"And Krystal!" August began to rumble toward the stairs.

Before he even knew what he was doing, Malcolm's free hand lashed out and gripped August's shoulder. "You lead the others downstairs; I'll get them."

August looked up at Malcolm. He looked small and childish under the older man's gaze. Malcolm knew the kid just wanted to help, and he also knew that August cared deeply for Paisley… but Malcolm had to be in charge, and Malcolm had to walk into the unknown territory.

He quickly glanced out the kitchen window. The strangers were closer now. Their skin was beet red, and they seemed to be carrying some bizarre equipment on their backs. What could have been two folded wings stuck out above their shoulders. If Malcolm tried to comprehend it, he would have been completely lost in thought and entirely useless.

"Lead them all downstairs." He handed Reece to August. She absorbed his hand without question.

Hollie was already holding the basement door open. Keegan had vanished into the shadows. Reluctantly but steadily, August led Reece down the stairs.

"Protect them," Malcolm said. "You still have your father's axe down there?"

Hollie gulped. "What is this, Malcolm?"

"I don't know. But I'm getting the shotgun. Whatever you hear, don't leave this basement. I'll come down once I've dealt with things."

The shotgun was in a locked cupboard in the

garage. The girls didn't know about it. Hollie hadn't thought it a necessity, and Malcolm had spent years convincing her that she should have a gun in her house, considering that—unfortunately—the world could be unkind to single females in isolated locations. Hollie was a pacifist and didn't even like the sight of guns. She had confessed on multiple occasions that having the weapon in the house scared her. It had been a form of compromise to have it locked up in the garage.

Malcolm went fast. He barreled through the garage door and skittered across the concrete floor and toward the locked cupboard. As far as Paisley and Reece knew, Malcolm kept some tools in this cupboard, and he kept the combination lock to himself just so no one was tempted to play with any of his sharp instruments. It was true, there was a toolbox on the bottom shelf, but the gun was the main attraction. A Mossberg with two-cartridge capacity. He broke the gun open and peeked inside. It was loaded, just as he had left it.

Malcolm's plan was to step out onto the porch and fire a warning shot over the heads of the strangers. There was a chance that their injuries were an elaborate costume and that one gunshot would send them scattering in different directions. If the first shot didn't scare them off, the second one would be more precise.

He realized he hadn't told anyone to call the police. Not that he had his doubts. Keegan was fast on the draw, and they would probably already be on their phone. Still, he wished he had thought of it just so he wouldn't have the idea clogged inside his brain.

He stepped out of the garage and back into the kitchen.

He was headed toward the front door when he heard the sounds of a struggle resonating from upstairs.

He had been so intent on the strangers, he had already forgotten about Krystal and Paisley.

*Stupid, Malcolm. Stupid! Stupid!*

Malcolm took the stairs two at a time.

# CHAPTER TWENTY-FIVE

Keegan was reminded of the drills they did at school. Every now and then, the fire alarm would go off and the students would be marched outside, unsure whether or not there was an actual emergency. It was even scarier when they did "active shooter" drills. Keegan hated cowering under their desk, waiting for the teacher to admit that this had been preplanned and was only intended to test the student body's readiness and seriousness in case of actual emergencies.

They felt, as they marched into the basement, that at some point, Hollie would grab their arm and say: "Hey, it's okay. It's just a test."

Keegan didn't know what was going on, but they couldn't help but be terrified. Their teeth were set on edge, and their fingers had become a knotted ball. They paced back and forth in the corner of the basement. Keegan watched as Hollie rifled through some dusty bins and produced an axe. The sight of the axe was enough to make Keegan's temperature rise. Their pits became damp, and their teeth furrowed into their lower lip.

"What's going on?" August asked aloud.

Reece had been silent. She clung to August's side and refused to be moved. Keegan couldn't help but wonder what internal traumas were being triggered by this event. Did Reece recall hiding in her bathroom while her mother slaughtered her father? Keegan couldn't begin to imagine. They didn't want to.

"It's going to be okay." Hollie's voice was trembling. She was trying to sound brave, and unfortunately, she was failing.

Keegan had to remain positive. There would be no use in worrying. They took a deep breath and studied their palms. The crisscrossing lines were barely visible in the basement's darkness. The only light was a swinging bulb that flouted overhead. Keegan hadn't noticed who had bothered to turn it on. Was it a good idea to even have a source of light right now? What if the people came down the stairs after seeing a line of white light pouring out from beneath the basement door?

*Malcolm won't even let them near the house. He'll make sure of it. He'll keep all of us safe.*

"I don't know, August." Hollie tested the weight of the axe.

Keegan had seen the tool before. It had belonged to Paisley's grandfather, back when the Karkoff property had sported a Christmas tree farm. There were other sharp implements in this basement too.

Keegan and Paisley had been warned from playing down here in their childhoods. Hollie worried that they would poke their eyes out.

"Trust me," Hollie had said with a giggle, "you wanna keep them both." She had tapped her black eye patch and made a funny face.

Keegan began to root through the mismatched items kept in the basement's corner. There was a box of soggy winter clothes they didn't recognize. There was a folder filled with old photographs. There was even a wooden rocking horse that Keegan vaguely remembered straddling as a kid. They thought they wouldn't find any means of defense …

And then they felt their hand slide across a sharp metal finger. Keegan balked and pulled their hand back. After waiting for their heart to restart, they reached back and pulled the rake out by its dulled tongs. It wasn't a perfect weapon, but holding it gave them confidence. A protective bubble had developed around Keegan.

"Mom!" A voice rang out from upstairs, in tears. "Mom!"

It was Paisley. Keegan felt their heart rise into their throat.

"It's Malcolm! I'm gonna open the door and send Paisley down!" Malcolm's voice shouted.

"Oh, thank God!" August released a heavy groan.

"We couldn't help Krystal." Malcolm's voice broke into a sob while the door swung open. "She's gonna lock the door behind her. Don't open it until the police show up, okay, gang? I'm going to deal with these punks! Everything is gonna be A-okay."

A pair of footsteps began to descend down the steps. They were wobbly and unbalanced. Whatever had happened to Krystal, Keegan already knew that Paisley had witnessed it. She was in shock ... and even worse, Keegan could already see that Paisley's shirt and face were coated in blood.

*Blood? Holy fucking shit. This is real. This is real.*

They heard the basement door didn't close. Light poured down from the kitchen and illuminated Paisley's figure.

Keegan felt like slapping themself in the face. They hadn't even considered locking the door! They needed to get their shit together, for Reece's sake. They took a deep breath and gripped the wooden surface of the rake tightly.

"God." Hollie set the axe down. "Come on down, Paisley! Momma's here!"

Keegan suddenly realized what was wrong.

Paisley was carrying something. She cradled it in her arms like a newborn. But it was the size and shape of a basketball. As Paisley took her rickety steps down the stairs and toward Hollie, Keegan let loose an aggressive shout.

"Hollie! Move!"

Paisley was carrying Malcolm's head.

And Malcolm's head was still impossibly alive.

"Hey, gang!" Malcolm said, as if nothing was wrong.

Paisley released a keening, whinnying laugh that sounded too mean-spirited to have ever been issued from her. Her eyes had gone dark red, and a pulsating thatch of tumors had developed like a goiter beneath her chin.

Reece was the first to scream.

Paisley lifted Malcolm's head and threw it toward Hollie. Hollie had to duck to avoid being smacked by the head. Hollie hit the floor and began to crawl back toward her axe, but the head was now soaring directly toward Keegan.

Keegan couldn't believe what they were seeing. Malcolm's lips and cheeks had been removed. All that remained was red tissue, pink gums, and fearsome rows of straight, white teeth. They looked horribly sharp and canine.

Keegan couldn't afford to think.

They swung the rake. The prongs skidded against Malcolm's scalp and sent him sailing across the room and into the farthest corner. Keegan had wanted the blow to land a lot harder than it had. They had managed to simply bat Malcolm away from themself, August, and Reece.

They wished that they could have somehow put him out of his misery. Malcolm had been a staple of the Karkoff house, and there had never been any reason to fear him. Not until now.

"Let go of me!" Hollie screeched.

Keegan reacquainted their eyes to the situation.

Paisley was grabbing Hollie's foot and yanking her toward the stairs. Her teeth snapped at Hollie's bare ankle. Keegan expected their best friend to take a big bite, but Hollie kicked hard and jostled Paisley backward.

"Get her, honey!" Malcolm crooned from the corner.

Keegan was appalled to see his head had a dent on the side of his brow, right beneath his widow's peak. Pink juices were oozing out of the depression.

"Let her go, Paisley!" August shouted.

"The axe!" Malcolm said. "She's going for the axe!"

"Shut up! Shut up!" August screamed.

"Shut up! Shut up! Shut up!" Malcolm returned in a bullying tone. It was a voice that didn't suit Malcolm at all. It sounded like the voice of a mean old man. It sounded as if it was incapable of good-natured laughter. "Kill her, Paisley! Kill her and make us proud!"

Hollie gripped the handle of the axe but made no move to swing it toward her daughter. She lurched to her feet and backpedaled until she was against the wall, sandwiched between Keegan, Reece, and August.

Keegan brandished their rake once again. They took a deep breath. In through the nose and out through the mouth. What was clear to them was that they had a responsibility to protect Reece ... even if it meant striking their best friend in the face with a rake.

There was clearly no logic to this scenario, and so logic was put on hold.

The thing that looked like Paisley but was obviously not her took a jaunty step forward. Her blood-shot eyes flicked back and forth along the lineup of potential victims. She was trying to surmise what her next move should be, it seemed.

"Paisley." August sobbed, still not acquainted with the strangeness of the situation, still seeking reason. "Paisley, it's okay! It's us! You don't have to hurt us."

Paisley's head snapped toward August. Her brows rose like the hackles of a wolf. She rolled her shoulders and snarled.

"You have to join us, Auggie!" Malcolm hooted. "You have to *give* to *receive*!"

It made no sense ... but talking heads rarely did. Keegan focused their attention on the Paisley-Creature. It was no longer their friend. It was a monster.

Paisley raised her painted nails and dug them into the bulbous meat sack that was ballooning beneath her chin. At first, Keegan thought that she was merely scratching at an itch. But Paisley's fingers dug in easily and left four red furrows in their wake. Following the quick expulsion of blood came a wet pound of white fluid. It looked as if Paisley had released a sack load of tapioca pudding onto the floor.

Now empty, the goiter hung like a wet towel from her throat.

Paisley should have been screaming with pain or alarm. Instead, she cackled. Her laughter reverberated through the basement and crawled underneath Keegan's skin.

As she laughed, Paisley's body began to change. First, a limb exploded out from her back. It tore fabric and skin as it went. It shot upwards, exposing itself to the wavering light swaying above them.

It looked like a featherless wing.

Its counterpart appeared closely afterward. With her two wings now flexing from her back, Paisley held her arms outward as if on display.

*Look at me and be afraid.*

Paisley's face began to contort. More tumors were bubbling up beneath her skin. Her cheeks were pushed out and up like the painted smiles of cherubs. Her red eyes began to swell as tumors grew beneath her lids. White pus began to squirt from her tear ducts. It looked as if two snails had held a race down her cheeks. The eyes themselves were suddenly forced from their sockets. They dangled on their ropes like marshmallows attached to strands of jerky.

Paisley began to advance, raising her hands and curving her fingers into dangerous claws. She was going to hurt them. There was no doubt. With Malcolm's decapitated head egging her on and with her laughter still booming out of her wide mouth, she was going to kill them with her bare hands.

Keegan saw Hollie's body stiffen. She wasn't going to use the axe against her own daughter, even if her daughter was ... what? Possessed? Dead? Mutated?

Paisley's face was still changing even as she strode toward them. Her teeth were being pushed out of her blackened gums. They skittered across the basement floor. Their replacements were yellowed, hooked, and fibrous. It looked as if her mouth had been filled with overgrown fingernails.

"Tear them up! Tear them up!" Malcolm cheered.

Paisley released an animalistic sound like the rumbling of a threatened bear.

Keegan threw the rake down and scrambled

in front of Hollie. "Give it to me!" They yanked the axe away from the older woman, but Hollie refused to let go.

"No!" Hollie balked and pulled against Keegan. "No … that's my daughter!"

The two played a quick game of tug-of-war before Paisley struck.

Keegan didn't even know how it had happened. One second, they were fighting for ownership of the axe and the next …

# CHAPTER TWENTY-SIX

August felt like fainting.

He didn't rightfully know how to grasp what he was seeing.

Keegan and Hollie were jostling back and forth beside him, trying to decide what to do with Grandpa Karkoff's old axe. The axe wasn't a very intimidating weapon. Its blade was dull and wobbly. There didn't seem to be much of a point in even using it against this … *thing*.

This monster that had taken Paisley's place.

This creature which was shedding her skin and replacing it with something crimson and slick.

It looked as if all the blood beneath her flesh had solidified and was now pushing its way out from its human-shaped cocoon. Her teeth were jutting outwards, a foot long each and as sharp as knives. Her eyes jangled back at the ends of their tangled ropes. The wings—for lack of a better word, that's what they were—on her back flexed up and down. They moved in jilted bursts, like the automatic popping of machinery.

August realized, all too late, that Reece had relinquished her grip on his hand.

Paisley released an animalistic screech, one that was fueled with the desire to kill. It was the sound of a rabid dog or a lost cause. It sounded less like a growl and more like a low bleat. There was a waver at its end, which filled August's heart with both dread and sadness.

Keegan tried to pull the axe away from Hollie, but Hollie was holding on tight.

"She's my daughter!" Hollie defended. "Don't you *dare* hurt her!"

"It's not *her*, Ms. Karkoff. It's not her!" Keegan whined. Their voice, much like Paisley's, ended with a tremble. "Please!"

The Paisley-thing was nearer. Her horrible mutations weren't finished. Her legs seemed to peel open, as if she had walked through a force field that tore her clothes and skin away and left it in a wet pile behind her. The tendon lashed stilts that remained were more skeleton than muscle, and they ended in what looked like a rounded hoof. Paisley's feet clopped as she progressed.

Malcolm's head was keening with laughter. The sick and psychopathic laughter of a drunkard. August didn't have the ability to focus on Malcolm. He was sure that his head was changing as well. It was probably ballooning with tumors, and his teeth had probably been replaced by the same fingernail mandibles that jutted from Paisley's mouth.

*Paisley's mouth* … August had just kissed her a few minutes ago. They had been laughing and watching the movie, and Paisley had quickly pulled him in and touched his lips with hers. His face had grown hot, and his tongue had rolled over his teeth.

"What was that for?" August had asked.

"No reason, dumbass. I just like you." She stuck her tongue out.

"You're so mean." He laughed and kissed her tenderly on her cheek.

"Eww," Reece moaned.

"Yeah. That's G-R-O-S-S." Malcolm had mocked them from across the room with a chortle.

"God." Keegan rolled their eyes. "Straight people."

Hollie tried to contain a mouthful of giggles.

Afterwards, Malcolm had sent Paisley up with a paper plate of pizza for Krystal.

And now … now, they were cornered by a demonic creature that had burst out from Paisley's body.

Keegan shouted in their sternest voice:

"Reece, get back!"

"Oh, God! Baby!" Hollie yelped.

August shook his head and refocused his attention on what was happening. Reece was walking toward Paisley with a bravery that couldn't be understood, much less emulated. August's back was glued to the wall, and he refused to budge.

"Paisley." Reece's throat was clogged with tears. "Paisley, come back!"

"Reece!" Hollie dashed forward with the axe

raised over her head. "Reece, get back!"

One of Paisley's arms lashed out and smacked into the underside of Hollie's jaw. August could hear Hollie's teeth clack together. It sounded like two coconuts being beaten together. Hollie stumbled back. The axe dropped from her fingers and smashed into the ground. Keegan was quick to scramble after it. Their hands grabbled with the handle and managed to heft it upward, but as they swung toward Paisley, Reece began to intercept the blade's swing.

August leapt into action. It was intuitive. He knew on a subconscious level that if Keegan accidently swiped Reece's little head off, none of them would be able to sleep at night. They all may as well die then and there.

"Let her GO!" Reece screeched.

August barreled into Keegan and knocked them off balance. They toppled to the floor. The axe skittered across the room and landed in the white and red slop that Paisley had left behind her.

August quickly crawled off of Keegan and went to retrieve the axe. His plan wasn't formulated yet. He could try and plant the blade into the demon's back ... but ... it was still Paisley. He could pass it back to Keegan and let them go to work. Keegan seemed to have all the nerve that August lacked, their timing was just off.

As he went, he looked back and saw Keegan was clutching their head and moaning. August had pounced upon them with too much force and had hit their head against the concrete floor. He flirted with the notion of apologizing, but there was no time.

"No! Put her down!" An irate voice boomed out from the corner.

August took a second to register that it was Malcolm.

"Put her down!"

August gripped the handle of the axe and yanked it toward him. Some of Paisley's white and red goop came with it. The gunk squeezed between his fingers as he tightened his hold on the wooden handle.

"Put her down right now, you bitch!" Malcolm shrieked, desperate to be heard.

August looked at Paisley. She had Reece by the throat and had lifted her off of the ground. Her bubbling skin had distorted her image so much that not even the memory of Paisley survived. Her hair hung in wet clumps on her scalp. Her bumpy skull was barely exposed beneath a membranous layer of scarlet skin.

Reece's feet were actively kicking against Paisley's chest. Her hands ensnared Paisley's wrist. Reece's face was growing purple.

Was there a piece of Malcolm left inside his decapitated head? Was that what was crying out for Paisley's mercy right now?

"He doesn't want *her d*ead!" Malcolm screamed. "Kill the others!"

August swung the axe. It sunk into Paisley's back for only a second. The flesh seemed to reject the axe, forcing it from its lodging with propulsive force. The weapon fell, dragging August with it. His knees scuffed the floor.

August reeled back, lifted the axe, and chopped again. The blade bounced against Paisley's spine.

*Oh God … I didn't want to do this. I'm so sorry, Paisley. I'm so sorry.*

"Kill him! Kill the boy and let Reece Brampton go!"

Malcolm would *never* use Reece's original last name. Reece was a Karkoff. Reece was not her mother's child anymore; she was Hollie's. Hearing Malcolm's voice say such a horrible thing and in such a disgusting way spurred more anger through August's body.

He yanked the axe out and swung again. This time, he beat the blade into Paisley's neck. Her head cranked sideways as her neck-meat was inverted. Her hooved feet clopped in unsteady beats, and her grip slackened. Reece dropped to the ground with a choking cough.

August pulled the axe free and took a step back. He expected Paisley to stumble helplessly before collapsing to the ground and dying. But that wasn't what happened. Paisley instead swiveled backward until her deformed face was pointed toward August.

"Kill him!" Malcolm jeered. "Fucking tear him to pieces!"

Paisley released an operatic wail toward August. She raised her left hand—

And it was met with the axe's blade.

August watched as the blade neatly sliced between Paisley's middle and index finger and dug into the wrist. Paisley pulled away, her hand flapping into two useless halves. She released a pathetic whimper and bumbled forward.

August swung the axe again, this time burying it into her shoulder.

But that didn't stop her. Paisley slammed into him, knocking the wind out of his chest. August faltered and felt his feet slide in the mucus pile behind him. He landed on his rear with a hard thump that instantly drew tears.

August watched as Paisley pulled the axe out from her shoulder with her left hand and tested its weight. Her face was beyond recognition. The teeth had grown into a thick cluster like a fungal growth. Her bobbing eyes bore no expression, and her nose had slid off in all the mayhem. All that remained was a hollow hole.

And still, August couldn't help but imagine that under all that mess, Paisley was smiling victoriously.

"She's gonna get you now, child! She's … knocking … you … *doooown*!" Malcolm whooped. "You're gonna suffer like us! You're gonna join the horde! Welcome … to the MEAT PIT!"

Paisley took a crude step forward.

She raised the axe above her head.

"She's gonna give you … what … you … got … *coming*!"

August closed his eyes.

# CHAPTER TWENTY-SEVEN

Keegan had decided that holding on to Reece would be the best route of action. After they recovered from August's hurdle, they crawled toward the young child and wrapped their arms around her. If Reece was going to die, she was going to die knowing that she was being protected with every breath in Keegan's body.

Reece was still struggling to calm her breathing down after being choked by Paisley. Her gasps came like desperate gulps, as if she was bobbing in and out of a tumultuous wave. Her neck had gone black and blue, and her eyes were squeezing tears. Reece responded to Keegan's embrace instantaneously. She wrapped her arms around Keegan's slender neck and pulled them close.

"It's okay." Keegan began to drag Reece back toward the wall. "We'll be okay."

Reece was crying. Sometimes, she was so quiet

and so stoic, Keegan tended to forget how young she really was. Reece was only ten years old. She had borne witness to tragedy before, and it had followed her here to this sanctuary. Keegan pitied her, feared for her, and wanted to keep her safe.

*Let me be a bubble. Let me be a shield. No one is going to hurt her.* Keegan wasn't sure if these thoughts counted as prayers or not, but they sent them upwards anyway. They could only hope that there would be a god and they would be all ears.

Keegan covered Reece's eyes and allowed her to curl into their chest. They were an armadillo, using their body to conceal the child as best they could. But Keegan couldn't help but look upon the horror show happening in front of them.

Hollie was stone-cold unconscious. Her lips were bleeding, and her good eye had gone white. The blow to her jaw had sent her right into the wall. In a lot of ways, Hollie was lucky. Keegan wished that they were unconscious, just so that they would wake up in a few hours and find that the storm had blown over in their sleep. But there was no calm and no hope for rest.

Instead, all Keegan could do was watch as Paisley raised her axe over her head and prepared to bring it down into August. Would he scream, or would all of his sounds be stopped short? Keegan wished they could help him too, but there was nothing they could do. They could beat Paisley with the rake, but clearly, Paisley would have only seen such a thing as a minor irritation. The gashes where August had hit her were all loathsome to behold. Each one looked like a black smile etched into her crimson flesh.

And they hadn't done a damn thing to stop her.

Even her broken neck didn't impede her.

Paisley was about to swing the axe down and strike a horrible blow into August. Her red skin shimmered in the swaying beam of light above her, and her whole arm seemed to crackle with anticipation.

And then, something happened. Paisley froze as if she had been caught in the stare of a gorgon. Her body seemed to seize up as she was gripped by an invisible hand.

August lay on the ground. He held his arms up to shield his face. His cheeks were saturated with tears. He seemed to have thought the blow had already fallen because his whole body jumped and he released a sound like a door creaking open. But upon realizing that he had suffered no damage, he lowered his arm and looked up at his aggressor.

Paisley craned her head backward with much strain and effort. She was looking toward Keegan. No, she was looking just beneath their face. She was looking—as best she could—at Reece. Both of her eyes dangled outside her sockets, but the direction of her preternatural gaze was honest.

She was looking at Reece.

Keegan followed suit.

Reece's face was buried into Keegan's chest, but her right arm was sticking out and aimed at the demon. Her fingers were splayed out like spider legs, and her wrist vibrated like a tuning fork. Keegan put a hand on top of her head and compressed it closer to their chest.

The demon's head snapped back and faced August. Keegan thought that the hesitation had been for dramatic effect, but then Paisley released a low whine, the sound of a broken radio slurring into static. The sound was obvious. It was the sound of defeat.

"What—?" Keegan started to ask before they were interrupted by a new noise.

"No! No!" Malcolm crowed. "No! You bitch! Killing her won't do anything! There are so many of us! You can't stop us all!"

Paisley clutched at her stomach and released a gruesome belch. It sounded like a dog preparing to vomit. It instantly filled Keegan with revulsion.

Reece turned her head, pushing against Keegan's hand, and looked at Paisley. Her outstretched arm became steadier the longer she held it. She was focusing all of her attention on the limb.

Keegan had no idea what was happening, but it felt advantageous. And so, they gripped Reece's elbow and held it steady for her.

As they did, they felt a static shock zap through them. Their whole arm felt hollow and ice cold. It was as if they had licked a battery. Or worse … as if they had been stabbed and gone numb. Reflexively, they pulled their hand away from Reece's arm.

"No! No! No!" Malcolm's head gnashed its gnarled teeth. "No! You can't do this! This isn't fair!"

Reece turned her arm toward Malcolm's head. Fixating her attention on him seemed to release Paisley from her hold. Paisley stumbled backward, dropping the axe at August's feet. August grabbed the axe and scuttled backward with it.

"You ... bitch!" Malcolm's head gurgled before it popped like a blister. Gray brains, snotty pus, and blood crawled up the wall and crept across the floor. Keegan released a sharp gasp and clutched Reece closer. They couldn't believe what they were watching.

As soon as Malcolm was smeared across the wall, Reece returned her attention to Paisley. It was as if she was seizing the demonic creature in a giant invisible vice. Paisley stood still, her arms upraised and her head tilted back.

Paisley's mouth was flooding with blood and inky fluids. They spurted and sprayed out as if bubbling up from a fountain's top. The blood coursed down her neck and splashed onto the floor between her cloven hooves.

Paisley's legs snapped back like a grasshopper. Her body jilted downward and wavered midair. She looked like a puppet being precariously held by limp strings. Her arms swung at her sides in an attempt to steady herself.

Reece gripped her hand into a fist.

And when she did this, Paisley's head completely rotated. It traveled backward so that it was affixed between her stumpy wings and then snapped downward into her body. A hard, crispy bone shot out from the sudden twist. The protuberance was followed by a swift spurt of black fluid.

Paisley collapsed.

A beat of silence passed between Keegan, Reece, and August ... before the boy spoke up.

"What the fuck?" August gasped.

Keegan noted that it was the first time they had ever heard him properly swear.

# CHAPTER TWENTY-EIGHT

Outside the house, the horde froze. Wylie, Sam, Chuck, Tanith, Moby, Krystal, Hurwitz, Liam, Darlene … even Chilton had been resurrected. The arrow still stuck through his throat. No one had bothered to remove it.

They had heard the death of two of their own and were unsure of how to proceed. Malcolm was spattered across the wall, and Paisley had been twisted like a dishcloth. Hearing it in their heads had been a terrifying ordeal. Krystal had started to whimper pitifully at the bottom of her tattered throat. Chuck couldn't keep it together and had started to unleash a volley of tears.

Tasting the blood of The Fallen One was like connecting to a beehive. What one demon felt, the others had to endure in equal measure. They felt the pain of every axe wound, and they felt the horror as Paisley's neck cracked. They had expected her to shake the pain and continue her assault, but they had all been surprised when she dropped to the ground and expired. It was as if a bulb had gone out in a string of Christmas lights.

*Reece did it. She killed one of us … it's true,* Hurwitz thought. *Everything The Fallen One said … it's all true. She is who he said she is.*

Not that Hurwitz had any doubts. He took The Fallen One at His word. And yet, it was reassuring to have proof. Even if that proof put him in more danger.

Krystal was standing upright. Her divided head lay like a pair of pads on her shoulders. She and Wylie were carrying the statue between them like pallbearers at a funeral.

They had all thought that Paisley would dispatch Hollie, August, and Keegan, and then they could take Reece to The Fallen One. But alas, Paisley hadn't even managed to take any of them out. She had knocked Hollie unconscious, yes … but not even a drop of Paisley's infected blood had landed on an unwilling tongue. No one had been converted.

"She's … dead …" Moby moaned around his broken mouth. A rope of blood seeped out of the hole behind his chin. His tongue had swollen between his teeth like a gruesome plum.

"Not … done … yet," Hurwitz rasped. "The Fallen One … is … waiting. Deliver … her … to him. By any … means …"

Tanith tilted her head sideways. Her face was unrecognizable. It looked like shredded cheese. Her mouth opened, and she moaned a quiet confirmation. As she did so, her wings puffed upwards, extending in length.

"Have … faith," Hurwitz gasped. "The … others … will … be here … soon."

The rain was still falling from overhead. Hurwitz could feel his skin sizzle under the moisture. He scratched at his cheeks with his claws. The talons had burst out underneath his fingernails. They were six inches long each, curved, and ink black. They were as thick as steak knives too. He felt as if he was transforming into a predatory animal. A lion, or better yet … a tiger. With one swipe of his claws, he'd ruin someone.

His chest was stilling yawning open, but even that hole was beginning to develop new means of defense. Upon the ridges of his injuries, little black studs were blossoming. They looked like the spiked undersides of a pair of cleats. With great strain and effort, he found that he was able to flex the cavernous hole open and closed like the chomping mouth of a fast-moving fly trap. But the motion caused him great amounts of pain. It was as if all of his bones were breaking over and over again.

His comrades were developing their own mutations. Not all of them, but most. Moby's tongue had grown even larger in the seconds following his last words. Its end was a hooked barb, much like the stinger of a wasp. A gray fluid shone like a diamond on the barb's tip.

Hurwitz watched Moby intently. He reached out and grazed his finger pad against the barb. It flexed backward like a turtle's head and then unspooled after Hurwitz backed away. Moby's head cracked backward, and the tongue wriggled loose from between his jaw. It flouted by his chest like an extraordinary tentacle before snipping at Hurwitz. Hurwitz stumbled backward, surprised and pleased by this development.

"You … and … me." Hurwitz moaned. "Inside. We'll take care of them."

The tongue bobbed approvingly before slinking back into Moby's mouth. His head snapped back into place. His eyes waggled in their sockets, moving but unemotional. They may as well have been fitted in a doll's head.

"I'm … different," Moby said.

"No." Hurwitz placated him with a reassuring hand to the shoulder. "You're gifted."

"I'm … gifted … too." Sam stumbled forward. His mouth hung open. His jaw had been broken by Chuck's fist. The bottom portion of his head swayed back and forth like a porch bench. Speaking was especially hard for him, and the words came out in burps. "Look."

Sam held up his left hand, displayed the bones protruding from his knuckles. They were rounded plates, and each one was topped with a hard nub. He curled his hand into a fist, displaying an armored club that was capable of braining a human skull with one swift punch.

Moby groaned. "To kill … and convert … the family."

Hurwitz turned toward his congregants and began to make demands. It seemed fitting that, even now, he was still a leader. "The rest … into …

the forest. Join … our Master. Wait … for us. We'll … bring … the girl."

Hurwitz's lips peeled into a vicious smile. He coughed and began to shunt toward the house.

One unsteady step at a time.

# CHAPTER TWENTY-NINE

Hollie woke up after two shakes. She rubbed at her eye single eye with the heel of her hand. "Wha-happen?" She sounded like a child that had fallen asleep halfway through a movie and needed to be caught up on the plot.

Keegan felt bad waking Hollie Karkoff up. She probably thought that the awful thing that had once been her daughter was part of an elaborate and horrible dream. They didn't want to be a bearer of bad news, but they had no choice. They needed to find shelter, and they needed to move fast. There was no time to even question how Reece had done what she had done. Or if Reece had even been at all responsible for the deaths of the two demons in the basement.

Keegan looked over their shoulder and at the stairway, where August and Reece were standing. August had a protective hand on Reece's shoulder.

They would have left without Hollie if Reece hadn't screamed, "We forgot Momma!" halfway up the stairs.

"Oh … oh god." Hollie's eyes had fallen onto the pile of guts, skin, and muscle that had once been her daughter. "Oh God!"

Keegan's brain spoke eloquently, conveying the things they wanted to communicate to Hollie in that moment. But they couldn't actually say the words. They felt like slabs of concrete being pushed through mud. Keegan thought: *So, Ms. Karkoff … it wasn't a dream after all. This is what has become of your only biological daughter … and my best friend. No one misses Paisley any more than I do, ma'am. I grew up with her. I had slumber parties with her. When I came out, I cried in her arms and she told me that she accepted me. But, I have no time to weep over her. Because there are more of what she became. Lots more.*

What Keegan said was a lot simpler:

"We have to fucking get out of here. Right now."

Keegan hated sounding so callous. They of all people should have been in tears and shambles. But their survivalist instinct was kicking in, as imperfect and as ignorant as it was. Keegan didn't know what they were supposed to do, all they knew was that they had to move. If they didn't, they'd be trapped in this basement. And they had a feeling that locking the door wouldn't be an effective method of fortification.

If one of those demons could survive as many injuries as Paisley took on, imagine what a crowd was capable of doing! It filled Keegan's heart and mouth with panic. Their pulse was thumping in their ears. A rhythmic beat that chugged endlessly away right in their mind, as if they were trapped in a hellish nightclub.

"Okay? We gotta go. Okay?"

"Okay." Hollie's words ebbed out drunkenly. "Okay." She needed help getting to her feet. The blow to her head had most likely caused a concussion.

"Can you walk?" Keegan asked while draping the woman's arm over their shoulder.

"Yeah. A little. Where's Malcolm's gun?"

"I don't know where it is. I don't think it would work here anyways. They … don't seem to be hurt by … weapons." Keegan wished they could sound like a cool and confident action hero, but their words were as jumbled as their mind was. How did tough guys come up with one-liners on the fly?

*They don't. They just follow the script.*

Keegan didn't understand why their inner narrative was following so many rabbit trails. Maybe it was their way of processing the events that they had just witnessed and participated in.

"What do we do?" August asked, looking at Keegan for leadership.

"I don't know. Fuck. Shit." Keegan rolled their eyes. Hollie was putting all of her weight on Keegan's narrow shoulders.

They lumbered up the stairs as slowly as they could go, hoping that their deliberation would pay off and they would have a plan by the time they reached the basement door.

Nothing came to mind.

"The axe." August hefted it up.

Reece was still holding his free hand, and she looked up at the axe with wide eyes.

"I could go out swinging. Clear room for you guys to book it to the van or something." His sacrificial offer was noble, but Keegan could tell he was hoping someone had a better idea.

"No," Reece mumbled. "No. We shouldn't let anyone go."

"Reece." Keegan grabbed the little girl and turned her face away from August. They hadn't realized that they had let go of Hollie. Hollie, thankfully, was awake enough to slump against the rickety banister and tilt her head upwards. She covered her single eye with her hand and released an exasperated huff.

"Reece," Keegan repeated, encompassing the child's full attention. "Did you do something to those things?"

Reece shrugged. "I think so."

"How?"

Reece didn't know. She was obviously looking for answers, but there were none to be found. "I just didn't want them to hurt you guys. And I-I don't kn-know."

Keegan set their forehead against Reece's. The child was sweaty and hot, as if she was running a fever. Her little hands were still trembling. "Whatever you did, it was very brave. Thank you."

Reece balked. "Did I kill Malcolm? And Paisley?"

"No!" Keegan and August said at once.

"That wasn't them. They both loved you very much and ... and they would never treat any of us the way they did. Whatever those things were, they took their shapes to hurt us."

"So, are they still alive?" There was a twinkle of hope in Reece's eyes.

Keegan looked up at August. His eyes were alight as well. She had almost forgotten that Paisley was his girlfriend and that he had truly and authentically loved her.

How hard had it been for any of them to defend themselves against a monster that took the form of someone they loved?

"I hope so, Reece," Keegan muttered. "I hope so."

Keegan looked up at August. His eyes were moist. He was struggling to hold back a sob.

*Paisley was his girlfriend and he loved her.*

*Paisley was Hollie's daughter and she loved her.*

*Paisley was my best friend and I loved her.*

Keegan swiped her hand across their forehead, brushing their hair aside. They reinstated their eye contact with Reece and pulled her into a tight hug.

"Reece, honey." Hollie was still slurring her words. "Are you okay?"

*What a dumb question.* Keegan felt a horrible spurt of anger rush up their throat. They held it back. There was really no such thing as a dumb question. All of them were in a position they had never envisioned. What else could Hollie ask?

"Go hug your momma." Keegan shuffled aside so that Reece could waddle across the stairs and fall into Hollie's arms. Hollie sighed aloud and nestled her head against Reece's.

*It's okay. Hollie's waking up. She got whupped pretty hard.* Keegan bit into their tongue and sidled up the stairs and toward the door. They pressed their ear against the door and listened closely.

Keegan could hear the rain pattering on the roof and bumping against the windows. They could hear bursts of thunder tearing the sky apart. They couldn't hear any intruders or stalking demons.

That didn't mean there wasn't a crowd of them silently waiting outside of the door, ready to pour in the moment the door swung open. The mental image that accompanied this thought was too gruesome to focus on.

"What do you hear?" August asked.

"Nothing."

"Did you hear what … the head said? When the monster grabbed Reece?"

"I can't remember."

"He s-said they weren't allowed to kill her."

"I can't even afford to think about it too much, Auggie." Keegan sighed. "If I stop and think about one thing, I have to think about all of it and … I'm not ready for that."

"Yeah. Of course. But, what if she's—I don't know. You saw what she did to them. What if she can do that to … the rest?"

All this postulating wasn't doing anyone any good. But Keegan couldn't help but think … what if they had an indestructible weapon by their side? A ten-year-old girl that was currently crying in her mother's breast. But Keegan felt wrong for using Reece as a weapon. Reece didn't even need to be seeing any of this, much less actively participating in it. But what could they do?

She had killed them. Both of them.

And she didn't even have to touch them.

Keegan pulled their head back. "What do we do? What are our options?"

"We could go for the car," August said.

"Fuck!" Keegan suddenly shouted and slapped a hand against their mouth. "We didn't even call for help!"

"Oh my god, are we idiots?" August asked.

"My phone was inside. I didn't bring it down." Hollie seethed.

"I … I don't have mine on me. It must still be in the living room. Shit."

Keegan reached into their back pocket and yanked their cell phone free. Their heart dropped as quickly as it had risen. The screen was smashed inwards. It had been broken during the fight with the demon and the tackle they had received from August.

Keegan tapped the on button, hoping that they could maneuver their finger around the broken glass … but the phone wouldn't even start.

"I have mine," Reece said in a whisper.

"Oh, thank god." Hollie squeezed her daughter tightly.

Reece pulled her phone out and scanned her thumb. After a moment's hesitation, she handed it to Keegan. "I don't know what to say."

"Neither do I." Keegan dialed an emergency line.

Keegan held the phone to their ear and waited for the line to click open. They recognized the voice on the other end. It was Sweet-Anne Sawyer.

"Kissing-Brooke Police Station! What can we

do for y'all?" Sweet-Anne sounded like she had just downed a mouthful of coffee. Keegan was comforted by the familiarity of her voice.

"Yes … this is Keegan Peterson!"

"Oh, Keegan! How's your dad? You know we miss him here!" Sweet-Anne obviously didn't understand that this was an emergency situation. Keegan didn't blame her. Nothing like this ever happened in Kissing-Brooke. "He was such a good cop, you know? Always so tender and kind. He didn't even like to give out speeding tickets."

"Listen, Sweet-Anne! Something bad happened. I'm at the Karkoff farm and … you need to send help immediately. We have … intruders."

Sweet-Anne didn't hear them. "Well, speak of the devil! Here's your old man now! Mr. Peterson! I've got your little girl on the line here!"

The misgendering didn't even faze Keegan at this point. They were more peeved that Sweet-Anne didn't even understand the gravity of a phone call to the police.

"Say hullo to your daughter, Mr. Peterson!"

There was a shuffle of noise … and then …

A low, coarse burble. Followed by the sound of a *splat*. It reminded Keegan of a tomato being dropped on the kitchen floor.

"Uhhhhhhh." The familiar sound of their father's voice leaked through the phone. "Kill … meeeeeeee …." There was another wet sound, like a nose being blown. The sloshing sounds that followed were too ghastly for Keegan to comprehend. "Kill … ME!"

"Daddy!" Keegan called.

"Kill me! Kill me! Why won't you let me die!" The sound of a bone breaking forced Keegan to hang up. They couldn't take any more of it. Keegan dropped the phone into their lap and buried their face in their hands. "It's everywhere. What's happening here is happening in town too."

"Oh, God," Hollie muttered.

"We're fucked. We're actually fucked." August breathed deeply.

"God … Daddy." Keegan sobbed. "Daddy …"

This wasn't helpful. Keegan wiped at their tears and tried to compose themself, only to collapse into violent, spastic weeping. They felt like a worm on a hook being dangled over a hungry pond. They felt trapped, and angry, and sad. Most of all, they felt like this whole situation was unjust and that none of them deserved to be here.

Reece didn't deserve this.

Paisley didn't deserve what had happened to her …

"What do we do?" August said. "No cops … no Malcolm … no one can help us."

God, Keegan hated this. They hated their own helplessness. Keegan wished that they had the ability to pop demon heads open the way Reece had. They hated that they were backed into this corner where Reece was their only option of survival.

"We need to make a run for the car," Keegan said. "Hey … Reece. Come here." Keegan stretched an arm out and took Reece's hand.

"What?" Reece asked with a whimper. Hollie's hands rested on her shoulders. Her lips were trembling, and her eyes were as large as saucers. Keegan had never seen such a small and terrified thing before in their entire life.

"That thing you did to the monsters. Can you do it again?"

Reece nodded but said: "No. I don't know what that was. I don't want to hurt anyone."

"They aren't people anymore," Keegan said. "They're …"

What were they? Demons had seemed to be the easiest place to land on, but Keegan didn't know if that was quite it. Despite the red skin, cloven hooves, and spiky wings, there had been something more like an infection to it. That goiter filled with pus that had popped on Paisley's neck reminded Keegan of a zombie from a gross-out horror movie. But still, demon seemed to fit, and so Keegan used the word.

"They're demons. I don't know if it's like the Bible or not, but … that's what they are."

"It wasn't Paisley. It wasn't Malcolm." August spoke through his teeth, more to himself than to the child that needed reassuring.

Keegan felt extra cheesy saying this, but they had to. "When you reached your arm out were you … praying?"

"No," Reece said. "I was just …"

Hollie's fingers went white from kneading her daughter's shoulders.

"Ow, Mom!" Reece yelped.

"Sorry." Hollie loosened her grip.

"What were you thinking?" Keegan asked politely and calmly.

"I was thinking about … my mom." Something in Reece's expression told Keegan that she wasn't referring to Hollie. "I was remembering how helpless I felt when my mom killed my dad. I was just locked behind the bathroom door … a-and I reached out and imagined breaking the door down."

"Oh, hun." Hollie moaned. "I'm so sorry."

"I imagined the door splintering through the middle, and that's when … Paisley started to … That's right when I got control." Reece shook her head. "But I don't know how it happened, and I don't know if I can do it again! Keegan, I'm scared, and I just want to leave!"

"We will." Keegan released Reece's hand. "And you don't have to do anything like that again. But … I want you to protect yourself, okay?" Keegan offered a small smile. "Don't worry about me or August or even your momma. All of us … all of us want to keep you safe, okay?"

"Okay." Reece sniffled.

"If one of those things starts coming toward you, I want you to break the door down, okay?"

"I won't let them hurt you." Reece moaned. "I'll try my best but … I just … I don't know what it was. I don't know why this is … happening."

With no coordination whatsoever, the four of them fell into a group hug. They lashed their arms together and shared a long and well-deserved sob. Reece was buried in the middle of their body knot, crying hard and leaking drool. Her little eyes flitted up to Keegan's and pleaded for her to wake them all up from this nightmare.

*Would that I could, kiddo,* Keegan thought. *Would that I could.*

Suddenly, the basement door was ripped away from its hinges. The movement was so fluid and loud that Keegan had mistaken the sound of breaking wood and popping hinges for a series of rapid gunshots.

August was the first to launch himself forward. He bravely swung Hollie Karkoff's grandfather's axe ... and was met with a punch to the face. His nose popped, and a gout of blood sputtered across the walls. The axe clattered to the ground between the assailant's feet. August wavered and tipped backward, threatening to tumble down the stairs, if not for the arms of Keegan and Hollie. Hollie had shoved Reece behind her back. The child was peeking out from behind her mother's legs. Her mouth hung open, and her knees knocked together.

The creature looked vaguely more human than Paisley had. He had dark hair and a long face. His jaw hung precariously open. His back was decorated with hard "wings," and his hands looked like rolled up pill-bugs with armored grooves.

The creature's hands uncurled, revealing that his fingertips were rounded studs ending in sharpened nubs. His skin had gone crimson red, and his left leg ended in a cloven hoof. His right leg was normal, but the skin breaking out from the seams of his jeans was purple and swollen.

"Want ..." The creature tried to annunciate his words despite his broken mouth. "The girl."

"No!" Hollie barked. "You can't have her!"

Keegan worked to stand August on his feet. His

face was covered in blood, and his nose tilted to the right uncomfortably. He was woozy, and he blinked slowly.

"Just hand us the girl!" An impatient and elderly voice squeaked from behind the creature. "Sam, move!" The monster stepped aside to reveal something even more hideous: an old man whose chest had been snapped open like a fearsome mouth. As he clopped forward on his hooves, Keegan saw that the fissure was lined with sharpened teeth. They were black needles that reminded them of a cluster of sea urchins. "Give us Reece Brampton!"

Sam smacked his clubbed hands against his chest. The beat issued forth a spout of blood from the back of his throat. Keegan also heard what she thought must have been a snapping rib. The demon named Sam didn't even care if he hurt himself!

"You aren't getting her." Hollie fanned her arms out in defense. "I swear to God, you aren't going to touch her."

"We don't want to hurt her, ma'am." The old man spoke surprisingly politely. "She needs to take her place by His feet."

Sam beat his own chest again. His ribs seemed to sink inwards, like a branch disappearing in a current. He released a wet laugh, which was followed by a blood-stained belch.

"Just give us the girl, and we'll make your deaths quick," the old man said. "That's the only mercy you will be afforded."

Keegan's eyes drifted to the axe. It lay between both demons now. They weighed their options. If they got the axe, it wouldn't do much, but at least they would be armed. If they missed the axe, they would land right in the demon's clutches. Keegan didn't want that. Their guts turned at the thought of being pummeled by Sam's massive fists … or caught in the giant mouth seared through the old man's chest.

"There are so many more of us that there are of you. Please, give us the girl. Just hand her over." Hurwitz seemed to relish this unbalanced bargain. He knew they had only two choices: defend Reece and die trying, or …

"You don't get to hurt my family!" Reece pointed her arm at the two fiends.

Nothing happened. Hurwitz and Sam both released a small snicker.

"No!" Reece seethed and flexed her fingers. "Don't take one step closer!"

"Or what?" Sam breathed. "Or … *what*?"

"You aren't in control here, child. He is." Hurwitz pointed a claw toward the Heavens. "The Fallen One controls us all. He even owns you. And He will not abide this world until you are sitting by His side … where you *belong*—"

Sam took a step forward, and his head exploded. It was like watching a watermelon be annihilated with an invisible hammer. His skull cracked open and then was forced downward into the space between his shoulders. His dislocated jaw twirled into the air before landing with a clatter. His eyes were squeezed out of their sockets and vanished from sight in the ensuing plumage of gore. As his shoulders were caped in blood, his hands raised as if to throw one last punch. They then flopped uselessly to his sides before his body slumped down and expired on the floor.

The old man seemed shocked. He looked at his dead comrade and released a soft whistle.

"I was really hoping this would be easier."

"I'll kill you too." Reece was unsure of her words. Keegan was too. They knew that Reece was re-experiencing her worst traumas just to defend her surrogate family, and that had to be taking a toll on her. Keegan wished once more that whatever abilities she had could be passed on. Keegan wished they could take this responsibility for the little girl and she could keep her eyes closed.

But if they weren't sure of it before, they were now. They only had one weapon. One source of hope and strength.

It was Reece Karkoff.

Not Brampton … Karkoff.

The old man raised his hands and took a small step backward. "You must sit by His side. Even if I don't deliver you, it is your destiny, girl."

"I don't care," Reece muttered. "I want to leave. I want all of us to leave."

"I will oblige." Hurwitz frowned. He obviously didn't like losing the upper hand. "But you won't get far."

Keegan took the first brave step out of the basement. They were followed by August. Hollie cradled Reece in her loving arms and was next out. The four of them slowly shuffled past the old man. Hurwitz kept his hands in plain sight. His mouth had broken into a disgusting smirk, and his tongue rolled around between his sharpened teeth.

"You won't get far."

Keegan wanted to tell Reece to just go ahead and kill the bastard. What use did a demon like this have in staying alive? But they wouldn't dream of using a child like a loaded gun. This was Reece's cross to bear, and Keegan wasn't going to assume they could tell her what to do and what not to do with her powers.

*Reece has powers … like … a superhero? No. More complex than that. I don't think she can pop just anyone's head. It has to be someone like these things. And what was it the old man had been rambling about? Who is The Fallen One?*

Keegan couldn't ruminate on their many thoughts for much longer. They gripped the doorknob leading to the garage, where they had parked the minivan. They were inches away from freedom now. All they had to was turn the knob and usher everyone out and then—

Then what? This wasn't just a localized threat. They had heard Sweet-Anne on the phone. Whatever it was, it had spread through Kissing-Brooke. Maybe it was global.

Keegan opened the door.

And was immediately face to face with another demon.

This one had long blond hair. His head was tilted backward like the lid of a cookie jar, revealing a horned slug between his jaws. It was his tongue. The muscle had grown to a horrible size and was as blackened as charred meat. Its tip ended in a sharpened stinger, which flexed and seeped with mucus. The tongue *thwipped* out like a chameleon's.

Keegan ducked down and watched as the slippery muscle whizzed over their head—

And implanted its stinger into Reece's neck.

Hollie was already backpedaling and screaming, trying to wriggle Reece away from the imbedded stinger. As Hollie went, her legs knotted together with Reece's. Together, the entangled pair toppled.

Reece flopped over … unmoving. Her eyes had gone white, and Keegan saw foam forming at the edges of her mouth. She didn't even twitch or shake.

The tongue was still attached to her like a malformed umbilical cord. The blond demon wheezed with laughter and grabbed a handful of Keegan's hair.

"I told you so!" the old man mocked them from the basement doorway.

Neither the demons nor Keegan had been paying much attention to August … until he slammed the axe's blade into the blond demon's tongue. The demon released a squealing cry as its tongue retracted back into its mouth, minus a third of its length.

August recognized that he only had a few seconds to act. He released the axe and fumbled to Reece's side, using his fingers to dig the stinger loose. He worked as he pulled her away from Hollie. Unfortunately, the distressed woman wasn't helping things. She was fighting with shadows and screaming hoarsely.

"She's alive! She's out cold!" August called as he extracted the stinger.

The blond demon released Keegan's hair and

clamped its hands over its mouth. Inky ichor shot out in ejaculatory stammers. Keegan made quick work to get to their feet and kicked the demon right in its pelvis. This didn't cause the demon much pain, but it did force him to lose his balance and tip backward into the garage.

Hollie screamed out once: "Reece!"

And then the old man chomped into the back of her head with his open chest cavity. It was as if he had snipped at her with a pair of scissors. The growing thorns that lined the walls of his slit were forced into the sides of Hollie's head and into the back of her neck.

With a forceful grunt, he pulled away. A substance that looked like melted bubble gum flopped out of the back of Hollie's head and smattered across the ground, adding to the mess Sam had left behind.

Hollie raised one of her arms toward Reece. Her eyes rolled into the back of her head, and she released a wet snivel.

Then she collapsed in on herself and lay dead at the old man's feet.

*Another one dead … another one … oh god. Oh god.*

Keegan found themself relieved that Reece had been knocked out cold before her mother had been killed.

The old man rolled a mouthful of spit around between his cheeks and then shot a dribble of blood into the bowl-shaped wound on the back of Hollie's head. As if to add insult to injury, he had spit on her corpse.

Hollie's fingers twitched. Her whole body seemed to seize up on the floor, curling in on itself and releasing a noise like an engine's falter. Her nails scratched across the linoleum surface of her kitchen floor. Her head beat itself into the ground. She looked as if she was throwing a tantrum. But that wasn't possible. Hollie Karkoff was dead.

Had to be.

A sharpened red bone split itself out of her back like the beak of a hatchling.

Keegan's head reeled backward. This was how they did it. They killed people and then planted demons in them … like seeds.

As if he was reading their mind, the old man offered a dark explanation.

"We are a legion of hosts … with only *one* soul. His blood purifies us. It strips us of our free will. It makes us *compliant*. The Fallen One doesn't want independents! He demands servitude! We drink His blood and are made *holy*! Hollie is part of us now. She's part of Him." His smile grew impossibly large. "Come on. Join the flock."

Hollie jangled up to her knees, swaying unevenly at her hips. Her eyes rolled like marbles around her sockets. Her mouth was dripping red syrup. Even worse, her skin was already inflamed. She looked as if she was blushing … but the blush was filling in the space beyond her cheeks and throat. It was consuming her from the inside out.

"Oh God!" August proclaimed.

"We abandoned *your* God!" Hollie moaned. "We left His Heaven … and came here!"

Keegan's back hit the garage door just before it swung open, and a muscular arm lashed around her throat. The blond demon had recovered.

"All shall witness us! All shall praise The Fallen One!" Hollie launched herself to her feet and stumbled toward Keegan. "Praise … Him! The true messiah!"

Keegan closed their eyes.

But nothing happened. Keegan thought for sure that Hollie would tear into their throat and hollow it out before spitting her infected blood into their wounds. They thought that this was where their journey ended.

But no. Keegan was given a second chance.

Because Hollie slammed against an invisible wall and careened backward. Her face was smashed inward, and her mouth filled with blood. Hollie landed on her back and began to squirm restlessly.

Keegan looked toward August. They saw that Reece was awake. One eye was half open, one finger was raised, and her mouth was moving slowly. A line of drool rolled out between Reece's lips.

*She doesn't have long. She'll be out soon. She's using what little she has to save you, Keegan.*

Hollie was already back to her feet and charging forward. She battered her fists against the invisible wall like an animal pleading to be loosed from its cage.

The old man's face had fallen. He seemed unsure whether he was allowed to participate in what he was encountering.

"Let go," Reece said.

Immediately, the arm around Keegan's throat loosened.

"Let's … leave." Reece's head bobbed backward

as she tried to stave off the unnatural narcotic that was forcing her to sleep.

Keegan ran toward August and took Reece from his hands. They knew they didn't have a second to spare. They had to leave while they had the opportunity.

They rushed toward the garage, pushing past the suddenly immobile blond demon.

They were almost free ...

# CHAPTER THIRTY

By the time the car had left the driveway, Reece was out cold again. She lay draped across Keegan's lap. Keegan was touching Reece's cheeks and prompting her to open her eyes. It seemed futile to August, but he didn't say anything. He simply tried to drive with stable hands.

"C'mon, Reece. It's okay. We're safe. We got out. We'll be okay," Keegan mumbled.

August took a deep breath. He couldn't afford to cry right now, but that's exactly what he wanted to do. None of the previous events had really hit him yet. It was like what he imagined a bad acid trip was like. His head felt swampy, and his nose was clogged from all the blood. He was also having trouble focusing on the road.

*Steady yourself, Auggie. Steady yourself.*

The road was mostly gravely slush at this point. The tires kicked up plumes of wet earth as they went. The wipers waved ecstatically back and forth, hypnotizing him and causing his vision to blur. The world seemed dark and threatening, and way too wet.

Briefly, his mind wandered to his own house, just across the road from the Karkoff property. He hadn't even thought of stopping by and picking up his mother. Did this make him a bad son?

No. They had all heard what had become of Keegan's dad. The gurgling sounds over the phone were so loud they had seemed to be leaking in from the other side of the door. It still gave him chills just thinking about it.

He knew, without having to see it, that the bastards had killed his mother. There was no way they wouldn't have. Despite her boisterous claims and combative nature, Charlotte Patch was easy pickings for—

*Dead. All of them. Everyone you know. Your girlfriend. Your acquaintances. Every single person. Your MOM. Your own mother is dead! Killed and more than likely transformed into one of those* things.

He still felt guilty. Even though time was of the essence, he wished he'd thought to go to his house, just so he could at least reclaim his mother's corpse.

August shook his head and watched the road. The rain was still pouring as if a spigot had been opened overhead. The windshield was blurry, and the wipers did little to expose the road ahead. He only got a few seconds of visibility to let him know he was headed in the right direction.

Lightning fizzed above them. It stretched across the sky and splayed its wiry fingers through the knotted storm clouds. The blue glow of it was like a stage light turned toward the road ahead.

August wasn't as surprised to see the crowd of people clustered on the road ahead of him as he supposed he ought to have been. But after everything that had already happened, this seemed less peculiar.

He couldn't catch any of their identities, but he was sure that that would have been impossible even if he had gotten a clear look at them. Each figure was swollen, red, and covered in malignant growths. And of course, each one was decked out with bony wings.

"Oh, God!" August stepped on the brakes. The van lurched to a stop. He kicked it in reverse and peered over his shoulder. He may as well have been driving blind. He couldn't see out the back window of the van. It was too far away and too waterlogged.

"What is it?" Keegan insisted.

"More of those things!" August shouted. He looked ahead once more. The massive crowd was moving sluggishly, like a herd of cattle. They had completely clogged the road.

"We can't go back." Keegan glanced over their shoulder.

"Well, where else can we go?"

"What if those other ones are waiting by the driveway?"

"How's Reece?" August asked offhandedly.

"She's still out." Keegan grimaced.

August didn't like it, but so far, that little girl was their only hope. He didn't mind pointing her magic hands at any foe that came their way if it gave them safe passage.

One of the creatures began to run toward the car. Its lope was long, and its flightless wings flapped impatiently by its head. August wished he could ram the car into drive and slam into the beast. But if one could survive so many axe blows, then a crowd of them could easily upend the car and tear them out of it.

There was no use in brute force. All they could do was escape.

Or try to, at least.

"Auggie, watch out!" Keegan cried.

August turned his head to see what they were pointing at.

He was too late to stop it from happening. The old man was colliding with the back window. His head ruptured through the glass, and his hands were scratching frantically at the back seats. His open chest was filled with shards of glass. Rain overtook him and poured in, soaking through the cushions.

"Give her ... to ... me!" The old man's proclamation was a guttural howl. His ghastly voice drew chills up August's spine.

"No!" Keegan returned. Their ability to even respond in such a situation was impressive. August wished he had their sense of awareness. He felt like a deer caught in the headlights.

August didn't know what to do, so he hit the brakes. The force of the car sliding to a stop sent the creature tumbling backward and away from the vehicle. Without a second's consideration,

August punched the van into drive and launched forward.

Keegan was screaming. They were clutching Reece close to their chest and watching the back of the van to see if the old man was going to pop back up at the window.

August was so distracted by the intrusion he had forgotten all about the demon that had detached from the herd and charged toward them. Until it was suddenly at the front of the van, that is.

The demon slammed into the hood of the van, wrinkling it.

The wipers drifted back and forth, clearing the glass and giving August a better view of the creature. He vaguely recognized the curly red hair and the police outfit. It was Tobin Marks, the young officer.

And to make matters worse, he had a shotgun held in his outstretched right arm.

"Oh … shit." August tried to swerve the van to tip Tobin off of them.

But all that did was prompt Tobin's trigger finger. The windshield exploded inwards after the front of the shotgun snorted loudly. August felt pellets skim over his cheeks, clawing at them. He clenched his eyes shut and tilted the wheel.

He felt the van hop off of the road and ram into the trees. It trundled forward, pushing through the thinner outcroppings before being lashed by bigger branches.

The trees revolted against the van's intrusion. They pushed the vehicle back and forth. It rocked forward against the pushing hands of the forest.

August wanted to open his eyes, but they refused his commands. He could only listen to the chaos around him. An unwilling witness. An inactive participant.

He heard the demon roll off of the van and smack into an oak. His yelp was cut in half quickly.

He heard the sound of something flying through the air toward him ...

August Patch felt a sharp burst of pain before everything went dark.

# CHAPTER THIRTY-ONE

When Keegan awoke, they were curled up on the floor of the van. The first thing they realized was that Reece was no longer in their arms. The second was that August Patch was dead. All it took was a moment to recognize that the liquid that covered Keegan's face and shoulders wasn't their own. It had pooled over them from the driver's seat.

When Keegan sat up, they were alarmed to see that the front of the van had been caved in, effectively pinning August to his seat. One of his shattered legs stuck out awkwardly toward the passenger seat. Even his ankle had fragmented. The bone shone out above his sock like a white fungus. Blood filled his sneakers.

A twisted branch had reached into the broken windshield and dug its fingers into August's face. The hard wood had stapled him to his chair through his neck and just between his nose and his upper jaw.

Teeth lay twinkling on the dashboard.

The nubs of the branch stuck out of the seat's back, bright crimson and splintered. August's hand swayed back and forth by his arm rest.

He was dead. At least he had not been killed by the monsters that had reanimated Paisley, Malcolm, and Hollie. In this new reality where demons existed, Keegan figured that dying a swift death at the driver's seat of a totaled van was about as equivalent to mercy as anyone would receive.

Keegan wished they didn't feel so cynical about the whole affair. But what other option did they have?

*I'm sorry, Auggie. You deserved better. So did Paisley. Hopefully … you two aren't very far apart now.*

The idea of an unending Heaven used to alarm them, but now it seemed idyllic. Keegan wanted nothing more than to be dead in that moment. They wanted to close their eyes and open them in paradise. They wanted to strum a golden harp and float through the clouds where their dad and their friends awaited them.

*Your mother is dead too. You haven't given that much thought. If they got Dad, then they definitely got Mom.*

*Fuck. Don't think about that, Keegan. Don't even think about that. It's just going to make you upset.*

But it was too late, and they were already crying. For every reason they had to cry, they let loose. Keegan took a gulping breath before releasing a flood of tears. They buried their face in their blood-soaked hands and began to unleash every emotion they had bottled up over this short period of intensity. All of their shivers caught up with them and wracked their body into a tiny circle. All of their nerves began to bounce like the lines on an oscilloscope. Their whole body felt super charged with grief, and fear, and anger.

Above all ... anger.

Anger at the cruelty and unfairness of it all.

And then, Keegan heard a small voice outside the van scream with terror.

Reece. They had Reece. And there was nothing Keegan could do about it.

Keegan looked toward the side of the van. The door was yawning open. With their prize in hand, the demons hadn't even given Keegan or August's body a second's notice. They had scooped Reece up and were marching through the woods with her. Keegan could see their forms in the distance. They looked less like a crowd and more like a living growth. Their bodies were mashed together, and even in the dark, they burned a bright red.

Reece was ensnared in their arms, being held above their heads like a sacrifice on an altar. Her legs were kicking and her arms were thrashing violently at her captors. She beat at their wrists and kicked at their fingers, but they were resolute. They refused to let her go now that they actually had her.

*Reece ... Reece ... kill them!*

She seemed to be trying to. Hard pops filled the forest as heads combusted and arms buckled, but with each demon that fell, a new one was there to replace it. And even the fallen demons were almost recycled into the meaty progression.

Keegan realized that their first glance had been correct. They were no longer a herd … they were a conglomerate. They were a winding tube of limbs and legs and heads, all connected by purple tubes and melting skin.

The rain sizzled on their hides, issuing plumes of steam into the air, gray smoke that was pattered apart by the swirling rain.

Keegan wrapped their hands around their chest and hopelessly watched as Reece was carted away.

*What now?*

Keegan felt another sob crawl up their throat. It was as if they were about to vomit up a handful of ice cubes. They leaned their head out of the van and cried into the rain.

They wished they had been awake when those demons had cracked into the car and pulled Reece out. They wished they had been able to fight them, at least long enough for their death to feel noble. They wished they didn't have to sit in this useless van, all alone save for August's corpse …

And here they were.

And they could do nothing but cry about it.

Until a voice chirped in their ear: "Don't cry, Keegan."

Keegan lurched out of the van and onto their feet. They whirled around, looking for the origin of the voice. It had sounded exactly like Reece. Keegan's eyes darted over the blood-soaked surface of the van, along August's ruined body, and over the seats. No one was there. It was as if Keegan had been communicating with a ghost.

"Keegan." Reece's voice erupted through their

head, igniting more fear, confusion, and panic.

"Reece?" Keegan asked. "Reece?"

"Shhh! They'll hear you! But they can't touch you. I won't let them."

"What do you mean?" Keegan spoke in a whisper.

"I don't know." Reece's voice seemed relaxed. The idea of being calm in this state seemed all but impossible. And yet Keegan didn't have time to question anything. They could only sit back and buckle in. "I hope you don't mind. As they were approaching, I thought it would be a good idea to try what they did."

"What do you mean?"

"I bled in you." Reece seemed to send a series of still images to Keegan. They experienced them like a dreamy slideshow.

There were only three images. The first depicted Reece peering through the windows and watching as the fleshy worm slunk toward the van. Reece's eyes were brimming with tears, and her teeth were bared. Keegan could see themself curled up on the floor of the van. Their arms and legs were jangled, and they were covered in August's blood, which was still trickling onto them. The blood which was currently gumming their eyes closed and flaking against their lips.

The next image showed Reece cradling Keegan's head while biting into the soft part of her palm. They could see a small, dark trail of blood forming between Reece's teeth.

And the last image showed Keegan laying on the floor of the van while the demons snatched Reece from her seat. They pulled her hair and twisted her arm. One scabrous hand even gripped the scruff of her neck as if Reece was a disobedient kitten and not a human child. But none of the demons seemed particularly interested in Keegan Peterson. They in fact seemed to be worming their way around them as if they had a force field around their body.

"Whoa." Keegan snapped their eyes open and closed and watched as the world faded into view once more.

"They're taking me to Him. They're talking about Him now. They say He's very old … and that they are connected to him. And now … *you're* connected to *me*," Reece said inside of Keegan's head.

"What can I do?" Keegan asked.

"I don't know." Reece huffed impatiently. "But whatever this is, they want me to be there to see it happen. They need me here for it."

Keegan placed their hands over their eyes and tried to focus.

"Keegan! Keegan, I'm scared." Reece let out a soft whimper. "I really don't want to go. Can you come get me?"

Keegan couldn't help but imagine this was what it was like for a parent to receive a phone call that their child didn't want to spend the night at their friend's house after all. They missed their warm bed and the familiarity of their room. *Mom? Dad? Can you come get me?*

"Yes, Reece. I'm coming. I'll find some way to get you out of this."

Keegan had to be careful with their thoughts. It was as if Reece's blood had acted as a key; it opened doors. Keegan's brain was wide open for Reece to pick through. Reece could probably see every memory in Keegan's head. Even the bad ones.

And Keegan didn't want Reece to lose hope.

No way.

Keegan began to trudge through the woods after the massive parade. The demonic cluster pushed through fallen trees and over shrubs, clearing a pathway in their wake. The path was slopped with blood, feces, organ parts, and little bone fragments.

Keegan didn't walk on this path. They worried that putting their feet anywhere the demons had would taint the neural hallway Reece had constructed between herself and Keegan. So Keegan walked beside the path.

Keegan used their hands to push through the thickets and burs. Branches slapped at their face. A few fingers of wood dug into their sides, spurring them forward.

Their ankles were torn by thorns and sticks. Their mouth had been lashed and their lips were bleeding. Their whole body was soaked in blood and gore. They imagined they looked about as crimson as the demons did … but thankfully, Reece's blood hadn't prompted any abnormal growths.

*As far as I'm aware.* They shuddered at the thought of peeling off their shirt and finding wings underneath.

Keegan reached over their shoulder and checked their back for lumps. Thankfully, none were to be found. Still, just because there weren't any immediate signs of change didn't mean that that wasn't a possibility.

"Reece," Keegan said, "I hope this is temporary."

"I'm sorry." Reece moaned in their head. "I wasn't thinking … I just … I thought it couldn't hurt. I was scared."

"No. No. You did the right thing. I'm sorry. Just thinking out loud. How are you holding up?"

"I see a light ahead of me. Something big."

"Okay. I'm with you. Every step of the way. I'm here, Reece. It's okay."

Keegan peered through the woods as best they could. Indeed, something was glowing in the distance. It looked like a bonfire. Flickering lights danced through the trees, dazzling them briefly.

Keegan couldn't even begin to envision what they were about to walk into. An unholy ritual? A giant sacrificial ceremony where the demons would serve Reece up on a platter to their overlord? Maybe even a good old-fashioned fireworks show.

"Oh, God!" Reece's voice screamed in Keegan's ear. "Oh, God … is that … Him?"

Suddenly, Reece's voice was cut away from Keegan. They felt as if a line had been severed.

"Hello?" Keegan whispered. "Reece? Reece?"

Keegan stood still. They watched as the worm slid out of the woods and into the clearing, vanishing from sight in the luminescent haze. It was as if all sounds had simply ceased to be.

Keegan braced themself up against the nearest tree. They pinched their eyes shut and took as deep a breath as their lungs allowed. They had to go forward and see what was ahead. All they had to do was look through the trees and see what it was that had blocked Reece's voice from them.

They began to move forward—

And heard a clatter as their feet dredged up a wooden instrument on the forest's floor.

Keegan froze. They looked down, expecting to have landed in a trip wire or a bear trap. Instead, they were relieved to see an abandoned weapon laying on the ground.

It was a wooden bow with a taut drawstring. And next to it lay a single wooden arrow. Keegan didn't hesitate to pick the weapon up. They weighed it in their hands and tested the string with their fingers. After some light strumming, they concluded that the bow was in fine condition, despite being dropped in the middle of the woods.

The arrow was hand carved and sloppy looking. Its shaft was almost veiny to the touch. Its head had been whittled to a fine tooth, and the tail was notched so that it fit perfectly against its string.

They drew the arrow back and held it upward.

Weapons hadn't worked against the demons thus far ... but still, it was comfortable to be armed.

Keegan used the bow's blunt end to rustle through the ferns, hoping to find more arrows. No such luck. It looked as if God was handing out miracles in single serving sizes tonight.

Keegan inched toward the light.

# CHAPTER THIRTY-TWO

Reece felt her connection with Keegan slice open and pour onto the ground like a hose draining water into the lawn and missing the garden completely. She was dropped onto the floor of the clearing and rolled forward. She hadn't gotten a good glimpse at Him. All she had seen were a few tents and the statue of Christ that they had found in the woods earlier that day. Sitting in front of the statue—His legs crossed together and His hands planted on His knees—was, obviously, the leader of the pack. He was tall and dressed in ratty clothing. His trench coat fanned out at his sides, pooling by his legs. His chest was bare and knitted with wiry hairs. His skin was, like the skin of his servants, bright red. So red it looked hot to the touch. Even worse were his nails. They were golden brown and curled. They looked less like nails and more like a hawk's claws.

His head was concealed behind a potato sack.

"Ahhhhhhhhhh." The Fallen One whinnied. "Reece … Brampton."

One of the demons grabbed her by the hair and lifted her face so she was staring directly at The Fallen One. Reece looked up at the demon and recognized the old man.

"Not so rough, Hurwitz!" The Fallen One snapped.

Hurwitz released Reece's hair and stepped back. His body melded back with the procession. "Sorry, your Grace." Hurwitz dipped his head down and sniffled.

"That's precious cargo you're tampering with." The Fallen One turned his attention back to Reece. "Now. It's been a long, long time since we've seen each other."

Reece looked around the campsite. Her eyes almost skimmed over the mouth that had opened up on the forest floor. The hole was as wide as a child's swimming pool. It was far more grotesque than a cave's entrance, though. Its rim was pink and dotted with white pustules. Its walls were dripping with oil and red blood. Reece wasn't close enough to look down the tunnel. She didn't want to know what was at the bottom of the hole. She could hear sounds emanating from its recesses. Screams of pain, brays of defiance, and weeping.

*That's Hell. That's a gateway to Hell.* Reece couldn't help but imagine Hell as she had known it in the cartoons. A dismal pit filled with tongues of fire and red-hot pokers. Sure enough, that was all she had experienced tonight.

The fleshy congregation began to trickle toward

the hole like a herd of ants returning to their queen. Reece recognized some faces in the midst of the storm of organs, arms, horns, and fingers. She saw Hollie. Her face was almost flattened against the surface of the horde. Her mouth was a vacuous depository, offering insight to the horde's inner mechanics. Pulsating intestines, shafts of bone, and gouts of blood all vied for attention behind her mouth. Some even found their way through. A long femur poked its way out of her mouth and rotated in the air before being pulled back into the meaty vortex.

*Don't look at it. Don't look at it.* But Reece couldn't pull her gaze off of the gory caterpillar as it trundled toward the pit.

The horde became divided as it went. Hurwitz seemed to step out from the meat herd as if he had simply hopped on the wrong train and was hopping off before the doors closed him in.

A slender girl with a pulpy face stepped out, as well as a young boy with a cracked jaw. All of them had seemed to have reached the ends of their mutations. Hurwitz with his chest-mouth, the boy and the girl with their scarlet red skin, flightless wings, and rams' horns. The horns curled around their ears like headphones. They were covered in bumps and sharp ridges. They seemed to have burst forth from their skulls, shattering the bone and tearing the flesh apart. Purple brains oozed out of their injuries and trickled down the horns' many curves and grooves.

They clopped forward on their cloven hooves and watched as their brothers sank into the hole, widening it and seeping into its sides. The hole grew open, swallowing the entirety of the parade and leaving them with more intimate company.

The screams from within could not be dulled. Reece clapped her hands over her ears and squeezed her lips together with her teeth.

"Painful, isn't it?" The Fallen One offered some solidarity. "Here. Let me take care of that for you."

The Fallen One clicked His twisted nails together, and the whole forest went still. Not even the sound of the hooves clopping on the mushy forest floor could be heard. Even the rain had muted.

The Fallen One made no move to speak first. Reece wondered if He, too, enjoyed the silence. Still, she needed to fill the air with something other than her own cries and tears.

"Who … are you?" Reece asked. "Why did you kill all of those people?"

Hurwitz released a chuffing laugh. "He didn't kill us, child! He made us stronger!"

The Fallen One clicked His nails together again. Hurwitz's tongue was immediately twisted in his mouth. He clamped his hands over his lips and bashfully ducked his head downward. Twice, he had spoken out of turn, it seemed.

"I am … who I am." The Fallen One held His arms out and mimicked the stance of crucifixion displayed by the statue of Christ looming behind Him. "I am the Angel of Blood."

Reece was confused. She hadn't heard this Bible story before. She doubted it was one that was taught in Sunday school.

"Are you …?"

"Jesus?" The Fallen One sneered. "No. But I've been in his court, and I called him a *fool*. And for that, God cast me out. I am The Fallen One, Reece. But I am not Lucifer. I am not Satan. I am not the Devil. And I did not bring a horde of demons with me. No. As you can see, I had to fashion my own out of what few materials I had. And unlike Lucifer—who was God's little pet—I wasn't given my own Hell to play in. I had to make my own. I'm making Hell out of *God's* most precious creation."

The Fallen One jumped to His feet and clutched the front of His potato sack mask.

"Do you want to see my face, child?"

Reece shook her head. She was not sure if that would be taken as an insult or not. She didn't really care. The last thing Reece wanted to see was this thing's face.

"The last person who saw my face—*really* saw it—fell in love with it." The Fallen One released His grip on the potato sack, thankfully keeping it over his head. "And her name was Becca Brampton."

Reece's breath froze.

"Yes. She nursed me after I fell. She brought me up like a child in the shed behind your house. None of you knew I was in there, hiding from the world and from my Father. None of you knew that she was worshiping me. And none of you knew that you were the first to carry my blood."

Reece's head felt as if it was going to catch on fire. Her eye swelled with fresh tears, and her teeth gritted together in defiance. "No. You're lying. You're lying!"

"You saw yourself. You have as much dominion

over my creations as I do. You are as much a God as I am."

"No!" Reece proclaimed. "No!"

"Becca Brampton is the Queen of my Hell ... and you, Reece... you will be our Princess." The Fallen One stretched out a hand. As He did, a flame caught between His fingers and swirled into the center of His palm. The image of a blue figure floated out of the surface of the fire. A stick with a V imprinted on it like a pair of upraised arms.

The same symbol that Becca Brampton had tattooed between her daughter's toes on her left foot.

*That way ... your Guardian Angel will always know where you are.*

"You were marked for this. I don't want to hurt you, Reece. We just want you to rule"—

With His other hand, He ripped the potato sack away.

—*"by our side."* Both Becca and The Fallen One's voices poured out from His divided head.

One half of the head was Becca Brampton, with one soft eye, tight gray lips, and a sallow cheek. Her flesh was pale, and the veins beneath thumped rapidly. Her teeth had grown yellow since Reece had last laid eyes on her, and her hair hung in strangled clumps from her bruised scalp. It looked as if her face had been peeled away from her skull and crudely fused to this monstrosity.

The other side of His face was red and muscly. His cheek sat right beneath His single emerald eye, and His eyebrow was thick with black hair. His mouth was filled with warthog teeth, curled tusks that protruded from His wicked smile. The mouths were separated by a thin line of flesh. It looked more like a gray jelly than actual skin.

Becca's mouth hung open. Her tongue rolled lethargically between her yellow teeth and lapped at the air like a weary dog's.

Both sides of The Fallen One's head were adorned with sharpened ram's horns. His scalp bore a twisted ringlet of thorns. The thorns dug into His brow. Blood streamed down into His and Becca's eyes and into their separate mouths.

*"Come to us, Reece … Come to us … Join us! Join us, and God's world will tremble at our feet!"* The dual voices growled the words. *"Come and explore the cave with us!"*

Reece didn't know what to say or do. So, she did the only thing she could do. She cried.

She cried aloud with fear and terror as The Fallen One raised His grotesque hands into the air and flexed His fingers. More fire plumed from His palms. It crawled up His arms and rested on His shoulders.

*"Be my third mouth! Be my third mouth! AND SING MY PRAISES! SING OF LOW BLASPHEMY AND HIGH HORROR!"*

The beast shucked His shoulders, and the flames arched off of His body and sat like a pair of orange wings by His sides. They expanded, flapping ruthlessly up and down.

*"All blood on Earth will be* our *blood! And we will remake the planet in* our *image. He will have died for nothing!"* The creature pointed a twisted hand at the statue of Christ. *"Nothing! He will watch*

*helplessly in his Heaven … and he will weep!"*

Reece's brain was filled with vile images. The blood trickling beneath the bathroom door. The sounds of her father being stabbed by her mother. The horrible sacrifices Becca must have made to this unholy abomination … this … *monster.*

She could see her mother kneeling at this thing's cloven foot. Her hands were clutched together in prayer. It was promising her the world. It was gently running its fingers through her hair.

*It lived in the shed behind your house. You didn't know it. But it was there. Your mother found it and fed it and kept it like a secret pet … like a secret lover. It's your father. Oh god, Reece … it's your real father!*

The Fallen One's chest began to yawn open. Inky blood coursed from the unwarranted hole. It sloughed between the creature's legs and pooled at His feet. His head began to crack in two. The divided eyes rolled in opposing directions. His split tongue waggled in His cavernous mouth. His teeth clacked together like hands against drums.

*"Come with us, Reece! Explore the caves with us. Three in one! Explore the caves."*

Reece imagined her face sitting right between The Fallen One and her own mother. She imagined the three mouths chomping into flesh and tearing it apart … passing judgment over legions of innocent, crying people. She imagined sharing her mind with these horrendous fiends. A hive mind dedicated entirely to the abuse of the masses.

And all Reece wanted to do was die.

*Anything … anything but this.*

And then an arrow smacked into the space

between The Fallen One and Becca Brampton's heads. The divided head bobbed backward harshly and released a hard yelp.

"Reece!" Keegan screamed from the woods. "Reece … kill it!"

"No!" Hurwitz clamored. "No! Stop her!"

Reece held her arm out. She felt a powerful eruption of energy fly through her fingers and wrap around the entirety of the arrow.

"Now, Reece! Kill it now!"

Reece screamed and threw her hand toward the ground.

The arrow ripped downward. It shredded through the evil entity like a knife sliding through a curtain. The sound of the beast being torn in half was as loud as a clap of thunder.

As He fell into two pieces, His fiery wings flopped inwards and coursed through the blackened blood like oil. It seared across the ground and leapt up the trees behind it.

When Reece's hand finally collided with the forest's floor, she watched as the arrow imbedded itself into the ground between The Fallen One's heels.

The Fallen One fell into two halves and collapsed into the fires.

The hole in the ground erupted in flames. A hot geyser of liquid fire poured like blood from a severed artery. Its heat was enough to sizzle Reece's hair and evaporate her brows. She was blasted backward as the flames vented into the sky.

"No! You can't! You can't!" Hurwitz cried and took a handful of Reece's hair. "You can't!"

Reece couldn't even struggle. She was in shock. She could only watch as a lasso of orange flames snapped over Hurwitz's head and jerked him backward. He lost his grip on Reece's hair as he was sucked into the middle of the flaming hole.

"You … *can't*!" Hurwitz screamed as he was blasted into ashes.

The next pair of hands to grab Reece belonged to Keegan.

Keegan screamed into Reece's ear: "Run!"

"Reece!" Becca Brampton squealed. "Reece! Come *baaaaaaack*!"

Reece looked toward the sound and saw her biological mother standing in the middle of the flames. Her hair was being swept upwards, and her clothes were alight. Her eyes were sizzling in their sockets, and her lips were frayed. The crosses she had sliced into her arms had become clotted and black, as if they were filled with chocolate stuffing.

"Come baaaaaaack!" the demented woman screamed.

A talon-tipped hand lashed out from the fiery pit and grabbed Becca's ankle. Reece watched as her mother struggled to stay afloat before she was pulled into the pit. As she descended, more hands clutched at her. Their sharpened nails pierced her skin. They shredded her back open and tore into her stomach. Her guts unwound and flopped into the hole beneath her. More hands clutched at the intestines and began to tug them.

Any blood that came out of her was immediately scorched by the roaring flames.

As she went, the skin around her face dissolved, revealing the bleached bones underneath. Still, she screamed for her daughter to join her.

"Come baaaaaaack!"

"Run! Just run!" Keegan screamed and jerked at Reece's arm.

Reece obeyed the command and followed her savior through the woods. As they went, the screams behind them grew quieter and quieter. The flames themselves seemed to curl back into the pit in reverse, as if they were merely cleaning up the mess that The Fallen One had left behind. They could hear demons being dragged into the mouth of Hell and falling into its torturous chambers.

Reece dared to look back.

The last thing she saw before the trees closed in on the scene was the statue of Christ toppling over to its side as the last finger of fire vanished into the earth … and the hole sealed itself up.

And then there was nothing, save for the gentle patter of rain and the hard sound of Keegan's panicked breath.

"We'll be okay." Keegan spoke to her as they approached the gravel road just beyond the totaled van.

Reece looked over her shoulder and back into the woods. The forest was still. She had expected it to be all aflame, as if Hell itself—or whatever Hell The Fallen One had created—had spilled upward and had filled the trees.

Instead, the forest was much as it had been that morning. Moist, humid, clustered, and ancient. Reece blinked and wondered if she was going crazy. Had she imagined all the fire and brimstone that had just moments ago filled the woods?

"We made it!" Keegan shouted. Their voice hitched with sobs. "We're going to be okay—"

The forest floor rumpled.

Reece clutched Keegan's hand tightly. The two stepped back in unison, watching with mouths agog as the dirt began to wrinkle like a disobedient tablecloth. Steam rose in gray tendrils from the creases in the dirt. Where the rain touched it, the earth seemed to sizzle.

"No. No. No!" Keegan blurted. "No!"

Reece said nothing.

She watched as a crimson arm bolted up from the dirt. Its curved, yellowed talons hit the ground and dug in, clutching the earth and drawing it close. Another arm shot from the dirt, spraying mud and grassy clumps as it broke through the surface.

"No!" Keegan proclaimed, as if they could stop what was coming.

The Fallen One lifted His head from the dirt. Stones, pebbles, and thick blots of earth tumbled down His crooked face and landed on the ground beneath His panting mouth. It was filled with curved teeth, and His tongue seemed to roil like a storm-cloud. Separated from Becca, The Fallen One now had only one face. Reece imagined this was what He had looked like when her mother found Him.

"Reeeeeece." The Fallen One drew her name out until it turned into a guttural gurgle. He began to worm His way out of the ground like a zombie from a freshly turned grave. His arms were rickety, and His back was bare. The orange wings had dissipated. He still wore the crown of thorns. They were so embedded into the flesh of His brow, Reece wondered if it was even possible to remove them!

"Reeeeeece!" The demon bared His fangs. "Three … in … *ONE!*"

He struck like a rattle snake.

One second, He was lying on the edge of the forest, and the next, He was sailing through the air. His arms were stretched ahead of Him, and His talons sliced toward Reece and Keegan. Reece held up her hands and screamed.

The Fallen One *detonated.*

It was as if He had stepped on a landmine. Blood popped out of his ruptured body. Bone chips leapt over the rocky ground. His talons swept across Reece's palms, searing them open, before clattering against the gravel road and skittering away like loosened cockroaches. Blood spattered across Reece and Keegan. The two sucked in surprised breaths, unwittingly inhaling the blood. It tasted sour and acidic. It filled Reece with revulsion and fear.

"Oh, god!" Keegan declared, swiping at their face with their soggy hands. "Oh, did it infect us?"

Reece blinked and looked down at the warped demon lying on the ground before her.

He looked like roadkill.

He didn't have organs, but instead, a fine mesh seemed to slip out between the fissures that had raced through His body. His head was split open, and Reece could see that His empty skull had long since decayed. The body of the demon began to deflate. It made wheezing noises as it evacuated its porridge-textured insides. Streams of blood and puddles of pulped tissue crawled across the gravel road.

"Are we going to become like … like them?" Keegan queried, fretting over the blood that had landed on their tongue.

As Reece watched The Fallen One collapse into a molten pool, she spoke in a whisper:

"No. I think … I think it's over now."

Somewhere deep below the earth, she could hear the townspeople of Kissing-Brooke exclaiming as their bodies fell apart and their souls were allowed to depart. Whatever hold The Fallen One had infected them with, it had been relinquished.

"Yeah." Reece looked back toward Keegan. "It's done."

In a matter of seconds, the last remains of The Fallen One were swallowed up into the ground. All that was left was a splotchy blood stain. And even that was washed away by the rain …

# EPILOGUE

Reece was twenty years old when she next encountered Keegan Peterson. Only Keegan had taken their partner's name. Now they were Keegan Marsh. They had been excited to share the news with Reece. The first thing they did was yank out their phone and give Reece a slide-show style presentation of the wedding.

"She isn't non-binary, but she's androgynous, so, like, she gets it, you know?" Keegan said. "I've never had to explain myself to her. She always just … she always gets it."

"Aww." Reece put her hands over her mouth. "Aww, she looks gorgeous! And you look very handsome!"

"Thanks." Keegan ran a hand through their tight black hair. "I honestly am surprised you recognized me. I dyed it black in college and just … kept it that way."

Keegan sat back in their bar stool and crossed

their arms over their chest. They looked different, Reece noted. Healthier. Their cheeks were full, and their eyes had a lively twinkle to them. Their hair was cut radically short, and their upper lip was decorated with light hairs. They looked amazingly beautiful. Reece felt an overwhelming urge to hug them, even though it had been about five years since she had last thought of her old acquaintance and her late sister's best friend.

Reece was surprised she had even recognized Keegan. Maybe it was a psychic thing. She had a lot of moments like that. Sometimes her intuition told her little things, like which side a coin was going to land on or which seat had gum left on it at the movie theater. Sometimes it could be more essential. Like when a date was going to lead to a disastrous relationship, or when she needed to skip taking a short cut to avoid getting in a life altering car accident.

And so, maybe it was intuition that screamed in her ear that Keegan was hanging out in the ratty little bar by the apartment she was sleeping at in New York City.

Reece was here to visit her boyfriend. They had met online, and this was their first time meeting each other. Things had been going really well, but she wasn't quite ready to give him a lot of details about her past. All he knew was that things had been rough for her.

"My mom was ... not very good to me. I was raised by my aunt, but when she disappeared, I kind of drifted around from place to place. I was a runaway orphan, if you can believe that. It took me a while to get my act together, but … now I'm in college and now I'm … I don't know. I'm studying fashion. I want to get into design. It feels like a pipe dream, but … I want to do it."

Chadwick had been more than open with her, and yet Reece didn't want to tell him the whole truth. And as she looked at Keegan's beautiful wife and marveled over how happy they looked—pushing wedding cake in each other's faces, popping the corks off of champagne bottles, and smiling with their friends—Reece couldn't help but wonder what Keegan had told their wife.

"What brings you to The Big Apple?" Keegan asked and scratched at their stubbly chin. "You here permanently?"

"No. It's spring break, and I'm visiting a friend," Reece admitted bashfully. "I can't even legally drink yet. I don't know why I'm here." She guffawed a little too animatedly. "I'm glad to see you. What are you doing with yourself, aside from settling down?"

"Well," Keegan mused, "we haven't really settled down. I don't think either of us is ready to take care of a kid, you know? We're just kind of … working on some fun stuff. She's a performance artist. I'm working as a mechanic right now, actually." Keegan popped their cheek. "A regular grease monkey. Turns out I have a thing for cars."

"Oh wow!" Reece admired them. "You've really made it, huh? You're happy?"

"Happy as a clam." Keegan scrutinized Reece. "Here. Step outside with me. Do you smoke?"

"Yes." Reece was lying, but she followed Keegan

toward the door.

Chadwick was on a food errand. He had promised to cook a real meal for her that night instead of taking her to some of his favorite greasy spoons. She had had a few hours to spare, and they had drawn her to the bar. They had drawn her to Keegan.

"Hey!" The shout came from a bald man in the corner. "Where you going?"

"Yeah, finish your story!" This from a small woman with heavy makeup. "You got us in suspense!"

"One sec, gang!" Keegan held up a wavering finger. "Old friend!"

"Well, introduce her!"

"I don't want her to get to know you, Kirk!"

"Eat shit!"

"Every day!" Keegan laughed. Their buddies responded with a collective chuckle before descending back into their own conversation. "Sorry. Pals from work. We meet up for drinks and beefy nachos every Friday before we go to a show. My wife is sick, so ... she's not joining us today."

They stepped out into the hot sun. Keegan was fast to flick their lighter against their lips. Reece hadn't even caught them putting the smoke in their mouth. When Keegan offered their open pack, Reece plucked a cigarette out and accepted the light. She tried not to cough.

"Have you told anyone?" Keegan asked bluntly.

"No," Reece said. "I'm kind of ... worried that people will think I'm crazy. You know ... you know what I heard someone call Kissing-Brooke?"

"What?"

"Roanoke Two." Reece sneered. "Isn't that a laugh?"

"I don't get it." Keegan took a deep draw as if they were sipping smoke through a straw.

"Roanoke was this town where, like, everyone just up and disappeared. It's like an urban legend. Kissing-Brooke is kind of the same deal. You know no one even found any blood left behind? The only dead body they found was August's." Reece sighed. "And that was because he was the only one that wasn't infected."

Keegan looked confused. "August?"

"Paisley's boyfriend."

"Oh. Sorry. Right." Keegan knocked their knuckles against their skull. "I kind of forget names sometimes. It's like a dream. I can't remember all of it."

"I can." Reece mumbled her reply. "I remember every detail."

"I remember … really worrying that you would," Keegan admitted. "I remember wishing I could cover your eyes the whole time. It eats at me. Just not being able to have done more."

"What could you do?" Reece flicked her cigarette into the gutter. The idea of inhaling smoke had triggered bad memories. She shouldn't have even accepted the offer.

"You should try to tell someone. Maybe. I don't know." Keegan sighed. "I told my wife. Ruth. Ruth … believed me. As much as she could. I kind of sold it as … you know … there's room for error. I told her what I remember happening, but I made it clear that's not what I think actually happened. Maybe you could do the same."

"Thanks. But … I don't know. It would have to be someone really special who hears about it."

"Right." Keegan tapped their ashes off and watched them fumble onto the pavement. "Of course. I wish I remembered more. I feel guilty for not remembering."

"Don't." Reece squeezed their arm. "I've gotta get going. My friend is coming back. I wanna see you again, okay? Let's not be strangers. You going to be back at the bar again tomorrow? If your wife is feeling better, let's meet up."

"Does eight work?" Keegan said through a mouthful of smoke.

"Yeah. That works. I'll bring Chadwick. He's … kind of my boyfriend."

Keegan's good humor returned. They flicked their tongue along their teeth and arched their brows. "Reece and Chadwick sitting in a tree … k-i-s-s-i-n-g!"

"Fuck off." Reece laughed and began to limp away.

"Whoa." Keegan stopped Reece with an upraised hand, taking note of Reece's precarious balance. "Are you okay?"

"What?" Reece froze.

"Sorry. You were walking like—"

"Oh. Right." Reece knelt down and lifted the right cuff of her jeans. She was proud of this development, and so she showed it off gladly. "It hitches up sometimes."

Keegan starred down, aghast. The prosthetic

foot had obviously slipped right past them.

"Did you … did you lose that during …?"

"No. This wasn't until a few years ago." Reece stood upright and shook her right leg. "I cut it off."

"Why?" Keegan asked. Their cigarette dropped from their mouth and landed on the ground between their feet. Instinctively, they crushed it beneath their heel.

"I …" Reece looked down at her right foot. She remembered the tattoo between her toes that had faded away. She had had the tattoo removed, but even the scar was too much for her to carry. And so, Reece had taken one last dramatic action before she felt it was possible to reclaim her normalcy.

"I took it off myself." She stated it proudly. "And honestly, Keegan, I've never felt better."

# WHO IS JUDITH SONNET?

Judith Sonnet (she/her) is a horror and splatter author from Missouri, although she currently resides in Utah... where she spends every day reading, writing, watching Italian horror movies, and listening to loud music. She's a trans woman, an abuse survivor, and is thankful to be involved in the horror community. Noteworthy publications include No One Rides For Free, The Clown Hunt, Something Akin to Revulsion, and Summer Never Ends

## More Books from

# Madness Heart Press

**Czech Extreme by Edward Lee**
isbn: 978-1-955745-06-2

**The Bighead by Edward Lee**
isbn: 978-1-955745-22-2

**Extinction Peak by Lucas Mangum**
isbn: 979-8-689548-65-4

**You Will Be Consumed by Nikolas Robinson**
isbn: 978-1-7348937-7-9

**Curse of the Ratman by Jay Wilburn**
isbn: 978-1-955745-19-2

**Trench Mouth by Christine Morgan**
isbn: 978-1-7348937-9-3

**Warlock Infernal by Christine Morgan**
isbn: 978-1-955745-24-6

**Addicted to the Dead by Shane McKenzie**
isbn: 978-1-955745-15-4

**Muerte con Carne by Shane McKenzie**
isbn: 978-1-955745-33-8